The Amazing

Mr. Howard

By
Kenneth W. Harmon

JournalStone
San Francisco

JOURNALSTONE
YOUR LINK TO ARTISTIC TALENT

JournalStone books may be ordered through booksellers or by contacting:

JournalStone

www.journalstone.com

ISBN: 978-1-942712-13-8   (sc)
ISBN: 978-1-942712-14-5   (ebook)

JournalStone rev. date: February 20, 2015

Library of Congress Control Number: 2015932363

Printed in the United States of America

Cover Art & Design: Cyrusfiction Productions

Edited by: Aaron J. French

To
Sarah
With love and gratitude
And
In Memory of
Nancy Reed
Who helped unlock the magic

He smelled her long before he could see her,
the metallic scent of blood carried on the warm breeze.

He accelerated his car, zeroing in on the smell like a shark after prey. She sat alone at the bus stop, her gaze on the sidewalk. In the glow of a streetlight, tears glistened on her cheeks. She was young, in her teens, with auburn hair that curled over her sloping shoulders. Something was wrong. Something had upset her. Why else would she be there on a deserted street in the middle of the night?

He would go to her, his words gentle and comforting, and she would surrender to his will... as they had for over three hundred years.

Chapter 1

The door creaked opened and two men wearing suits slipped inside the classroom. Their jackets flared briefly to reveal pistols in shoulder holsters. Mr. Howard stopped his lecture on the Shurale, an ancient demon of the Tatars. He knew they had come about the missing girl. Eventually, they always came to him regarding such matters. One of them was his old friend, Chandler Killgood. A most unfortunate name for a homicide detective.

Killgood pressed his back against the wall and gave a quick nod. The other man, whom Mr. Howard didn't recognize, stood straight, arms folded across his chest. A scowl resided on his angular, pock-marked face, which reminded Mr. Howard of the creature in William Blake's *The Ghost of a Flea*.

Mr. Howard glanced at his Rolex. Five minutes until class ended. He strolled to the window. Outside, a soft summer night painted the campus black. Lamps cast circles of white light across the sidewalks. Midges flittered through the brightness. Warm air passed into the open window. He breathed in the fragrance of a summer thunderstorm—the rain-soaked grass and the musty earth. *They have come sooner than I expected, not that it matters. When I am ready, I will give them what they seek, but for now, they must wait. The process has a certain order, like the passing of seasons and the earth traversing on its course through the heavens.*

Mr. Howard faced the class. Everyone's attention was on the detectives. The male students squirmed on their seats as if trying to remember something illegal they had recently done. The young women viewed the cops with a primal yearning. Mr. Howard sighed. In this world, all that mattered was the size of one's gun.

Back at the podium, he cleared his throat to recapture the students' attention. Karen Webster, the leggy blonde who always sat in the front row, uncrossed and crossed her legs like a young Sharon Stone. He felt dirty, and in need of a cigarette, yet found himself smiling. *So the blonde is actually a brunette. Why am I not surprised?* He brushed long silver hair away from his eyes and focused on the textbook before him.

"As we have learned from our reading"—he paused—"and I know each of you spent your weekend doing your homework, the Tatars believed the Shurale to be a demon that lived where, Miss Johnson?"

Blood rushed into the cheeks of the freckled redhead. "In Hell?"

"No, Miss Johnson, Hell is where students reside who fail to do their assignments." He used a black marker and created a crude depiction of the beast on a drawing board. "Furry body, elongated fingers, and a horn in the center of his forehead. This is our friend the Shurale. Forest demon of the Tatars."

"Looks like Mr. Howard," Brian Spriggs shouted from the back of the room.

He shook his head and turned around. "Actually, Mr. Spriggs, this will be you in ten years if you continue to use shrooms."

Laughter erupted throughout the room. Spriggs slouched in his seat, his gaze on the cops. Mr. Howard returned to the book. The small print slid before him like a fuzzy caterpillar. A soft groan rose in his throat as he retrieved his reading glasses. He pushed the glasses onto his nose. "In addition to the Shurale, there are other forest-dwelling creatures in Tatar myths—the Seka, a dwarf known to make mischief, and the Abada, a benign spirit who resembled an old woman. The Siberian Tatars believed in the Pitsen, which also lived in the forest, but preferred to inhabit derelict buildings. They are closely related to the—"

The bell rang, announcing end of class. Students sprang from their chairs and pressed toward the exit.

"Don't forget to read chapter ten in your texts on Slavic mythology. You may be questioned on the Svarog."

The detectives watched Karen's ass as she disappeared through the door. Killgood whistled softly. "How in the world can you stay focused on teaching?"

Mr. Howard stashed his textbook inside a leather attaché case. "Perhaps if I were a younger man, it might affect my concentration, but at my age, I'd need a double martini and a big dose of Viagra to have a chance with a girl like Karen."

Killgood extended a hand. "It's good to see you again."

Mr. Howard shook the detective's hand, calloused in the upper part of the palm from swinging a hammer. Killgood was always building something for his kids or his church. "How is the family?"

"They ask about you. When Susan heard we'd be working together again, she wanted to invite you over for dinner."

Mr. Howard offered a polite smile. "So, we are to be working together?"

The other detective's eyebrows pulled down. "He doesn't know why we're here?"

"Mr. Howard prefers as little information as possible before jumping into a case. Isn't that right?"

"Chandler, you do know me well." He held out his hand to the other detective. "I'm afraid I didn't catch your name."

The detective glared at his hand without moving.

What a well-mannered fellow. He must have been raised in a bordello. Mr. Howard brought his hand down.

Killgood jerked a thumb toward the burly detective. "This is Detective Willard from the Colorado Bureau of Investigation."

"Detective Willard." Mr. Howard dipped his head as a courtesy. "You must like rats."

The detective's eyes narrowed. "What's he talking about?"

Killgood grinned behind a fist. "Beats me."

Willard lifted a pack of cigarettes from his jacket pocket and tapped one out.

"I'm sorry," Mr. Howard, said, "smoking is not permitted in the school."

The detective smirked as he lit the cigarette. "Go figure." He stashed the cigarettes and lighter back inside the jacket, and took a long pull. He blew a cloud of smoke at Mr. Howard.

Mr. Howard snatched the cigarette from the detective's mouth and tossed it down, grinding it into a black smear. Willard didn't react until the cigarette was a distant memory.

"What the—?"

Mr. Howard continued to smile. "In my classroom, Detective, even policemen must follow the rules."

Blood rushed into Willard's cheeks, turning them the shade of Chateau Latour breathing in a glass. He grunted. "Now you got me riled, but I'll let you have your moment... this time."

"How considerate of you."

"So you don't want to learn anything about the girl?" Willard asked. "Surely you've heard something on the news?"

"I don't watch television or read the news on the Internet. Why waste my time when they only talk about lunatics blowing things up and imbeciles in government who will bankrupt us all. No, I would rather spend my time listening to Rossini. Have you heard *La scala di seta*?"

"Not lately."

Eyes closed, he moved his right hand through the air as if conducting a symphony. "It tells the story of the beautiful Giulia and her teacher, Dormont, who insists she marry Blansac. A short comedy, but the music is superb. You are probably more familiar with Rossini's *The Barber of Seville*." Mr. Howard looked at the detective.

Willard shrugged. "I'm more of a Johnny Cash man."

"Johnny Cash... yes, of course. Perhaps one day, if you decide you need some culture, I can play Rossini for you."

From the accent you try so hard to conceal, I would say you were raised in the South. Louisiana or Mississippi. Probably backwoods trailer trash. Still, you possessed the drive and determination to obtain an education and leave the bayou behind. You must be proud to work for the Colorado Bureau of Investigation.

"I'll think about it."

"I am sure you will," Mr. Howard said.

Killgood maundered to one of the desks and sat. He glanced around the room. "So, you're still teaching ancient mythology?"

"Yes, it is not often a professor gets to teach others about oneself."

"Oh come on," Killgood said. "How old are you? Sixty?"

Mr. Howard erased his drawing of the Shurale. "A little over sixty." He turned to Willard. "I apologize if I seem enigmatic, but it has been a long day and I am starved."

"You figure yourself a mystery, Professor, but I know quite a bit about you."

"Is that so? Enlighten me."

Willard walked to a bookcase. He traced a finger across the spines of several titles. "You've written several books."

"Very good, Detective. I have written two novels, and three nonfiction books on mythical creatures. The last was about vampires. Are you familiar with them in your line of work?"

"Should I be?"

Willard's intellect exceeded what he had gleaned from a first impression. He might come across as folksy and slow, but he had the mind of a good detective. Willard trusted no one. He looked beyond the obvious and questioned everything. Mr. Howard would need to watch him with a keen eye.

"Have your books sold well?" Willard asked.

"Why do I feel as if I am providing answers you already know?" Mr. Howard took off his glasses and returned them to their case. He pinched the sides of his nose where the eyeglass pads had dug into his flesh and gently massaged. "My novels never sold well, but such is the case in this age of instant gratification. How can one compete against the siren song of the Internet?"

Killgood wiggled out of the desk, which screeched on the linoleum floor, and stood. "Mr. Howard, we're not here to waste your time talking about books."

"No, I should think not."

Killgood moved alongside Willard. "Could you do a psychic reading for us?"

"Is this in regards to the girl Willard referred to?"

"Sorry I didn't call to let you know we're coming. This girl might be in danger."

Mr. Howard glanced at his watch to give the impression he was in a hurry. "I wish I could help you, but I have a dinner date, so tonight is not good for me. And besides, on such short notice, I could not provide useful information."

"Can you come to the station tomorrow afternoon?"

"Afternoon?"

"I realize it's hard for you to go out during the day."

"And still you ask." Mr. Howard pulled his car keys from a pocket. "Very well, Chandler. When should I be there?"

"One o'clock work for you?"

"I may lose sleep, but anything to help my friends in the department."

Killgood smiled and started toward the door. Willard glared for a moment before turning to walk away.

"Detective Willard," Mr. Howard called.

Willard stopped and looked back.

He pointed at the crushed cigarette. "Littering is a crime in this state."

Willard shot him an angry glare. "I'm not the one who put it there."

Mr. Howard fought off a grin as Willard stamped out the door. He picked up the crushed cigarette, tossed it into the trashcan, and stepped to the light switch near the door. "And so our game is 'in book,'" he said, and turned out the lights.

Chapter 2

The clouds that brought the rain moved east, leaving behind a black sky dappled with stars. Mr. Howard drove with the top down on his Mercedes. Warm air rushed over his cheeks and his hair flew straight out behind him. He imagined himself Odin, creating verse on the way to battle, Gungnir at his side, or Jim Morrison, writhing on stage in tight leather pants, lighting the fire of desire in female admirers. Most of the kids in his classes wouldn't know who Jim Morrison was, but he didn't care. Mr. Howard knew a god when he saw one.

The road twisted into the foothills. Below, the lights of the city spread toward the eastern horizon. He turned onto a dirt road and stopped at a gate. A few taps on a security pad and the gate swung open with a groan. Gravel pinged against the undercarriage as he started up the long driveway. His house nestled against the rocky hillside, barren except for an occasional Utah Juniper. Built in the style of Frank Lloyd Wright's *Fallingwater*, it had sharp angles and a large deck out front. When the sun went down, he sat on the deck and suffered in isolation. The house was far too big for one person and he spent many hours wandering through its passages like a ghost in search of a purpose.

The garage door opened and he parked beside a black-panel van. He slipped inside the dim house, ears attuned for unusual sounds. "Lights," he said, and color flooded the rooms. He entered his office, furnished with an eighteenth-century Georgian style desk, Arts and Craft sideboard, a burr walnut bookcase that once belonged to Sir

Arthur Conan Doyle, and a file cabinet that held Bram Stokers papers in the Lyceum Theatre.

At his desk, a few keystrokes on his computer keyboard and the monitor crackled to life. He opened the webpage of the *Coloradoan* newspaper, put on his reading glasses, and leaned toward the screen to read an article about a missing teenager, Stephanie Coldstone. The seventeen-year-old had vanished following an argument with her parents. Authorities speculated she headed to her boyfriend's house, but never arrived.

He sat back in his chair and stared at the girl's picture. Terrible image. Probably taken at the DMV. Notebook and pen in hand, he started toward the basement. There was much work to do before he met with the investigators. His shoes pounded down the unfinished steps. He flipped a switch and the darkness became a yellowish glow. The girl's head snapped up and her eyes opened wide. He strolled over to check the ropes that kept her splayed upright against the wall like a butterfly on a spider's web.

"Good, good, everything is secure." He gently peeled off the duct tape covering her lips. She gasped. "There, there Stephanie, everything will be all right." Her eyes were red and glassy. "Why must you cry?"

"Please don't hurt me." She had been sweating. A rancid stench lingered beneath her armpits and between her legs.

"Why do you think I am going to hurt you? Have I hurt you so far, other than the little prick on your arm?" He patted her clammy cheek and she flinched. "Do not worry, child, I have no intention of sexually abusing you. That would be rude. Do I strike you as a rude man? I should hope not."

He drifted past shelves that held his wine collection and went to a cabinet filled with record albums. "Let me see," he said, moving a finger over the sleeves. "Ah yes, perfect." He pulled out a record and placed the vinyl disc on a turntable. Soon, the haunting refrain of a piano filled the room.

A smile formed on his lips and he turned toward the girl. "Rachmaninoff. Very nice, yes? Did I tell you I saw his First Symphony premiere in Moscow? Back in eighteen hundred ninety six… no, seven. Not everyone recognized Rachmaninoff's genius. The nationalist composer Cui said only inmates of a music conservatory in Hell would admire it. Damn fool."

He pressed a hand over his heart, the other out to the side, and whirled across the floor in a waltz with a spectral partner. "Beautiful, just beautiful. You may have heard Rachmaninoff's music before. Have you seen the romantic movie with Superman, what is the actor's name? Ah yes, Christopher Reeve. Anyway, he falls in love with a woman played by Jane Seymour. He travels back in time and wins her heart by sharing Rachmaninoff's *Rhapsody on a Theme of Paganini*. When I watch the part where she lets her hair down, fireworks explode inside my brain and there is a tingling in my pants. If I could be with her, we would make the earth move off its axis."

He stopped dancing. "Now for our business." Opening a small wooden box, he withdrew a glistening needle.

"No more pain, please."

He moved before her. "There is a trick to controlling one's rage. When you are with someone you do not wish to hurt, you must think of them as you would the one person in the world you are least likely to harm. For example, some men may think of their mothers. However, this will not work in my case for I killed my mother and chopped her up with an ax. I dumped the pieces in the Danube and watched them sink like stones. But do not fear, dear Stephanie, she was a wicked woman and most certainly deserved it."

He gently turned her right arm until the veins came into view. "When I look at you, I think of my cousin Astrid. She had skin like cream and skinny legs, hair the hue of strawberries, and sea-green eyes. She gave me my first kiss, but we were not in love, no, not like that. We lived in a world of dark passages and forbidden rooms, where dreams and reality merged. We admired, yes, but from a distance. There was a line we could not cross."

He positioned the needle over a vein. "You should feel honored. This needle has drawn the blood of nobility. Josephine herself surrendered to my will in her chateau of *Malmaison*." With a quick thrust, he pierced the skin, and a line of blood trickled down her forearm. He brought his mouth to the wound and gently sucked, the metallic flavor of blood overwhelming his palate. He drained her for only a minute. Upon finishing, he pressed a thumb against the wound to stop the bleeding, and bandaged it. "All better," he said.

The color left her face, leaving it almost as pale as his. "What are you… some kind of vampire?"

He returned the needle to its case. "You say that as if you believe there is more than one kind." He brought over a chair and placed it in front of her. For a brief moment, he considered turning her. She could be his companion. Someone to understand the thoughts inside his mind.

No, she deserves better. She deserves peace.

He retrieved the notebook and pen from his coat pocket. "Let us talk now. When we are finished, I will give you supper, agreed?"

"Why are you asking me all these questions?" she asked with a frail voice.

"I need to know all about you," he said.

"There must be more than that."

"Are you afraid?"

She nodded.

"Put your mind at ease. I have talked to the police and tomorrow I will see them again and explain how to find you."

She blinked several times. "Why would you do that?"

"This is what I have always done. The police are my friends and I want you to be my friend too." He opened the notebook to a blank page. "Now let's see, we have already discussed your family, your childhood, and your friends. Let us concentrate on more intimate details. Tell me what makes you the person you are. Tell me about your hobbies and passions. Who was your first love? What are your dreams? I want to know *everything*."

Chapter 3

The alarm clock went off like a ringing bomb. Mr. Howard rolled toward the sound, fingers probing to find the off-switch. Alarm silenced, he brought the clock close to his eyes. "Eleven o' clock," he grumbled and swung his legs over the side of the bed. "What kind of fool wakes up this early?"

He padded across the cool wooden floor toward the bathroom. Heavy drapes kept his bedroom as dark as a catacomb. The bathroom light caused him to squint. When his eyes adjusted, he turned on the shower and slipped out of his clothes. "Ah," he said. The water snapped him awake, and in his mind, he went over his schedule for the day. Meet the police, come home and eat, off to the campus for a class, come back home, eat again, then take care of the girl.

A smile crept over his lips. The girl's blood invigorated him invigorated and made him whole. He felt alive, the way he did as a boy walking the streets of Vienna, back when the Danube ran clear and free to the sea, before the Black Death stole the joy from the world and the Turks returned with dreams of conquest.

His smile vanished as quickly as it came. He liked this girl. Not in a sexual way, but rather how she carried herself. Despite all he put her through, she retained a measure of pride that put him to shame.

He was so deep in thought, he failed to register the click of the shower door followed by a rush of cool air. A soft body pressed against his back. He turned to stare at his new companion, taut and tanned from hiking in the mountains. Only the lines around her eyes and sagging breasts betrayed her age. She slithered up against his pale frame. In their Eden, she played the role of serpent.

"Dean Harris," he said, "what a pleasant surprise. I thought you would be on your hiking excursion until tomorrow."

"Consider this a perk," she replied, and softly kissed his chest. Her lips moved down his stomach as she knelt before him.

He had known women of all sorts during his long life. Frail creatures ashamed by the pleasure they gave and received. Wild ones whose welcoming thighs made the troubles of the world vanish with each thrust of their hips. Leslie Harris belonged amongst the wild ones. She had a photographic memory and he swore she used it to memorize every page of the Kama Sutra.

Her mouth gave him an erection. She stood with a satisfied smile. "From the look of things, maybe I should start dropping by more often."

***

She sat at the kitchen table, dressed for business in a gray skirt, white shirt, and matching gray jacket. She wore her shoulder-length blond hair in a partial ponytail, a style he considered much too informal for a woman in her fifties who ran a university. Leslie didn't care what people thought because she could still pull off any look she desired. Even the college boys watched her walk past, their thoughts drowning in a sea of fantasies.

He shuffled to the coffee maker. "Thank you for a most enjoyable shower."

"I'm glad you liked it." She brushed a strand of hair behind an ear. "I do wish you'd invest in a mirror. Makes it hard for a girl to fix her hair."

"Why have mirrors when there is nothing to see?"

She frowned. "You're an attractive man for your age."

"For my age," he said, and forced a smile. He scooped coffee into a filter. "Care for a cup?"

She sprang out of her chair, slapped her palms together, and bustled toward the basement door. "If we're going to be drinking, it should be champagne. I'll grab a bottle."

He dropped the scooper, coffee grounds spilling across the counter, and dashed over to block her path. "I am afraid I cannot let you go downstairs."

She pulled back, her eyebrows drawn down. "Why not?"

"Because you would find evidence of a crime so vile, you would never want to see me again."

She rolled her eyes. "And what crime would that be?"

He put a hand on her shoulder and steered her toward the kitchen. "Remember the bottle of Dom Perignon I was saving for us? I drank it."

She settled in the chair. "You drank our Dom? Someone should call the police."

He swept coffee grounds off the counter into his palm and dumped them in the sink. "Yes, it was terribly impolite. Another time perhaps?"

"Since we won't be having champagne, I'll take coffee."

When the coffee finished brewing, he brought two mugs to the table. Steam curled from the cups like the smoke of distress fires. "So, what is the occasion?"

"Occasion?" she said, from behind her raised mug.

"To want champagne, you must be celebrating something."

Her cup clanked onto the table. "I've decided to retire."

The news sobered him in an instant and he tried to hide his disappointment. "You are much too young to retire."

A laugh floated from her chest. "I've been at this for over thirty years. It's time I moved on."

"Move on, as in Florida?"

Her daughter, Melanie, who lived in Jacksonville, recently had a baby. It was Leslie's first grandchild and she talked of wanting to live closer to her family. He just never took her seriously. The prospect of her leaving made him want to kick something. His gaze lowered to the table.

"Now don't pout."

"You will miss the mountains," he said, recalling a moonlit hike into the foothills. Sex beneath the stars, it was a perfect date.

She took hold of his hand, her fingers coiling around his. "Come with me. You're eligible to retire."

"What, and leave all this excitement behind? Besides, sunny Florida is no place for someone like me."

"We can swim naked in the ocean," she said, the words soft off her tongue.

"We can swim naked in a mountain lake."

Her hand left his. "I'm leaving. My mind is made up. So stop trying to talk me out of it."

His jaw clenched. He missed her already. "When will you go?"

"Two weeks."

"That soon?" He weaved his fingers through his hair, onto the back of his neck and sighed. "Who will take your place? Do not say Luther Van Adams. The man is a jackass."

She smirked. "A Harvard-educated jackass."

"It does not matter where they forged his degree. Van Adams has the mental capacity of a flea. I suppose he will try to cut my position once more."

"He'd like to see you gone."

He slammed a fist onto the table. "And I will make him gone!"

She leaned back in her chair and blinked several times. "I never knew you had such a temper."

He took a deep breath to calm his nerves and held out the sugar bowl. "For your coffee."

She hesitated before accepting the bowl. "No need to fret, Van Adams will only be the Acting Dean. The board has already found my replacement."

"Who did they hire?"

"Jennifer Tolliver, dean at Medford State. I met her once. Mid-thirties, black hair, long legs, just your type."

"Perhaps your type as well."

Her eyes sparkled for a moment. "Perhaps."

He held back a response. She would be gone soon and start to fade in his mind like an old photograph exposed to sunlight.

"I heard the police visited your classroom last night." She looked at him with an expression that suggested she understood their relationship was burning down to embers.

"You heard correctly."

"They must have come about the—"

"Please," he said holding up a hand.

She chewed her bottom lip. "That's right. You don't like to know about them ahead of time." Several seconds of awkward silence followed before she said, "It's really amazing what you do. You have a gift."

"A gift," he said, the words trailing off to a whisper, a vision of poor Stephanie in the dark basement inside his head. Would she consider what he did amazing? He took a sip of coffee and glanced at his watch. "I need to leave soon."

She rolled her cup between her palms. "You're angry with me."

"No, not at all… well, perhaps. I will miss our moments."

She pushed out of her chair and stood. "You can always come visit me in Florida. I'm buying a condo near the beach. I will put aluminum foil over the windows."

He rose from his chair and went to her. "You have always accommodated me."

She touched his cheek. "And now I desert you."

"You have your reasons, and so you are forgiven."

Chapter 4

As he sat in the hallway outside the homicide office, an idea came to Mr. Howard. Over a hundred years before, he had sat in the hallway of Scotland Yard, waiting to talk to Inspector Abberline about the Ripper—nasty fellow, no manners at all, tearing apart women and leaving their bodies on the street for everyone to see. Given his history of assisting in difficult investigations, it was no surprise Abberline came to him. Of course, he had nothing to offer them and the killings continued. Tired of reading about the case in the papers, he decided to put an end to the nonsense. He failed to save Mary Kelly, but when he discovered the identity of her killer, he taught the Ripper a thing or two about ripping. It was one of the few times he took pleasure in killing.

Hunched over a black notebook, he studied the information Stephanie provided the previous evening. She was a good kid. Too good for him. He traced the page with a finger as he read to himself. *Mother—Janet. Father—Carl. Two siblings—brother, Steven, and sister, Mary. Rides horses, plays soccer, likes Johnny Depp movies.*

"Deciding who to call for a date?"

Killgood and Willard stood before him. Killgood smiled. Willard did not.

"My days of pursuing the fairer sex are long over."

Willard motioned with his chin. "Why are you dressed like that?"

To protect himself from the sun, he wore a heavy trench coat, scarf, leather gloves, sunglasses, and a fedora. His exposed skin glistened with sunscreen.

"Mr. Howard has a skin disorder," Killgood said.

"Is that why your skin's so pale?"

Mr. Howard stood and put away his notebook. "I have PMLE."

"What's that?"

"Polymorphic light eruption, which is a fancy way of saying I am allergic to sunlight."

Willard squinted, his face a stony mask. "And that's why you only teach at night?"

Killgood waved toward an open office. "Come, let's talk inside."

He followed the detectives into the office. The small space felt suffocating despite having a window that looked out onto the hallway, and another with a view of the distant foothills. It was the kind of office you'd expect a cop to have, all business, with a cold metal desk, and dented steel filing cabinet covered with sticky notes. His gaze fell on the only clue of humanity in the room, family photographs displayed on the desk. "Your children have grown into beautiful young people." He took a seat. Willard sat in the chair beside him. His clothes reeked of cigarette smoke.

With his wavy, auburn hair and lively blue eyes, Killgood had managed to retain his boyish good looks. He eased into a chair behind the desk, the vinyl rippling, and picked up the frame with the photographs. He smiled. "They are beautiful, aren't they?" He pulled out his wallet, opened it, and held it toward Mr. Howard. "My granddaughter, Gail."

Mr. Howard put on his glasses and leaned forward. The photograph showed a little black-haired girl with big blue eyes. "She looks like her mother."

Killgood returned the billfold to his pocket. "You're right."

"Reann has always been lovely."

"Jesus H. Christ, can we get on with it?" Willard said.

Killgood gestured toward the agitated detective. "Detective Willard doesn't believe in any of this."

Mr. Howard peered at Willard from the corner of his eye. The detective grimaced as if he suffered from constipation. *Someone really needs to get the poor sod some prune juice.*

"Is it psychic ability you don't believe in or just me?"

Willard lit a cigarette. He took a long drag and blew smoke at Mr. Howard. "I'm familiar with the work of so-called psychic detectives. Frauds if you ask me. Look at Hurkos in Boston. He didn't do a damn thing to help catch the strangler other than provide a series of false leads. The same thing happened with the coed murders in Michigan."

Mr. Howard tapped his chin as he considered the detective's words. *I will need to win the man's trust and soon, or at the very least throw him off by providing information that could be verified. Since Willard thinks so little of Peter Hurkos, it is best to reaffirm his suspicion rather than challenge it.*

"Yes, Hurkos sought publicity and fame. I, on the other hand, do not. You are the ones who came to me for assistance."

Willard's line of smoke drifted toward the no smoking sign on Killgood's desk. "What powers do you claim?"

"Powers?"

"You know, psychic abilities. Retrocognition, psychometry, or does God whisper the answers into your ear?"

"God does not choose to whisper into my ear, Detective, but if he whispers in yours, I know a good psychiatrist who can help you with that."

Killgood smirked and shook his head.

"I do not try to categorize my gift," Mr. Howard continued. "What I do is what I do. If I can help the police, I will, but I make no guarantees."

"Have you had any visions lately?" Killgood asked.

Mr. Howard pressed his hands against his temples and massaged the skin. A little show to fool the cops. To add to the effect, he hummed softly. The cops always interpreted this as some form of meditation. He hummed for several seconds before stopping. "I had a vision as I drove home last night."

Killgood leaned across the desk. "What did you see?"

Mr. Howard closed his eyes tightly to cause the skin around them to gather in fine wrinkles and pretended to concentrate. "Rocks."

"Rocks?" Willard said.

Mr. Howard's lips parted and he sucked in air between his teeth, the wet sound adding to the illusion of concentration. "No, not rocks... more like stones... river stones... glistening." He looked at Killgood. "Does this mean anything to you?"

"Glistening stones... hmm. Why did they glisten?"

Mr. Howard stopped massaging his temples and tapped knuckles against his forehead. "The sun... yes... it glistened on the stones as if they were covered in..."

"What?" Killgood asked. "What were they covered in?"

He sighed. "Ice. I believe it was ice. Sorry, this is not much."

"Hmm, stones covered in ice." Killgood looked at Willard. "Stones covered in ice. Cold stones."

Willard groaned.

Mr. Howard turned toward Willard. "What have I said?"

"A girl went missing over the weekend," Killgood said. "Her name is Stephanie Coldstone."

"And that is why I am here?"

"I have no clue why you're here," Willard said.

Mr. Howard faced Killgood. "Detective Willard is in charge?"

Killgood nodded. "She doesn't live in the city."

"Why are the State Police and not the sheriff's office handling the investigation?"

"Her father has money," Willard answered, "and powerful friends."

This revelation came as a shock to Mr. Howard. Stephanie had given no indication her family was wealthy and there was no mention of her father's position in the newspaper. He tried to target low-profile victims, prostitutes, runaways, not wealthy men's daughters. "You think the girl is dead?"

"Why would you say that?" Willard asked.

He gestured toward Killgood. "Chandler is a homicide detective."

"I was asked to get involved because of our past association," Killgood explained.

"I see. So, you believe the girl may still be alive and you want me to help find her?"

"I don't want you to do anything," Willard said, "but the family is desperate."

Mr. Howard massaged his chin. "I will do what I can, but there are things you must do for me."

"You'll need a case file with the girl's photograph," Killgood said.

"Case file yes. Photograph no. Let me see if I can develop a mental picture of the girl on my own. Black out anything in the report that pertains to her description." He wrung his hands on his lap, another trick meant to demonstrate his psychic abilities. "Do you have any of the girl's personal items?"

"So you can make a relevant association with Stephanie?" Killgood asked.

"Yes."

"This is bullshit," Willard said.

"Mr. Howard's helped us in the past," Killgood said.

"Fine," Willard answered. "I'll play along for now. I'll talk to the girl's family. What do you need?"

"Personal items. Articles of clothing. Journals. Favorite stuffed toys, anything with a strong association."

"I'll contact the Coldstones as soon as we're done here," Willard said.

Mr. Howard sprang out of the chair, pretending urgency. "I must go home and ruminate. When can I get the case file?"

Killgood lifted a stack of paper-clipped pages and held them out. "Here you go."

He took the papers, nodded at both detectives, and opened the door. Mr. Howard paused in the doorway. "Last night, I kept thinking about Johnny Depp. Does this mean anything to you?"

The detectives shook their heads.

"Hmm," Mr. Howard said. "How about the word Bethord? I kept seeing the word Bethord."

Killgood glanced at Willard and then back at him. "I will call you when we have those personals."

Mr. Howard stepped out into the hallway, a big grin on his face. Bethord, Ohio, was Stephanie's hometown.

Chapter 5

Willard's shoulders sagged as he stared at the Colonial-style house. Lights burned in every room. Gears turned inside his head like the wheels on an electric meter. *Damn family costs me a fortune.* He stomped up the sidewalk toward the front door. A pair of scooters lay on the lawn. *Little shits never take care of anything.* He grunted upon discovering the front door unlocked. How many times had he told Doris to keep it locked?

He stepped inside and a chill crept over his skin. A low growl rose from his throat. He checked the thermostat, which was set on 68.

Bitch thinks I'm Donald Trump.

Laughter floated from the kitchen. He made his way toward the sound. Doris sat at the table behind a plateful of pancakes smothered in syrup. He estimated the stack to be at least four inches tall. Six slices of bacon shared a nearby plate with three fried eggs. His kids, Dave and Margo (he hated that fucking name), sat behind similar feasts. *No wonder they look like a family of hippos. If Doris's butt gets any bigger, I'll have to widen the goddamn front door.*

She picked up a piece of bacon and chewed. The bacon hung from the side of her mouth. "Hey, hon, how was your day?"

He resisted an urge to punch the wall. *If this is the American dream, wrap me in a flag and put a fucking bullet in my head.* "Great, just great." He grabbed a beer from the refrigerator.

"Hey, Dad," Dave said. "I'm trying out for the school wrestling team."

"Isn't that fantastic?" Doris asked.

"I didn't know middle schools had sumo wrestling," he said on his way out of the kitchen.

Inside his office, he slumped behind the desk. He couldn't shake the image of the smirking psychic from his mind. The son of a bitch nailed the girl's hometown, but he could have obtained that information from public records. Just because Mr. Howard claimed not to follow the news meant nothing. His vision of stones covered in ice was total bullshit. The only thing he said of interest was the part about Johnny Depp.

After leaving Killgood's office, he had contacted Stephanie's parents. When asked about Johnny Depp, her mother's eyes grew big and blood rushed into her cheeks. "Johnny Depp is Stephanie's favorite actor," she said. "Why do you ask?" He had considered lying rather than admit the information came from Mr. Howard. As expected, when he explained, both of her parents became excited. "Can he help us?" Mr. Coldstone asked. Upon hearing Mr. Howard wanted to see personal items belonging to Stephanie, they tore out of the foyer like teenagers on a scavenger hunt.

Alone in their mansion, he looked around the grand façade they had so carefully constructed. The rich paintings on the wall suggested culture. The polished marble floor implied a status he'd never enjoy. His twenty plus years on the job taught him to see past the window dressing. Mr. Coldstone inherited several thousand acres from his grandfather. Oil and gas deposits gave him money. The advice of a good broker turned him into a wealthy man. Without a bit of luck, he'd probably be living in a doublewide trailer with a wife like Doris.

They rushed down the stairs. Mr. Coldstone carried a box. He held it out. "Some of Stephanie's things."

"Thanks," he had said, even though he didn't mean it. Working with Mr. Howard was like having hemorrhoids he couldn't scratch.

On the drive home, he rummaged through the box. Inside he found a pink, fuzzy sweater, a stuffed panda bear, and a sketch book. He lifted the sweater and noticed a pair of white panties stuck to the wool. He held up the panties. What was that stain in the crotch? After checking to make certain no one watched, he pressed the panties against his nose and breathed in a faint metallic odor. Blood. He brought the panties down to his lap. His fingers worked the silky material like a pottery maker molding clay as he imagined her wearing the panties. His breathing became rapid. His penis tingled with the arrival of blood. He tossed the panties back inside the box and wiped sweat from his brow. *What in the hell is happening to me?* The smell of Stephanie's blood remained strong in his mind all the way to his house.

Willard opened the Internet on his computer, fingers rushing to type in the address of a search engine. He pulled up the webpage for the college. "Let's see what I can find out about you," he said, clicking on a link to the facility bios. He scrolled down the list until spotting the name "Mr. Howard, professor of ancient mythology." Opening the bio, he leaned close to the monitor and read:

Mr. Howard has been a member of the staff since 1990. He has a PhD in History, Applied Human Sciences, and Cognitive Psychology.

He leaned back in the chair. "That's it? Come on, there has to be more information. This prick has to have a first name. Where did he earn his degrees?" He next tried searching "Howard professor." Nothing came back. He typed in, "Howard psychic." Still nothing. He sighed and tried one more time. "Mr. Howard psychic detective." A link appeared to an article from the Baltimore Sun dated July 1988. The title of the article was, "The Amazing Mr. Howard."

"Yeah right." He opened the link and started to read.

College Professor Helps Solve Murder Mysteries

Six months ago, nineteen-year-old prostitute Janet Harking vanished from Baltimore's waterfront park. Despite a massive search conducted by the local police with the assistance of hundreds of volunteers, no trace of Harking was found until now. Thanks to Mr. Howard, a professor of History at The University of Maryland, police were able to recover Harking's body on Saturday from a grave in the woods near Sharpsburg. According to an anonymous source in the Baltimore Police Department, Mr. Howard told authorities that he experienced recurring dreams of a Civil War battle and saw Harking in those dreams. When Mr. Howard, who is a Civil War history buff, saw Burnside's Bridge in a dream, he recognized the location as the Antietam Battlefield. It was here that the Union Army commanded by General McClellan drove back the Army of Northern Virginia commanded by General Robert E. Lee on September 17, 1862. Later visions helped Mr. Howard pinpoint the exact location where Harking's body was discovered. According to the source, Mr. Howard has helped the police on several murder investigations in the past. When contacted, Mr. Howard had no comment.

Willard pulled on his bottom lip as he thought. *So, he has a history of helping the cops in Baltimore, but nothing shows up in Colorado, and he's been here over twenty years.* He would need to contact the Baltimore homicide unit. *I also need to press Killgood about his experience dealing with Mr. Howard. Psychic detective my ass. There's something strange about this son of a bitch.*

More laughter carried from the kitchen. He stared at the closed office door and sighed. The world was shrinking around him. He felt connected to no one and nothing. Why did Doris have to let herself get so heavy? What happened to the woman he married? She'd become a stranger to him. A fat Goldilocks who ate all the porridge and still wanted more. He had stopped attending police functions because other detectives joked about Doris behind his back. How could he ever hope to advance in his career with a wife that looked like a beached whale? Lord knows he'd tried to help her lose weight. He'd spent a fortune on diet books. Looking at Doris, he saw his roly-poly Mama tending the hogs, Mississippi mud painting the hem of her dress mahogany, sweat beading across her wide face. After a while, it became hard to tell person from hog. "Sooie, Sooie, little pigs." He slithered into the cellar, down in the shadows, hands over his ears to block her voice. *Make yourself small enough and soon no one will notice you're gone.*

Digging into his pocket, he retrieved the panties. Holding them out of sight, he massaged the crotch. *I'm pretty sure it was blood I smelled. Maybe not. Could be an important clue to the investigation. I don't want to overlook anything.* He eyed the door and brought the panties to his nose.

Chapter 6

Mr. Howard drove east, the lights of the city fading in his rearview mirror. From time to time, he stole glances at Stephanie, who sat in the passenger seat staring out the window. She was quiet as he passed through farm towns whose single traffic lights flashed a yellow warning—the buildings dark and sidewalks empty. As he drove away from the last town, the sky deepened and countless stars flamed overhead. A waxing moon painted the surrounding fields a soft gray. The hum of the tires floated through the open van window. Warm air carried the stench of manure.

Stephanie turned to look at him. "I've been on this road with my family."

"Oh, when was that?"

"Back when I was..." Her words faded in the wind whistling through the open windows and her attention returned to the passing scenery.

She shimmered in the pale glow cast by the van's instrument panel. A ghostly hue settled around her. He longed to apologize for all he had done and was going to do to her.

After driving a little over an hour, he arrived at the exit for the grasslands. He drove north, past the entrance sign. Steel rattled as the van traveled over a cattle guard. He made a mental note of the cattle guard. The road ran straight and flat. He cut the headlights and the passage became a black smudge.

"Have we arrived?"

He gripped the steering wheel so hard his fingers ached. "Yes, we are here."

Mr. Howard spotted a lone cottonwood tree. It marked the location he'd chosen on his previous excursion into the area. He stopped the van and jotted notes in his journal. Welcome sign, cattle guard, barbed wire fence, cottonwood tree.

"What are you writing in your book?" she asked.

"Information for the police."

"About me?"

He shut off the engine and looked out the window, unable to meet her gaze. Without answering, he exited and walked to the back of the van. Opening the door, he reached inside to grab the zippered plastic bag. With a grunt, he hoisted the bag onto a shoulder and lumbered toward the tree. His shoulder ached as the weight of the bag settled. He pushed through an opening cut in the fence.

At the tree, he eased the bag onto the ground and returned to the van for a shovel. On his preceding visit to the park, he prepared the spot by digging a hole. Since then, the dirt on top had baked into a crusty layer. Beyond this, the earth remained soft and easy to turn with the shovel. The moon slipped low on the horizon as if creeping closer to spy on his activity. In the distance, a coyote howled. Sweat bubbled across his back as he dug. Muscles burned with each thrust of the shovel. By the time he finished digging the hole, his damp shirt clung to his shoulders, and a deep ache took root in his bones.

Mr. Howard knelt beside the bag. He unzipped it and pulled the plastic aside. Moonlight washed over Stephanie's face. In a fairy tale, this would be the part where he leaned over to kiss her awake, but this was no fairy tale. No kiss could stir Stephanie from her deathly slumber. He bowed his head. Tears welled in his eyes and he tried to massage them away without success.

Her spirit moved alongside him and rested a hand on his shoulder. "Do you think I was beautiful?"

He nodded. "You were a most beautiful girl, yes, and I am heartless and cruel. You are a giver of life and I take it away. One day, Stephanie, I will burn in hell for my crimes, of this I am certain." He brushed a strand of hair from her forehead. "You did not deserve this fate."

Moonlight revealed bruises on her neck. He remembered her soft skin compressed beneath his fingers, her body writhing in agony as she struggled to survive. He rocked back and forth, hugging himself, a soft groan rising from his throat.

"If I was not such a coward, I would take my own life to spare the innocent their pain, but I am afraid, yes, I am most definitely afraid. The door to Heaven is locked for me and rightfully so. Damn you, Lenhard."

A scene came alive inside his mind, a memory from his distant past. Vienna was a city of rats then, a filthy shit hole. No sewers, garbage piled in heaps everywhere, a place of religious intolerance hidden behind crumbling medieval walls, where a dozen languages were heard on the streets—German, Italian, French, Spanish, Hebrew and more. His home was in The Regensburg Hof at Lugeck in the Inner City, with a view of the Danube and a private courtyard where his wife, Sophie, spent her afternoons reading. He'd been married a number of years and fathered four children who had children of their own. His shipping business made him a wealthy man, and now in his later years, he had much to be thankful for. When the Black Death arrived, cries of agony and desperation filled the air both day and night. One man drank blood from a recently decapitated head hoping it would protect him. Others drank the urine of plague victims for the same purpose. Across the city, church bells rang constantly in the belief the movement of air would disperse the infection. The bells performed a strange requiem to remind people what had been lost and to warn them of the suffering still to come.

He kept his family secure behind locked doors. This failed to save them and one by one they succumbed to the disease. First his oldest daughter, Romy, followed by his youngest son, Franz, and daughter Heidi, who held him in her gaze as if expecting him to save her. Sophie was the last to die, silent beneath her sheets, her body like a piece of fruit left to rot in the sun. He wanted to cry when her eyes closed to the world, but his own body had already began to decay and he had nothing left to give.

Fever, yes, his body on fire as if tied to a burning pyre. The Brotherhood of the Holy Trinity carted him to their hospital. Doctors administered an emetic, some kind of thick brown syrup that made him vomit into a pail. They drained his blood in order to balance the "humors" inside his body. Nothing worked. He grew weaker by the hour, the world around him turning to shadow. Night arrived. He tried to focus on the moon shining through the window, but his vision became clouded. It was then his oldest son, Lenhard, appeared next to his bed, body pale, lips as red as cherries. How could this be? Word from his fellow priests at St. Stephens was that Lenhard had the plague. He should be dead. "Are you a ghost?"

Lenhard shook his head. "I have been given a second chance and now I will give it to you, Father. Because of me you shall live on." Lenhard knelt beside the bed and used a dagger to open a vein in his arm. Black blood seeped from the wound. Lenhard brought his arm to his father's mouth.

"Drink this and live." It took but a moment for Lenhard to complete the task. He stood with a smile, bowed his head, and walked toward the doorway, vanishing in the shadows. *What did Lenhard do to me?* This question weighed on his mind throughout the night and he could not sleep.

He rolled in the sheets, a fire igniting inside his chest and spreading across every nerve. An invisible hand gripped his heart and squeezed. Sweat erupted from his pores and pooled beneath him. Dawn arrived with sunlight streaming through the tall windows. A ray beamed down upon him. A thousand needles pricked his flesh. The light, he had to escape the light.

Scrambling out of bed, he stumbled from the ward, oblivious to the suffering around him. Inside the dark basement, he curled into a ball of insignificance, safe from the burning sun. Time inched forward, slowed by overpowering hunger that twisted inside his gut like worms in a corpse. And then he calmed, his body still, the heat in his body fading to a winter's chill.

He ventured into the night. The clang of church bells vibrated through his brain. *Dong-dong-dong.* Hands clasped against over his ears, he staggered onward. Passing clouds obscured the light of the moon, but he saw the world as if a blazing sun shined upon it. His hunger intensified, ripping and tearing at his insides. He spotted a man asleep on the riverbank. An old drunkard whose alcohol-laced breath charged the cool night air. Murder was wrong; he knew this, but having spilt blood before, it came more easily for him. He fell upon the man, fangs ripping apart his neck before he could scream. Warm blood flooded his palate and his pain subsided. He was alive, and yet, a part of him had died. The part created by God—his humanity.

"What are you thinking?" Stephanie asked.

"I am thinking I have become the beast of a thousand nightmares. I live if you die, that is my curse." He worked an arm under her body and lifted her head onto his lap. "I can never love, not as a man is meant to love, but realize this, in the still chambers of my heart, I have love for you. The way a father feels love for his daughter, yes, this is what I feel for you. I have caused such heartache. Your parents will never stop grieving your loss." He brought her against his chest and leaned down to rest his cheek against the top of her head.

"I don't want to stay here by myself."

He took in the radiance of her spirit and sighed. "I will keep my vow and tell the police how to find you. But first, I must return you to the earth and this takes time. When all that remains are bones to mark your passing, I will lead them to you."

He wrested her body from the bag and gently laid it inside the hole. He whispered a prayer as if God might actually take an interest in what he had to say. Leaning into the shallow hole, he softly kissed her on the forehead. "Good-bye, dear Stephanie. Rest in peace, child. I beg you."

She floated past him and eased into the grave. "Do not forget me."

"I could not forget you even if I wanted to."

Her eyes closed as she disappeared inside her body. To the west, lightning flashed over the distant mountains. He grabbed the shovel and, with trembling hands, went to work.

Chapter 7

Evening arrived with the rumble of thunder. Fat, gray clouds blew over the mountains and broke open. Rain and hail hammered the roof of the house. Mr. Howard checked the clock on the wall.

Damn it.

He would need to leave within fifteen minutes in order to make it to class on time.

The hail stopped before he climbed into his Mercedes, but rain continued to fall in wind-driven sheets. The pattering rain and squeaking windshield wipers performed a seasonal melody. There was one blessing in the rain—no crazy bicyclists to dodge. They invaded the town like parasites, weaving in and out of traffic and popping up in blind spots. A year before, he hit a bicyclist named Harvey Langford. Poor Harvey, he would have ridden away with a few bruises if he hadn't threatened to file a lawsuit. Good thing the accident took place with no one around to witness it.

Mr. Howard often recalled Harvey as he drove past his unmarked grave in the foothills. "How is that lawsuit coming, Harvey?" he would shout out the window and smile. But in the end, Harvey had the last laugh. His spirit appeared inside Mr. Howard's house, tearing through the rooms on his phantom bicycle. "I'm still going to sue your ass," he'd shout. Someday, he would need to find a way to return Harvey's bones to his family out in California.

The rain ended by the time he arrived on campus. He parked and set off toward Van Adams Hall. Lamplight reflected in puddles on the sidewalks. Raindrops glistened on blades of grass. Brian Spriggs ran past, carrying the sweet fragrance of cannabis. "You're gonna be late, Professor."

And you are going to dead in five years. Mr. Howard waved. "Keep running, Brian, but you will never catch up to your dreams."

"Mr. Howard, Mr. Howard," a voice called behind him. He cringed and turned around. Van Adams jogged in his direction. Pudgy and balding, dark eyes hidden behind thick black spectacles, he projected neither confidence nor authority. To Mr. Howard, Van Adams was the kind of man you'd like to kick in the nuts, if for no other reason than to wipe the stupid grin off his face. He was a clown in need of a circus, a monkey in need of a hurdy gurdy man. Despite his Harvard education, he only landed his job at the university because his wealthy grandfather donated vast sums of money to construct monuments to himself such as Van Adams Hall. Van Adams passed himself off as a righteous man. He dragged his millstone to church every Sunday morning, gaining forgiveness before the ink dried on his check. But he was no saint, as evidenced by his licentious behavior at the last faculty Christmas party. Mr. Howard made it a point to gather information on anyone he considered a threat. He had enough dirt on Van Adams to bury him.

"Luther, you are out of breath. Have you been chasing sorority girls again?"

Van Adams grimaced. His attraction to female students was a poorly kept secret, not that it bothered Mr. Howard. A rumor whispered amongst professors told of a naked coed who ran bleeding from Van Adams's home. It took a million persuasions to ensure her silence. Mr. Howard didn't give a damn what inspired the bumbling academic as long as he stayed out of his business.

Unfortunately, this was not the case. Three years prior, when Van Adams name came up for the position of assistant dean, Mr. Howard protested the promotion most vigorously. "There are candidates who are better qualified," he told anyone who would listen. His advice went unheeded and Van Adams got the job. Now he made it his mission to get Mr. Howard's position eliminated. Twice, he proposed letting him go due to budget constraints. Twice, Leslie had saved his job. Who would save him after she left?

"Mr. Howard, you are a pompous ass."

"Come, Luther, you did not run after me just to tell me that."

Van Adams gestured toward the building. "We'll talk on your way to class."

He grunted under his breath and fell in alongside Van Adams. "So, what are we to talk about?"

"By now you are aware of Dean Harris's retirement."

"Yes, most unfortunate. Are you planning to retire as well?"

Van Adams eyebrows pulled down. "Of course not."

"Also most unfortunate," Mr. Howard said.

Van Adams held the door open for him. "There will be changes at the University with a new Dean."

"You are referring to budget cuts."

"I'll discuss your position with Dean Tolliver."

Mr. Howard stopped outside his classroom. "Luther, let us be frank. You do not like me. I do not like you. That is the way of things. You will try to convince Dean Tolliver that my position is expendable. She will discover after spending five minutes in your company that you are an asshole. Let us hope she has the good sense not to be swayed by your lineage."

Van Adams pulled back, chin toward his chest, lips quivering. "What are you suggesting?"

"We understand each other too well to dance around the truth, yes? Either I stay on in my current position, or I leave. Is that not how it goes?" He opened the classroom door but paused. "Tell me, Luther, considering your education and family background, why do you think the Board of Trustees decided not to promote you? Perhaps they too share my doubts regarding your capabilities? I will leave you to ponder that question. Good evening." He stepped into the room and closed the door before Van Adams had an opportunity to reply.

Mr. Howard smirked as he walked to the desk. The students stopped talking and followed his movement. They never felt totally comfortable in his presence and how could they considering his appearance? Skin the hue of a snow-covered field. Wavy silver hair that hung to his shoulders. Grey eyes capable of such intensity; the bravest soul withered under their glare. To compensate, he did his best to make the class enjoyable. He employed the motto of "no one left behind" long before the idiots in Washington stole it. Open book tests and grading on a curve ensured all of his students passed the course, which in turn made him one of the most popular professors at the college, another sore subject with Van Adams.

He sat at his desk and sorted through paperwork. Karen fidgeted in her seat on the front row. She wore a black mini skirt that left little to the imagination, not that he needed to use his after her previous peep show. She held a paperback on her lap. He smiled at the title. "I see you are reading about vampires, Miss Webster."

She stopped fidgeting. "Uh, yeah, I guess."

"Perfect sparkly vampires."

"Yeah." She shifted in the seat. "Edward is sexy."

He resisted the urge to roll his eyes. "And what makes him sexy? Because the author tells you he is?"

"He sounds sexy."

Soft laughter filled the classroom. She stared at her lap and flushed.

"Do not listen to them. Vampires are sexy creatures, yes? Even old ones, I do believe."

She looked up at him and flashed dazzling white teeth.

"Would you not think me sexy if I were a vampire?"

She continued to smile. "Very sexy."

One day he might have to find out if she was serious. He pulled a textbook from his attaché, stood, and strolled to the podium. "As I recall," he said, putting on his glasses, "you were to read the chapter on Slavic mythology."

A groan went up.

"Now, children, why do you complain if you fail to do your assignment? Could it be you were too busy making mischief of some sort? Were you using drugs? Binge drinking? Or perhaps your libidos ran wild." He shook his head. "Very well." Moving out from the podium, he walked straight to Karen. "May I see your book?"

She held up her textbook.

"No, the other one."

She looked to her left and right before sheepishly pulling the novel from her backpack. "Do you want to read it?"

"No," he said, taking the book, "I know all I need to know about vampires." He remembered Stephanie, alone and afraid inside his basement. If only real life could be like fiction. "This novel is about sacrifice, yes? Does not the protagonist sacrifice her life in order to be with the vampire? Maybe not in a literal way, but she is willing to change herself. Humans have sacrificed other humans since the dawn of time. The Incas favored the sacrifice of children in a practice known as Capacocha. Fattened up on a diet of llama meat and maize, they were sacrificed at high altitudes to be closer to the gods."

Several of the students squirmed on their chairs.

"Terrible, yes?" he continued. "The Aztecs held ceremonies involving human sacrifice at least once a month. Their first recorded sacrifice was that of King Coxcox's daughter, who they killed and skinned while creating Tenochtitlan. They believed sacrifices were necessary to pay a blood debt to the gods, who had sacrificed themselves to create the world for men." He closed the book and brought it against his forehead. "A blood debt to the gods. What god could demand such a toll? The same one who created vampires?" He lowered the book. "It is a curse to live through the death of others, would you not agree?"

"You talk as if vampires are real," Spriggs said.

"I am a vampire."

"What kind of drugs are you taking?" Spriggs asked.

Mr. Howard went to Karen and held out the book. She stared up at him through half-closed eyes. Bedroom eyes. "Our friend Mr. Spriggs does not believe me a vampire. Who would like to see me kill Mr. Spriggs and drink his blood?"

Hands shot up around the room. He chuckled. "It seems, Mr. Spriggs, you are not popular with your classmates. Unfortunately, I do not consider you worthy of a sacrifice. Perhaps if I were an Aztec, I would cut out your heart and skin you."

Spriggs slouched in his seat in an effort to become as small as possible. Mr. Howard returned to the podium. He cracked open his textbook and thumbed through the chapters until coming to Slavic mythology. He looked up from the book. "Excuse my wandering introspection. My mind is far away I fear, but I will do my best to battle through these distractions. Now for our friends, the Slavs."

Another groan went up and he smiled. Spriggs held his book in front of him with his eyes peeking over the top.

It is right that they fear me.

When class ended, Karen was the last to leave. She stopped in front of him, the scent of musk wafting from a spot on her neck. Her jugular pulsated with the rush of blood. "I do think you'd make a sexy vampire."

Her words played inside his head like Chausson's *Poeme*. It took all his fortitude to keep from touching her. "Why, thank you, Karen. You have made my day."

She held him in her gaze for several seconds before walking away. When she disappeared out the door, he took a deep breath and held a hand to his chest. "I am much too old for this."

He returned to his desk and read the *Apology of Socrates*. He had no reason to stay, but found himself not wanting to return to an empty house. If Stephanie was there, they could talk. If Stephanie was there, tied against the wall, her life fleeting with each passing second. She had never been his friend. No. He must remember the reason she had been his guest.

Footsteps approached in the hallway outside. Two people. Heavy footfalls. Probably grown men. One carried the stench of cigarette smoke. The handle on the door rotated with a click. Killgood and Willard stepped into the room. Willard carried a box. "Good evening, Detectives. I did not expect to see you again this soon."

They walked to the desk. Willard dropped the box with a thud. "Stephanie Coldstone's personals." He squinted like an Old West gunfighter.

Mr. Howard snapped his book closed and turned to Killgood whose eyes betrayed quiet desperation. "Still no word on the girl?"

"We wouldn't be here if we knew anything," Willard answered.

Killgood flattened his hands on the desk and leaned forward. "We may be running out of time."

"I understand." Mr. Howard's attention moved to the box. "Did you ask the girl's parents for these items, Detective Willard?"

"I did."

"That must have been difficult for you."

"More than you know."

Mr. Howard brought the box onto his lap. "Let me see what you have brought." He rummaged through the items. "Yes, yes, this might do."

"What do you mean by might do?" Willard asked.

"This is not an exact science, Detective. If scientists could understand and control my abilities, then even men of your limited capacity would be able to use it."

"You haven't shown me anything yet."

He smiled at the detective. "Did my previous visions turn up anything?"

"Yeah, stones covered in ice." Willard folded his arms across his chest.

"And what of Johnny Depp and Bethord?"

"Bethord, Ohio, is Stephanie's hometown," Killgood said.

"That means nothing," Willard said. "Anyone could have obtained that information from public records."

"And Johnny Depp?" Mr. Howard asked.

Willard shrugged.

So you have taken us to a dead draw. Well played, Detective. "If you believe I am a fraud, why are you here?"

Willard glared at him. "It doesn't matter what I believe."

"You are right," he answered. "All that matters is the girl."

Willard took several deep breaths. Air whistled through his nose. "So, are you going to get started?"

"These things cannot be rushed. You should take a seat."

The detectives retreated to the front row of chairs and sat. Killgood leaned back, hands behind his head. Willard rested his chin in one hand while the fingers of his other hand softly tapped on the table top.

Mr. Howard lifted a pink sweater from the box. He touched the soft material and grimaced as the memory of Stephanie's dead face flashed through his mind. Teeth clenched, he struggled to drive the image away. Massaging the sweater, he brought it against his cheek. His eyes flared as he pretended to be in a trance.

"I see a large house. Mediterranean... no, French. A bedroom, yes, a girl's room. A high picture. On the ceiling... above her bed. A man in the photograph stares down. Black eyes. No, black around his eyes. Old clothes. Strange hat. Tricorn style, black. Pirate Hat. I see many animals on the bed. Unicorns, bears, and dragons. Pink bedspread with white flowers." He wrung the sweater faster. "Two people in a room. A pool table. Man and woman. Both middle-aged. Curt and Janice... no, not Curt... Carl. Carl and Janet. Their names are Carl and Janet." Willard's mouth gaped open. Inwardly, Mr. Howard smiled. Others are in the room. Three people. Younger. A boy and two girls. Teenagers. Boy is..." He stopped wringing the sweater and tapped his knuckles against his forehead. "Stan... no, not Stan... Steve... Steven, yes Steven. Girl is Mar... Marga.... no, Mary... yes, Mary, and Steven."

He paused to give the detectives time to register the information. Killgood would need no convincing for he had long accepted his abilities as real. He needed to toss Willard a few bones to chew on other than names of family members. If Willard asked Stephanie's parents about the Johnny Depp poster on the ceiling above her bed, his resistance might weaken, but the detective probably wouldn't bother asking.

"What else do you see?" Willard asked in a voice that exposed his skepticism.

"You shouldn't ask questions while he's making a connection," Killgood said.

"Why not?"

"I don't know, but you shouldn't."

Willard scowled.

"This other girl," Mr. Howard continued. "Reddish-brown hair, fair skin... I believe she is your missing Stephanie."

He tossed the sweater onto the desk. "Let me see something else in the box." He grabbed the stuffed Panda and began to run his hands over it. "I see a young man. Tall, slender, but broad in the shoulders, an athlete perhaps. He plays football... no, soccer. Daniel... no, David, his name is David. He spends time with Stephanie, yes? He kisses her. They are happy together... No, wait... I hear shouting. They are angry. Why are they angry? She is crying. He has hurt her."

Mr. Howard sat the Panda on the desk and reached for the sketch book. Opening the book, he examined her drawings. The majority depicted unicorns. No surprise, many young girls fantasized about unicorns. Several of the drawings were of Johnny Depp. From his conversations with Stephanie, he knew the picture of a young man was her boyfriend David Rice. Arrogant, conceited, the son of doctors, all-state soccer player, and all around asshole. He did not deserve her.

Mr. Howard closed his eyes. He rocked on the chair to give the illusion of a trance taking over his body. He drew in a breath and released it slowly, the air escaping in an, "Ahhhhh." Opening his eyes, he watched Willard lean back and shake his head.

"Anytime, Professor."

Killgood glared at him.

"I see a car. Red, fast, no... not red... white... has red stripes. Two door. Loud engine. Boy is driving. Stephanie's inside the car. Not on front seat, no... stretched... on her side... backseat. Eyes closed.

Perhaps she sleeps. There are mountains. Snow on mountains. Boy drives too fast. He seems nervous. He sweats. Looks around as if watching for something. She still sleeps." With a loud sigh he pretended to snap out of his trance. He blinked several times. "That is all I have for now. Perhaps if you could bring me more of her personals."

Willard squeezed out of the desk. He hurried over and gathered Stephanie's items into the box. Anger and frustration hardened his countenance. "I don't see how bringing you more of her things is going to help. The information you've provided is available to anyone willing to investigate."

Killgood joined him. "Isn't Stephanie's boyfriend named David?"

"That's right. David Rice. We've already talked with him."

"Have you given him a polygraph?"

"On what grounds? He has an alibi for the night Stephanie went missing."

"What kind of car does he drive?" Killgood asked.

Willard hesitated. "A white Shelby Mustang."

"Does it have red stripes?"

Willard picked up the box. "That doesn't mean a damn thing."

"Have you asked him about a trip into the mountains with Stephanie?"

"I came here hoping for information that might help us find her. All I heard was a bunch of mumbo jumbo."

Mr. Howard lowered his head and massaged his eyes to give the appearance of fatigue. "I am afraid these things can take time."

"Time is one thing we don't have," Willard said.

He looked straight at Willard and nodded. "If I come up with anything, I will notify you right away."

Willard considered him for a moment through narrowed eyes and started for the door. He paused in the doorway. "I heard you are something of a Civil War buff."

"Checking up on me, I see. Have you contacted the Baltimore police yet? They must have dozens of files pertaining to me."

Willard grunted before disappearing into the hallway.

Mr. Howard turned to Killgood. "Your friend does not like me."

"No surprise. There's not a police department in the world that will acknowledge working with a psychic."

"He considers me a threat."

Killgood shrugged. "We haven't talked about you much. Willard's under a lot of pressure to find this girl."

"Detective Willard seems to be a most unhappy man."

Killgood walked toward the door. He stopped. "Are you doing anything on Saturday night? We're thinking of grilling swordfish."

"What time?"

"Just come on over when it's dark enough."

"Very well. I will see you on Saturday."

He waited until the door closed behind Killgood and then stood and walked to the window. In the distance, Willard trudged toward the parking lot, hunched over the box.

I will have to keep an eye on this one. Doubting my psychic ability is one thing. Investigating my background to make a connection between me and homicides is something else entirely.

He loved the tranquility of the campus at night after the students were gone. Crickets chirped in the shadows. Thunder rumbled over the mountains with the promise of rain. He breathed in the smell of grass and roses planted near the benches. As he walked, he called to mind the false clues he provided Willard. Would they buy him time? It would take a couple of months for Stephanie's body to decompose. A couple of months to wipe away the stain of his crime.

The tires on the Mercedes squealed as he peeled out of the parking lot. He became so absorbed in calculating the decomposition cycle of a body he failed to notice a car following him. When he finally spotted the car, it stayed back, weaving in and out of traffic as the driver struggled to keep up. In his rearview mirror, the car turned west to pursue him into the foothills. Arriving at his turnoff, Mr. Howard waited at the security gate. A black sedan picked up speed as it approached. The driver looked away when he drove past, but Mr. Howard had seen enough. He smiled while tapping in the security code. "Goodnight, Detective."

Chapter 8

Willard accelerated past ninety on the freeway entrance ramp and never slowed. He swerved in and out of traffic, hands squeezing the steering wheel. *Son of a bitch knew he had been followed. Why does an uppity college professor need a security gate, and how can he afford to live in a mansion on the side of a mountain?* He found himself more interested in learning about Mr. Howard than finding the girl.

Reaching across the front seat, he snapped open the locks on his briefcase and reached inside. He brought Stephanie's panties to his mouth and licked the crotch. For a moment, he imagined he could actually taste her. He let out a breath and tossed the panties aside. Nothing, it seemed, would clear his mind of the mysterious Mr. Howard.

How did he know about the Johnny Depp poster on the ceiling in her bedroom? And he nailed David Rice's car. I don't think that little prick has anything to do with Stephanie's disappearance, but I'm covering my ass just the same. I'll set up another interview with David right away. His daddy can bring a lawyer along for all I care.

He smacked the steering wheel. Cases involving the wealthy were a pain in the ass. He foresaw hours of sitting in the courthouse if this thing ever went to trial while high-priced lawyers argued over legal technicalities.

He'd been a cop long enough to anticipate the outcome of almost any investigation. Stephanie was dead, of this he was certain. She might have become angry with her parents and taken off to go see David, but she wouldn't run away, not with so much to live for. Good looking, captain of the volleyball team, honor student, cheerleader, scholarship to Stanford. Stephanie Coldstone had everything. And now she had him licking her panties.

He arrived home to a dark house—a blessing. The last thing he needed was Doris sitting down in front of him, stuffing her mouth with Ding Dongs while telling him about her exciting day at the real estate office. He opened the front door as quietly as possible and slipped into the family room. His heart sank when he saw a light on inside the kitchen.

I hope she didn't wait up for me.

A smile slowly moved over his lips upon discovering the kitchen empty. She had left a sack of fast food and a soda large enough to quench the thirst of an elephant on the table along with a note.

Honey,

I bought you a happy meal to make you happy. When you're done eating, I have a surprise for you in the bedroom that will make you smile.

Love
Doris

He crumpled up the note and shot it into the trash can.

The only thing that would make me smile is if someone filled you with helium and you floated away.

He imagined little kids pointing into the sky as Doris sailed past. "Look, Daddy, there goes a blimp." After his unhappy meal joined the note in the trashcan, he walked to his bedroom. Doris lay on her back, lips quivering as she snored. *How would she sound with a pillow pressed down on her face?* She rolled onto her side away from him, taking the sheet with her. Wearing thong panties, her Jell-O butt glowed brighter than a full moon. His stomach dropped as if he'd just gone over the first big hill on a rollercoaster and he made a hasty retreat.

Inside his office, he entered his computer password. Soon the website of Swingers Just Wanna Have Fun opened. He scrolled to the link for women seeking men. Leaning close to the screen, he scanned the photographs of desperate women who would do anything to get laid, girls who looked like high school freshmen, women old enough to be their great grandmothers, white girls with nasty tattoos on their butts, black girls sticking their junk in the trunk close to the camera and skinny Asians who could almost pass for boys.

What's wrong with these people? Don't they have any pride?

He pulled up his profile page, which featured a photograph of him standing sideways in the nude, with an erection. Everything cropped out above his shoulders because he didn't want to be thought of as an exhibitionist. Clicking on the inbox, he frowned upon discovering no messages. Three weeks on the website and not one offer for his services. He'd used the money he inherited when his father died and worked part-time jobs for nine years to secretly buy a foreclosed house to use for sex adventures. It was time to finally put the house to use, if he could just find someone willing to accompany him.

He scrolled through the profiles until coming to the one which had previously caught his eye. His tongue ran over his top lip as he focused on her photograph. She was perfect, exactly what he was looking for. Not beautiful in the traditional sense, but unusual, like the woman from his youth. The strange woman from the circus who haunted his memories. Should he send her a message? What if she didn't respond? Blood rushed into his penis. He unzipped his pants and reached inside to pull himself out. An image of Doris's big ass popped into his mind and his erection begin to melt away. He stared at the woman on the screen and the blood returned.

Fuck it, I have nothing to lose.

As he masturbated, he used his free hand to type a message to the woman. He hesitated for only a moment before hitting the send button. Eyes closed, he pictured himself with her. A low moan escaped from his throat as his hand moved faster. Everything was perfect. And then he recalled Mr. Howard sitting inside his classroom, massaging Stephanie's sweater as he spun another tale of bullshit. "Goddamn it!" he said.

He shoved his penis inside his pants and zipped them closed. The woman on the computer screen beckoned. He longed to drift back into his fantasy, but Mr. Howard held on like a leech.

I've got to learn more about that son of a bitch. You can't hide behind your security fence forever, Professor.

Chapter 9

Willard entered the Detective Office holding a case file in one hand and a cup of nasty convenience store coffee in the other. Heather, the young secretary with sexy eyes, looked up from her work and smiled. "Good morning, Detective."

He grunted as he passed. Detective Sanderson approached from the bathroom, tucking in his shirt over his round belly. "How's that Coldstone investigation coming along?"

Willard grunted again. "It's coming," he said, and ducked inside his office. He let out a sigh after closing the door. Sanderson shook his head on the other side of the glass and continued walking toward Heather. He stopped behind her and placed his hands on her shoulders. His fat fingers dug into her flesh like tarantulas making a kill. A clear case of sexual harassment. Instead of complaining, she closed her eyes, head rolled back, lips pursing as she started to sway from side to side like an exotic dancer riding a pole.

That son of a bitch gets the sexy girl and I get Doris. Willard looked to the ceiling. *Thanks a lot, God.*

He tore into work but couldn't stop thinking about the drama at breakfast. Doris had marched into the kitchen, the muscles in her face taunt, eyes ablaze. She pulled a gravy bowl from the cabinet, banged it onto the counter, and poured in Lucky Charms until they spilled over the top. He considered asking if she really believed they were magically delicious as she plopped onto a chair at the far end of the table. They ate in silence for several minutes before she announced,

"Why didn't you come to me last night? I got all dolled up for you. Am I not good enough for you anymore?"

The last time they had sex felt like rolling around on one of those exercise balls. By the time it was over, he was battered and bruised.

"I'm tired," he said, without looking up. "This case I'm working on is… difficult."

"You think I'm stupid. You think I'm a stupid, fat pig."

"I never said you're stupid."

She pushed out of her chair, which screeched across the linoleum floor. "If you were half the man you think you are, then maybe, just maybe I'd try keeping myself in shape. In a world of foot-longs, I ended up with a cocktail wiener."

Now inside his office, his gaze traveled to his lap. "Cocktail wiener my ass."

He picked up the phone and dialed Baltimore PD. The phone rang five times before a woman answered. "El-oh, Baltimore Homicide."

"This is Detective Willard from the Colorado State Police. I left a message for Investigator Hollingsworth to—"

"Ol-on hon, I'll patch you through."

A man answered in a deep voice. "Hollingsworth."

"Investigator Hollingsworth, this is Detective Willard from—"

"I know who you are. What can I do for you?"

Willard spread his notes across the desk. "I'm working on a missing person case." He tapped a photograph of Stephanie Coldstone and let out a breath.

"What does this have to do with Baltimore?"

"Are you familiar with a professor who claims to be a psychic?"

"Mr. Howard."

Willard felt like a child on Christmas morning. "Yes, you remember him."

"What do you want to know?"

"I found information on a case where he helped locate the body. A girl named…" Willard pushed through his notes looking for the printout.

"Janet Harking—discovered buried on the Antietam battlefield."

"That's right. Did you ever make an arrest in that case?"

"No."

Willard leaned onto his thighs and massaged his forehead. "Did Mr. Howard ever provide information that led to an arrest?"

"Never."

He waited several seconds before asking, "Did he assist your department on more cases?"

"On the record, no. Off the record, nine."

"Nine? Wow, that's more than I expected. Any missing person cases?"

"As I recall, they were all missing until they turned up dead."

Willard picked up a pen and turned it between his fingers. "What do you know about Mr. Howard?"

Hollingsworth laughed softly.

"What did I say?"

There was a moment of silence. "You'll drive yourself crazy, Detective, trying to find out about Mr. Howard. What I can tell you is he's a brilliant man. He worked at the university for a number of years."

"What's a number?"

"Ten or twelve, I think."

"And before that?"

"I couldn't say. The son of a bitch is a phantom. No background. No records."

Willard stopped turning the pen and clicked the button several times. "He has an accent... European... maybe German or Austrian."

"Yeah, I seem to remember that as well."

"Was he much assistance in your investigations?"

"Mr. Howard helped us find their bodies. We might not have done that without him."

"So he provided clues that led to their bodies, anything else about the victims or a possible suspect in their murders?"

"The M.E. was unable to determine the cause of death."

Willard used the pen to scratch behind an ear. "I'm not following you."

"By the time we found their bodies they were skeletons."

"But they were murdered?"

"I would think so, unless they figured out a way to bury themselves."

Heat crept up the back of his neck into his cheeks. *Hollingsworth must think I'm a moron to ask such a question.* "Did Mr. Howard give you a lot of information about the women, other than about their burial sites?"

"Sure, he told us all kinds of things, but we couldn't use any of it."

Willard tossed the pen on the desk. He picked up his notes from the last interview with Mr. Howard. "Was he able to provide the women's names before you mentioned them to him?"

"Yes and the names of their family members."

"Boyfriends?"

"Boyfriends, male acquaintances, names of co-workers, teachers, shall I go on?"

"And none of them ever checked out?"

"We never liked any of them as suspects." Hollingsworth sighed. "Don't waste your time trying to figure out how he does it. Psychics don't think like the rest of us."

"You're assuming he's really a psychic," Willard said.

"Have you ever come up with information that led to the discovery of nine graves?"

"No."

"Well, he has, so that qualifies him as a psychic to my mind."

"To your knowledge, has Mr. Howard ever been in trouble with the law?"

Hollingsworth sighed again. "Detective Willard, I've already warned you not to try figuring out how he does it."

The door to the office opened and Captain Tate stepped inside. He went straight to one of two chairs positioned in front of Willard's desk and sat, arms folded over his chest. With his salt and pepper hair, thin mustache, and black eyeglasses, he looked more like a banker than a cop. His chiseled face a grim mask. Willard had more questions to ask Hollingsworth, but this wasn't the time. "I'm going to have to let you go, Detective, but perhaps I can call again at a later time."

"You can call, but you'll never get the answers you're looking for."

"Thanks again." He hung up.

Tate gestured toward the phone. "Was that about the Coldstone case?"

He straightened the paperwork on his desk. "No."

Tate frowned. "You saw the psychic last night?"

"I took him some of the girl's things."

"And?"

"He made a few statements."

"Such as?"

"Most of the information was useless. He named her family and David Rice. Mentioned something about Stephanie riding in David's car on a trip into the mountains."

Tate twirled one end of his mustache. "Interesting. Did he describe Rice's car?"

"He called it a white car with red stripes."

"And is it?"

Willard chewed the inside of his lip. "Yes."

"You consider that information useless?"

"Anyone with an interest in the case could have learned what kind of car he drives."

Tate stopped twirling his mustache. "You're assuming Mr. Howard has a reason for doing this. It's my understanding he's assisted in prior investigations without seeking publicity."

"I found an article about work he did in Maryland."

"But you have no evidence he contacted whoever wrote the article."

"That's right," Willard answered.

"And has he contacted anyone in the media here?"

"Not that I'm aware of."

Tate's tongue clicked on the roof of his mouth. "Then we should assume Mr. Howard's only interest in this case is to assist us."

Willard slumped in his chair.

"Did Mr. Howard tell you anything not available to the general public?"

He ran a hand through his hair. "He described a poster on the ceiling in Stephanie's room."

"So, you would say it's possible Mr. Howard does, in fact, have psychic powers?"

"I couldn't say at this time."

"Because you don't want to believe he does." Tate stood. "The Coldstones have powerful friends. Powerful friends who can make life miserable for this department. You believe she's dead, don't you?"

"She's not the kind of kid who's going to run away."

"Do you think Mr. Howard can help us find her?"

"He has helped other departments find bodies."

"Are you scheduled to interview him again?"

Willard shook his head. "He asked to see more of Stephanie's belongings. I hate to ask her parents, they're pretty torn up about her. It feels like I'm giving them false hope."

"Unfortunately, Detective, we're in the business of giving false hope. Go see the Coldstones." Tate left the room.

When the door closed behind him, Willard slammed a fist onto his desk.

Chapter 10

Mr. Howard parked and turned off the engine. Bottle of Romanee Conti in hand, he climbed out and strolled up the sidewalk. Killgood lived in a modest two-story house in an older neighborhood on the west side of town with mature shade trees and weed-choked lawns. The kind of place you'd expect to find a veteran cop. This wasn't his first time visiting the Killgood's, but each occasion felt like an adventure. Other than faculty events, he didn't get out much.

He rang the bell three times before Reann answered the door in a pair of sunglasses. Tall and slender, she had a body you wanted to coil around and squeeze. If Michelangelo were alive, he would create a marble statute in her likeness and rub up against it. Shoulder-length black hair framed a heart-shaped face. Full lips eased into a seductive smile. "I was wondering when you were going to get here." She stepped aside.

He moved into the entry, noting a bruise hidden behind her sunglasses and a generous amount of makeup. To his left, a small room served as Killgood's office. He painted the walls blue as a reminder he had never visited the ocean. He was in love with the idea of the sea and often spoke of living in a beach house. Paintings on the wall depicted ocean scenes. The wallpaper border featured nautical flags. Models of sailing ships sat on the desk and bookshelf. He even had a lighthouse in a glass bottle that made the sound of a foghorn and a ship's bell when you lifted the cork top.

"I do wish your father would make that trip to the ocean."

She sighed. "Me too."

"Do you still investigate ghosts?"

A few years back, Reann accompanied high school friends on a ghost hunt at a local cemetery. She swore the ghost of a woman appeared between the headstones. After that, she became obsessed with spirits. She launched her own ghost hunting group and they traveled around the state, spending the night in haunted houses and graveyards.

She looked down at the floor. "Not as much. Ryan thinks I'm crazy."

His eyes narrowed as he tried to remember where he had heard that name before.

"My ex-boyfriend," she said as if reading his mind. "Dad hates him."

He nodded. "I see. So, how is your ghost book coming along?"

Her head came up. "I write when I have time." She gestured toward the back of the house. "Everyone's outside."

"I smelled the swordfish grilling when I arrived. Your father is an excellent cook, yes?"

Reann walked past him. "Sure, when he's not burning the food."

He followed the sway of her hips as she led him into the kitchen. "Your father showed me a picture of Gail. She is a beautiful child."

She peeked over her shoulder and smiled. "Thanks."

"Is she here?"

"She's with Ryan, but he's supposed to drop her off soon."

They already act like a divorced couple and they never married. "I am anxious to meet her."

Reann opened the sliding glass door. "Look who's joined us."

Porch lights cast a white glow over the deck. Midges and gnats swarmed around the bulbs. Susan sat beside sixteen-year-old Michael at the table. She beamed upon seeing him. "Hello, stranger, it's been years."

Killgood stood near the grill wearing an apron. Gray smoke swirled around him. Five swordfish steaks sizzled nearby. He turned and smiled. "There you are. I was starting to think you wouldn't show up."

Michael pushed out of his chair. "Hey, Professor, what's happening?"

Mr. Howard shook his hand. "The last time I was here, Michael wore diapers. Now look at him, taller than me."

Susan glided over and held out her arms. He brought her close, her breasts pressing against him through the thin fabric of her shirt. "You're as pale as one of Reann's ghosts."

"Mother," Reann scolded.

"I am not offended," he said. "I am what I am and will not apologize for that."

"Nor should you," Susan said, pulling back.

"I brought wine." He held out the bottle.

Susan took the bottle from him. Her left eyebrow arched. "How much did you pay for this?"

"More than I should have."

"Then we must drink it slowly." She glanced at Reann. "Could you—?"

"I know, I know," she grumbled, "get some glasses."

Mr. Howard smirked as he watched her sulk into the house. Children would always be children in the eyes of their parents, no matter what their age and they resented their parents for this, as he resented his mother for attempting to turn him into a priest. Three hours of praying each day while his friends roamed the city learning to be men. It was enough to drive a boy to murder. Strange that his own son should travel a road he resisted so violently.

"Take a load off," Killgood, said.

He eased onto a chair. "Do you have a bottle opener?"

Susan turned to Michael. "I'll get it," he said, while pushing out of the chair.

"Children are so much fun," she said. "Why didn't you ever get married and have a few of your own?"

His wife, Sophie, had been a slender flower he nourished for almost forty years until the plague took her life. The daughter of an Italian merchant who migrated to Vienna, she had the smooth olive skin of her people, thick dark hair, and eyes the color of rich earth. He remembered making love to her on the bed, an afternoon sun streaming through the open window, curtains dancing as a cool breeze blew past. Her lips tasted of mountain berries. He looked straight at Susan and smiled. "If I had found a woman like you, then perhaps."

She dismissed him with a wave. "Did you hear that, honey?"

Killgood walked over and sat beside her. He put an arm across her shoulders. "Should I be jealous?"

"Of course," Mr. Howard answered, watching Reann and Michael return. "One day I might come along and steal her from you."

Michael clanked five glasses onto the table.

"I believe you have one too many glasses there, chief," Killgood said.

"Come on, Dad, just a taste."

"I began drinking wine when I was much younger than Michael," Mr. Howard said.

"Yes, and look how you turned out."

"This is true. You do not want to follow in my footsteps, young man."

Michael slumped onto a chair. "I can't wait until I'm twenty-one."

Mr. Howard snatched the bottle off the table and held out his hand. "I believe you were sent to fetch a bottle opener, yes?"

"Oh yeah," Michael said. He reached into a pocket and pulled out the opener. "Here you go."

Reann took a seat beside her brother, her attention on Mr. Howard. "You know a great deal about wine, don't you?"

"I am not an expert per say," he answered as he worked the opener into the cork, "but I have some experience buying and selling wines." He recalled a warm sun on the back of his neck as he strolled through the vine-covered slopes northwest of Vienna. The smell of grapes carried on a breeze blowing in from the Alps.

"And the tasting," Susan added.

The cork popped out of the bottle. "Yes, that too." He poured wine into four glasses. "Best to let it breathe for a bit."

Killgood picked up his glass and drank the wine in three long swallows. He wiped wine from his lips.

"Or not," Mr. Howard finished.

Reann lifted her glass and sniffed. "It has a lovely bouquet."

Killgood reached for the bottle. He refilled his glass and offered a mock toast. "To better days." He slurped as he drank.

Susan watched her husband with a forlorn expression. It was obvious he suffered, but why? Could it be job related? Being a homicide detective had its stresses no doubt, but in their town, he probably didn't work more than one or two murders a year. No, something else consumed his thoughts like a dancing flame. Reann stared into her glass of wine, seemingly oblivious to her surroundings. *Yes, of course, it is because of her bruise. Ryan has hurt her and she won't admit it. Knowing the truth without being able to prove it drives a cop crazy.*

Time to lift the dark veil that had fallen over them. "So, Michael," Mr. Howard said, "tell me about your girlfriends? You must have many young women chasing after you."

Susan and Reann both laughed softly. Killgood traced the lip of his glass with a finger.

Michael's chin sank toward his chest. "Come on, Professor, it's not like that."

"Why? Do you not want the young women to chase after you? Or would you rather chase them?"

"He's in love with a cheerleader," Reann said, the word cheerleader slipping off her tongue with disdain.

"Hey!" Michael protested.

"Wendy Pepperidge," she continued.

His eyes narrowed and a soft growl rumbled in his throat. "Thanks a lot."

Mr. Howard hid a smile behind his glass. "Nothing to be ashamed of Michael. I am sure young Wendy is beautiful. She must make your heart beat like a drum." He took a sip of wine and sat the glass on the table. "Do you know the origin of the name Wendy?"

Michael stopped glaring at his sister. "Please don't tell me it has something to do with one of your ancient monsters."

He shook his head. "No, nothing so romantic I am afraid. The writer J.M. Barrie created the name when he wrote Peter Pan."

"Is that true?" Michael asked.

"It is."

Reann snickered into her free hand. "So, I guess that makes you Peter Pan." She took a sip of wine.

Susan jumped out of her chair. "Honey, the swordfish!"

Everyone looked toward the grill where smoke poured from the charred fish.

"Not again," Reann groaned. She slouched in her chair.

Michael stood and turned to his mother. "Backup plan?"

She looked at Killgood hunched over his wine glass, sighed, and then at Michael. "Backup plan."

***

Mr. Howard rubbed his stomach. "I have not enjoyed delivered pizza in years. Thank you."

Susan offered a furtive smile. "As I recall, we ordered pizza the last time you came over for a barbecue."

"Yeah," Michael said reaching for the last piece of pizza, "we love when Dad cooks on the grill."

Killgood offered a weak grunt.

When everyone finished eating and cleared the table, Susan steered the kids inside the house. "I'm sure your dad and Mr. Howard would like to visit on their own." She paused in the doorway. "Shout if you need anything and thanks again for the wine. It was delicious."

He dipped his head. "You are most welcome."

A smile flashed over her mouth before she disappeared inside the house. He had always considered Susan Killgood a kindred spirit because they both were teachers. She had taught at a middle school for almost twenty years and somehow managed to keep her sanity. Young adults in their early teens were most disagreeable. They thought only of sex and mischief, but were too young to truly understand sex, and too old to be making the kind of mischief they wanted. Pimple-faced boys stared in mirrors and imagined themselves modern-day Valentinos. Beautiful young women did the same thing and imagined themselves ugly and unworthy. No, he most definitely could not tolerate the obnoxious behavior of middle school students. At least half of his class would disappear under mysterious circumstances in the first week.

Silence moved between them. Killgood stared into the darkness where crickets chirped. A bug zapper crackled at the neighbor's house. Mosquitoes buzzed around Mr. Howard's ears, but would never land on his skin. They seemed to comprehend his stolen blood wasn't what they needed. The air smelled of smoke and mowed grass. After perhaps a minute, Killgood turned to him and sighed. "It's Reann."

He nodded. "Yes, I noticed the bruise. Very brave of you to have me over considering the circumstances."

"I trust you'll keep this to yourself."

"You can count on it."

Killgood ran a hand over the top of his head. "It's her fucking ex-boyfriend Ryan. I never liked the scumbag."

"You are a policeman. Arrest him."

He guffawed. "I'd like to do more than that."

An image of the detective digging a grave in the moonlight popped into his head. "What does Reann have to say about it?"

"She's confused."

"As to be expected. She must love him to have had his child."

Killgood smiled. "You possess the chivalry of a knight in a modern world that respects nothing. Young people fuck and have kids all the time without understanding what love is." He massaged his eyes. "We managed to talk her into moving back home."

"That is a positive step."

He stopped rubbing his eyes and cast a hard glare. "Now she's thinking about returning to him."

"And you worry he will hurt her again?"

"It's not a matter of if, but when. I've spent most of life protecting people and now I can't protect my own daughter." He smacked a mosquito on his forearm. "Sometimes when I'm worrying about Reann, I think of Stephanie Coldstone. I won't let that happen to Reann."

"So, you believe Stephanie Coldstone is dead?"

"She had no reason to run off."

Mr. Howard tapped a finger against his lips while absorbing this information. The only thing which would dampen an investigator's passion for a case was the passing of time. The longer he delayed the investigation, the better. But this case was different. As Killgood correctly pointed out, she had no reason to run from home. Her parents did not abuse her. She wasn't pregnant or feeding a drug habit. She came from a wealthy family and they would pressure the investigators until the discovery of her body. Perhaps even the discovery of her bones wouldn't satisfy their need for vengeance. Coercion would continue. The investigation dragging on, months, maybe even years. He'd stepped into a pile of dung with no way to clean it from his shoes. "Detective Willard must be under tremendous stress."

"Yeah, he is, so take it easy on him."

"What do you mean?"

Killgood finished his wine and reached for the bottle. "I realize you don't like Willard. I don't care for him myself. And he sure as hell doesn't like you."

"Is that what he told you?"

"Isn't it obvious?"

Mr. Howard lowered his gaze and to pretend humility said, "I am only trying to help."

"Yeah, I know you are, but Willard thinks you're full of crap."

"Because I am a psychic?"

Killgood smiled. "Yeah, that too."

He suspected Willard wanted him off the case but was meeting resistance from Killgood and possibly his own superiors, who tried to deflect the heat coming from Stephanie's rich family and the media. Time to test his theory. "If Willard wants me to stop, I will stop. You may be right about the girl. She may be dead and if that is true, there is nothing I can do to help her. I do not claim special powers, nor do I seek publicity. If Willard is somehow threatened by me, if he believes his job will be easier with my absence, then perhaps, I should step away."

"He can't get rid of you even if he wanted to."

"What does he intend to do?"

"He's consulting an FBI profiler."

"So, Willard also believes she is dead."

"We're investigating as if she is still alive."

Mr. Howard raised his glass until the remaining wine captured the glow of the house lights. A yellow flare settled over the blush like a Barcelona sunset melting upon the Mediterranean Sea. "As you should."

Killgood shifted uncomfortably in his chair. "You haven't had any more visions about her have you?"

"Are you asking if I have seen anything that would lead me to believe she is dead?"

"Yeah... I guess I am."

"No," Mr. Howard answered. "To my knowledge Stephanie Coldstone is alive and well."

"You will tell me if you experience anything?"

"Indeed."

The doorbell rang. Killgood twisted that direction, his jaw set. Reann's voice carried outside. She spoke quickly as if trying to make a point. The muffled voice of a man responded. A child called out for Mama. Killgood pushed out of his chair. "I'd better see what's happening."

Mr. Howard followed him toward the backdoor. The quiet conversation inside the house exploded into shouting.

"Damn you, bitch. I do everything for you and this is the shit I get?"

Reann offered a quiet reply.

"I don't give a damn if your daddy's a cop."

Killgood pushed open the door. "What the hell is going on?"

Susan rushed into the entry ahead of them. A tall man in his twenties hovered over Reann, who clutched a little girl with wide, terrified eyes. His right arm was cocked and ready to deliver a blow. "Get away from her!" Susan shouted. She grabbed Reann by the arm and pulled her toward the family room.

The man lunged at Reann. Mr. Howard rushed to block him. The man blinked twice, eyes flaring at the sight of an old man in his way. "Who the fuck are you?"

"You must be Ryan," Mr. Howard said, gauging the anger in his eyes.

Ryan ignored him. "Reann, get your ass back here."

Killgood flew past Mr. Howard. He pointed a revolver at Ryan's head. "Give me a reason to pull this trigger."

Ryan smirked. "You don't have the balls."

Killgood's hand trembled as he cocked the trigger. "Let's find out."

Mr. Howard smashed a fist into Ryan's gut. He doubled over and clutched his stomach. "Son of a bitch," he groaned.

"Get out of this house," Killgood said, pressing the barrel of the pistol against Ryan's forehead.

The young man glared at him for a moment before straightening. "You'll get yours." He pointed at finger at Mr. Howard. "Same for you, freak show. I don't give a damn how old you are. I'll fuck you up."

Killgood growled under his breath. "You heard me, asshole."

Ryan kicked over a coat rack. "You'll see me again." He stomped out the front door, slamming it behind him.

Killgood eased down the hammer on his gun. He pressed against the wall and swallowed hard. "Jesus Christ, I thought I'd actually have to kill him."

Susan and Reann peered out from the family room. "Is he gone?" Susan asked.

Killgood nodded. "For now."

Reann hurried to her father and embraced him. Tears welled in her eyes. "I'm sorry, Daddy, I'm so sorry."

"Do you still want to live with that loser?"

She shook her head. "No way."

Gail clung to one of Susan's legs as she surveyed the scene, fear and confusion etched on her face. Mr. Howard went to her and bent down. "You must be Gail. I am Mr. Howard, a friend of your granddad."

She scooted behind Susan.

"It's all right, sweetie," Reann said, wiping tears onto the back of her hand. "Mr. Howard's not going to hurt you."

"She has every right to be afraid given everything that has happened. Besides, I am a stranger to her. A very odd stranger at that. Yes, she is wise to show caution." He turned to Killgood. "I should be going."

"Don't run off," Susan said. "You haven't tried my cheesecake."

"If I eat more food, I will most certainly grow fat. Thank you for your kind offer."

"I'll see you out," Killgood said.

They walked to his Mercedes and stopped at the edge of the yard. The air was hot and sticky. Sweat beaded along Mr. Howard's hairline. Two cats battled in the darkness, hissing and screeching. Someone shouted for them to shut up followed by a bottle shattering against pavement. An orange cat ran through the glare of a streetlight. "I hate cats."

"I could have killed him," Killgood whispered.

"You may still get your chance."

"I'm sorry you had to see that."

"Think nothing of it."

Killgood massaged his jaw. "What am I going to do?" I can't let him hurt Reann."

"No, that is a given." Mr. Howard looked to the west. A thin band of golden light stretched across the top of the mountains. "What do you know about this Ryan?"

"He works at a tire store near the college."

"What is the name of the store?"

"Jackson's Discount Tires."

Mr. Howard nodded. "I have never given them my business, but I am familiar with the establishment. What is Ryan's last name?"

"Logan."

"I am certain you have already checked his criminal background."

Killgood smiled in the faint light. "That's the first thing I do with all of Reann's boyfriends."

"I take it he is clean or their relationship would never have gone so far."

"Actually, he was arrested several years ago for PI and criminal mischief."

"PI?"

"Public intoxication."

He placed a hand on Killgood's shoulder and squeezed. "Do not worry, my friend. Reann still has her wits I believe"

After Killgood returned to his house, Mr. Howard sat in his car for a long time, staring at Reann's silhouette in a bedroom window. Ryan would kill her. It was only a matter of time.

Chapter 11

Mr. Howard labored through his Monday class, his mind on Reann and the FBI profiler Willard intended to bring into the investigation. He had dealt with FBI profilers in the past. Robert Janssen grilled him for hours at Quantico about statements he'd provided Baltimore homicide detectives. Not that it did him any good. Janssen had nothing to determine offender characteristics. The only crime scene evidence was bones. Autopsy reports proved inconclusive in every case except one, and all they discovered was the cause of death. Victim profiles told Janssen the girls were either prostitutes or runaways, which placed them at high risk. There were no witnesses. Police reports offered bare facts that led nowhere.

Janssen went crazy trying to classify the murderer. He must be an organized killer, Janssen announced, since he left little or no forensic evidence or clues and appeared to plan his crimes in advance. With the lack of evidence, Janssen's behavioral sequence of the crimes proved useless. The only thing he gleaned from the location of the girls' bodies was the killer moved about easily without drawing attention. Mr. Howard laughed whenever he heard a television show touting the crime-solving skills of the FBI profilers. In the real world, none of them were Will Graham. A profiler could only use what a criminal left behind. A smart killer could keep a profiler up at night for the rest of their lives trying to figure out their *modus operandi*.

He contemplated a dozen solutions for Reann's problem, but found none of them satisfactory. Something needed to be done about this Ryan and soon.

When class ended, Mr. Howard stood at the window, hands locked behind him, lost in memory. He recalled riding into the woods, daughter Heidi in front of him, braided pigtails bobbing as the horse trotted. Her high-pitched squeal carried through the shadowed valleys. Her tiny hand merged with his as they walked the river's edge and discussed the yellow butterflies that melted over wildflowers like warm butter. His hands tingled at the thought of holding her. She had been gone over three hundred years and he still missed his little girl.

I would have done anything to keep her safe. Now I have become a wolf that steals the joy from others. I am a cancer to the world.

"You must have a lot on your mind."

He whirled toward the voice. Leslie stood nearby, entrancing in a pale green dress that brushed her knees. "I apologize for not hearing you come into the room. My thoughts are as distant as the stars."

She pattered over and leaned into him as a cat seeks affection. "It's nice out tonight."

"Indeed."

"I was wondering," she said, her left breast rubbing against his arm, "if you'd like to go for a walk?"

"A walk?"

"Down by the river."

He'd miss his excursions with Leslie. Who else would sit on a blanket with him in a frost-covered field during a cold autumn night to watch the Leonid meteor shower? Who else would make love to him as the heavens wheeled and the ancient light of the stars bathed them in a soft glow? The essence of him that remained alive slowly died at the prospect of her leaving.

"The river, yes, we could do that."

"Can you drive?"

He steered her away from the classroom window. "Too fast for my own good, but yes."

They drove to the river without speaking, the tires humming over the asphalt. Parking near the locked gate of a riding stable, he put up the top on his car. Leslie waited for him at the trunk. He helped her navigate the dirt trail down to the paved river walk. The river slipped past like a black road that led to the boundaries of imagination. Moonlight beamed along the riverbank, turning the shadows of gnarled trees into strange creatures of the night. There was magic here.

They strolled without speaking, serenaded by the tapping of their shoes and the soft rustling of leaves. He gestured toward an opening to the water. She nodded. Mr. Howard weaved around the trunks of fallen trees until coming near the river's edge. Leslie eased onto one of the trunks, the wood creaking. He sat beside her. On the water's surface, light and shadow merged and flowed under the direction of moon and passing clouds.

"How are things going with the police?" she asked.

"They have not tried to ply me with coffee and doughnuts yet."

A muted laugh stayed in her throat. "Have you had any... visions?"

"About the girl?"

She nodded.

He hated her questions. Why couldn't they discuss something more enjoyable such as the plainsong of the passing river? Why were people so fascinated by the action of Satan when angels held the curtain line? Criminals were such a bore. He would know.

"No, but I fear they are yet to come."

She took hold of his hand and squeezed. "It must be terrible for you to see those things. I can't imagine it."

The memory of their faces floated through his mind like evening fog. Always young, so very young, some worn beyond their years from poverty and toil, all of them wide-eyed and frightened, clinging to their last moments of life, sending out silent prayers that went unheeded.

"It is a nightmare from which I can never awaken."

They drifted into silent repose, the sounds of nature amplified in the absence of talking. The river gurgled around rocks and against the shore. The wind fluttered through the trees like the flute in Mahler's *Das Lied von der Erde*. Wings stirred the air as an owl glided through the moonlight. He tilted his head and breathed through his nose. The musty smell of damp soil trapped in roots came back to him and the lavender scent of Leslie's perfume. "I do think it is rude of you to take all this from me."

"I was wondering when you were going to bring that up," she said. "I must admit it hurt the other day when you seemed to dismiss my leaving so easily."

"You caught me off guard."

She draped an arm over his shoulders. "I will miss our adventures. I still think you should come to Florida with me."

"Are there any universities in Jacksonville?"

She pulled back. "Are you serious?"

"It is a simple inquiry."

"You wouldn't have asked if you weren't considering it."

He bent to pick up a stone and tossed it into the river. "I consider many things without acting upon them. Besides, we could never live together."

"Why? Good things happen when we're together."

"Trust me. I am not an easy man to live with."

She twirled strands of hair around a finger. "There are several colleges in the area, Jacksonville University and the University of North Florida. Florida State has a campus downtown."

"And do they offer night classes?"

"All colleges offer night classes these days, plus I happen to know the deans from those schools. I'd put in a good word for you."

He tossed another stone. "I will have to think on it." He turned toward her. "Why would you want me to move to Florida? You can do so much better than me. There must be a thousand young men with tan, muscular bodies running around on the beach who would love to rub sunscreen all over you."

"Perhaps you're right, but could they sit down with a glass of wine and debate why the Roman Empire fell?"

"The split into an eastern and western empire governed by separate emperors."

She smiled and leaned into him. "You just proved my point."

"All I proved is I am a ridiculous old man whose head is stuck in the past."

"I've got a place you can stick your head." She flattened a hand against his back and massaged his shoulders.

A quiet moan rose in his throat. "Aren't they throwing you some kind of farewell party?"

She stopped massaging and looked straight into his eyes. "Didn't you hear? They are having a surprise party for me Friday afternoon at the student center."

"Let me guess, Van Adams is organizing the event."

"As a matter of fact—"

"Damn him."

"What's wrong?"

"Why do you think he arranged to have it during the afternoon?"

She glanced at the river for a moment and back at him. "To make it more difficult for you to attend."

"Luther is a shrewd little bastard. A rat that hides behind walls, waiting to scurry out when no one watches and steal the cheese."

She poked him in the chest. "Don't worry. I'll try to find a way to get the party moved to the evening. You really should come. The new dean will be there. Not that it matters if you're serious about moving to Florida. You are serious, right?"

He hesitated in answering. His gut told him it might be time to relocate. His intuition had always been right in the past. Kill just enough to survive, that was his motto, but he could only kill so many before suspicion turned on him. Killgood never considered him a suspect because he didn't want to believe it was possible. Willard, on the other hand, was suspicious from the beginning. He would exhaust all leads in an effort to understand his involvement in Stephanie Coldstone's disappearance. Fortunately, those leads went nowhere.

Mr. Howard offered a patronizing smile. "Yes, of course I am serious."

"Excellent." She lifted off the tree trunk and looked both directions. "The water's calm here."

"Indeed."

"We could skinny dip."

"Are you going to do something about rescheduling your retirement party?"

"Yes, I promise."

He stood and peeled off his jacket. "That is what I wanted to hear. Now let us remove our clothes and proceed with copulating."

"Mr. Howard, you are such a romantic."

Chapter 12

Mr. Howard sat at the writing desk inside his dark bedroom, staring at the phone. Stephanie lounged at the foot of his bed, looking bored. Apparently the spirit world did not agree with her teenage sensibilities. Or perhaps she grew tired of Harvey exploding from the wall as he bustled past on his bicycle shouting, "See you in court, Mr. Howard!"

Under normal circumstances, he would wait at least three months before contacting the police with more information. Willard's dogged investigation pushed up the timetable. He must give them something to deflect attention from him. But he wouldn't contact Willard directly. Not yet. Instead, he would share his lies with Killgood. He had a history with Killgood that counted for something, but he hated to dump this on him given what he was going through with Reann's boyfriend.

Killgood answered on the fourth ring. "Homicide, Killgood."

"Chandler, Mr. Howard calling."

There was a pause. "This is a surprise."

He detected stress in the detective's voice. "Am I catching you at a bad time?"

"When is it ever a good time in Homicide?"

"Good point." He switched on a table lamp and fanned open the book containing notes supplied by Stephanie. "I had a new vision."

"Anything we can use?"

"Despite my many years assisting law enforcement officers, I am a rather poor judge when it comes to understanding what you can and cannot use for your investigations. I apologize for that."

Killgood chuckled softly. In the background papers shuffled. "No need to apologize. Hold on a sec and I'll grab a pen. All right, go ahead."

Mr. Howard scanned through his notes. "These visions are like dreams, you see. Sometimes they feel quite real. Other times I cannot be sure."

"I understand, just give me what you've got."

"I fell into a trance-like state an hour ago after waking up. It was a very strange sensation, yes, most strange."

"But you've experienced these trances before, right?"

"Yes, but it has been a long time since the last one, and I had forgotten how they affected me. Anyway, I was sitting in my room reading *The Iliad*. Have you ever read Homer?"

Killgood sighed. "Back in high school, I think."

"So, Achilles was attacking the Trojans with rage and grief over the death of Patroclus, and had driven a great number into the River Skamandros—"

"Mr. Howard."

"Oh, please forgive me, I find Homer's work enthralling. Anyway, Achilles was killing the Trojans and the next thing I knew, it felt as if I left my body. Like those people who die and claim to see Jesus. I found myself watching a young girl. She was arguing with someone. At first I did not recognize her, until I realized it was the girl you are looking for."

"Stephanie Coldstone?"

"Yes, Stephanie Coldstone."

"What did the man in your vision look like? Was he a young man?"

"He was not the same man I saw driving with her in my previous vision. No, this man was older, more mature. Perhaps middle-aged."

"Anything else?"

He paused for several seconds to make the detective believe he was thinking. "His hair was brown, not long, and he was thin in the face."

"Did they do anything other than argue in your vision?"

"She was crying and seemed to be in pain." He snapped the notebook closed. "I am sorry, but that is all I have at the moment. I know it is not much to go on. Is it possible the man I saw is Stephanie's father?"

Killgood slurped some kind of liquid, probably coffee. "I haven't met the man, but I can pass this information to Detective Willard. He's met Stephanie's parents."

"To obtain the girl's personals?"

"That's right."

"I asked him for more of her things. Will he be bringing them?"

"I couldn't say," Killgood answered. "He's working hard on this case, I can tell you that."

Mr. Howard hesitated on purpose, wanting to give the impression he was in deep reflection, and said, "Chandler, I am trying my best to come up with something that will help in your investigation. I hope you understand."

"I know."

"It is a struggle, you see, trying to sort through all of my visions. To be perfectly honest, it is a gift I sometimes regret having."

He'd used this technique before, making the police believe he suffered with his psychic ability. Normally, this won their sympathy, for even the most hardened homicide detective couldn't imagine being plagued with horrific visions of death. Visions that defied explanation. Cops wanted control of everything, including their emotions, and the way he presented himself made them think he had no control over his own life. This wouldn't work with someone like Willard, who charged into an investigation like a bull after a red cape.

"We appreciate everything you do for us."

"I am grateful to hear that." Mr. Howard opened the silver heart locket on a chain that had belonged to Stephanie. Inside were photographs of her and a young man he assumed was her boyfriend. Not a bad-looking boy. Curly blond hair. Green eyes. He snapped the locket shut.

"How are things with Reann?" He hated to ask, but speculating her fate was driving him insane.

Several seconds passed before Killgood answered. "Not good, I'm afraid."

The smart thing to do would have been to say something like, "I am sorry to hear that, let me know if there is anything I can do to help," but instead he said, "tell me what is wrong, my friend."

Killgood sighed heavily. "After you left the house, we found bruises on Gail. I'm not saying Ryan beat her, but he definitely spanked her too hard."

He wanted to reach through the phone, grab Killgood by the neck, shake him and shout, "What is wrong with you? Why isn't the bastard already dead?" Once again, he said words that belonged to someone else. "That is terrible. What can you do?"

"Reann's afraid to file charges and rightfully so. I talked with detectives in child abuse and they said with no more evidence than a few bruises, there's not a lot the courts will do. If we don't do something, Ryan might hurt her worse next time. He might even..."

Mr. Howard listened as Killgood took several deep breaths. "Chandler, everything is going to be all right. You must believe me. These things have a way of working out for the best, you'll see."

"I worked in child abuse for several years," Killgood said, his voice rising. "I've stood over the battered bodies of children and stared into their lifeless eyes. Don't tell me these things have a way of working out for the best."

He had crossed a line with Killgood that wasn't meant to be crossed and regretted his decision. Time to retreat and regroup. "You are right, of course, and I apologize."

"No need to apologize. I shouldn't have lost my temper. I just don't know how I can keep Reann and Gail safe. That crazy SOB showed up at our house three times last night. Susan's terrified that he'll come over while we're at work."

"Is there someplace safe Reann can go?"

"We don't have relatives close and I can't ask our friends to get involved. I've thought about getting a protective order, but they're not worth the paper they're written on."

An idea came to him. He turned it over in his mind, weighing the pros and cons. It was risky. Perhaps too risky. But it would serve two purposes. Reann and Gail would be safe and it might help slow down Willard's investigation. How could Willard continue to suspect him if Killgood entrusted him with the lives of his daughter and granddaughter? "Chandler, let Reann and Gail come and stay with me. My house is private. It has a gate and security cameras."

"Mr. Howard that's a generous offer but I don't—"

"Let me do this for you, my friend. No harm will come to Reann here, that I can promise."

Killgood hesitated before answering. "I'll need to talk with Susan."

"And Reann."

"Yes, and Reann. Thank you for your offer."

"You can thank me by letting me help you."

"I'll call later."

"Please do," Mr. Howard said. He stared at the phone after Killgood hung up, wondering what he had gotten himself into.

Chapter 13

Willard hated the FBI—everything about them. A bunch of skinny-necked accountant assholes. He sat outside the office of Profiler Dave Hartley, leaning onto the arm of a painfully stiff chair, chin in hand. He'd been waiting for forty-five minutes and was bored out of his mind. From time to time, the agents in their cubicles popped up their heads like the moles in the game Wackamole. If he had his Maglite, he'd walk over and whack the crap out of them. Snot-nosed, fresh-out-of-college punks. One of them had the audacity to ask if he was there to fix the copy machine. It took all his fortitude to keep from popping him in the mouth.

The minute hand on the wall clock crept like an old man. He squirmed in his chair and looked at his watch to confirm the time. *Screw this*. He pulled out the case file for the third time since he sat down and started to read.

Stephanie Coldstone was as cold as her surname, probably buried in a shallow grave, a buffet for beetles and worms. Still, he couldn't fault her parents for holding out hope. If someone kidnapped his kids, he'd feel the same way… well, maybe not quite the same. In fact, he would enjoy the savings on his grocery bill and not listening to their alternative music crap. What was that shit? The alternative to good music? He just wished his supervisors would get off his back. He wasn't a goddamn miracle worker. If she's dead, she's dead. He didn't have the power to resurrect her.

His imagination drifted to the woman from the Swingers Just Wanna Have Fun website. She had answered his email. Hallelujah and praise the Lord. Now he could try out the device. Would she enjoy it? Hell yeah she'd enjoy it, why wouldn't she?

"Detective Willard?"

Willard looked up from his notes. A man who appeared to be in his fifties stood nearby. He wasn't wearing a jacket and the top button on his shirt was undone. His necktie was clipped to a pocket. He looked like an angry drill sergeant with his closely-buzzed grey hair. A half-eaten sandwich occupied his left hand. Before Willard could answer, the man took a bite.

"Yes, I'm Willard." He put away the case file and stood with his hand out. "Are you Hartley?"

The man shook his hand with a firm grip. "So they tell me."

Willard followed him into a small office. Hartley closed the door and moved behind a desk cluttered with loose papers. Wood paneling covered the walls like a bedroom in a white-trash singlewide. Outside of his folk's trailer, Willard hadn't seen a room with paneling in years. The walls were barren. No photographs, no certificates, not even a clock. He'd expected to see them covered in crime scene pictures, but that was the Hollywood FBI. A can of air freshener sat on the desk and the room held an odd scent of flowers and soap.

"You're probably wondering why there's nothing on the walls," Hartley asked as Willard sat. "Helps me concentrate. Sometimes I like to dim the lights, put on my headphones, listen to a little Pink Floyd, and relax."

Hartley motioned with his chin toward one of the chairs in front of his desk. "So, what did you need to see me about?"

"I'm working on a case."

"Yeah, I didn't figure you came here about your prostate. What kind of case?"

"Missing person. Teenage girl named Stephanie Coldstone."

Hartley pressed into his chair, the leather rippling. "I'm familiar with it. Disappeared after arguing with her rich parents."

"That's right."

"And you think she's dead?"

He tossed the file onto Hartley's desk. "What do you think?"

"I haven't studied the case."

"But you believe she's dead."

Hartley's cheeks bulged as he worked his tongue against the inside of his mouth. "That's pretty damn perceptive of you, Detective."

"Not really. I think any investigator with half a brain would come to the same conclusion."

"Unfortunately for me," Hartley said, "about half the people working around here have shit for brains." He leaned over the desk. "You, on the other hand, are old school. You don't rely on computers to tell you what to do. You trust your gut. Am I right?"

Willard smiled at Hartley's assessment of him. "I need your help."

"Yeah, I imagine you do."

"A psychic was brought into the case."

"Oh Lord." Hartley rolled his eyes.

"He has a track record of helping in investigations. Several during the eighties around Baltimore, and a few here after he moved west." Willard took out a packet of cigarettes but noticed a no-smoking sign on the desk.

"Ignore it. The sign's for show whenever a tour group comes through. Hand me one of those cancer sticks."

Willard gave him a cigarette and lit it for him. Hartley sat back in the chair, his cheeks sinking in as he took a long pull. He blew out a wavering smoke ring that melted into the overhead fluorescent lights. "What kind of information has this psychic given you? Anything useful?"

"Well, he identified the girl and her family by name, supposedly without reading about the case."

"Bullshit. He read about it in the newspaper."

"He knew the girl's hometown and what kind of car her boyfriend drives."

"All in the public records."

"And he knew about the Johnny Depp poster on the ceiling in her bedroom."

Hartley pressed his lips together and pulled them apart with a pop. "Now that is interesting. Any reason to believe he knows the girl's family?"

Willard shook his head.

"Has this psychic worked with anyone from the Bureau?"

"Actually, he was interviewed by one of your colleagues, a fella named Janssen."

Hartley's eyebrows pulled down and he smiled. "Robert Janssen? The man's a legend among profilers. What'd he say about your psychic?"

Willard shrugged. "I've been hankering to get my hands on one of his reports, but Janssen's retired."

Hartley's right index finger shot up. "Ah-ha." He pulled a Rolodex in front of him and started to flip through it. "I happen to be friends with Janssen. He was my mentor in Behavioral Sciences." Hartley stopped on an index card. "Here we go. Let me give him a call."

Willard couldn't help but grin at this turn of events. As badly as he wanted to solve this case, exposing Mr. Howard as a fraud had become more important to him. There was no victory in finding Stephanie Coldstone's body, and his odds were better against the house in Vegas than learning who killed her.

Hartley brought the phone close to his lips. He became animated and giddy like a child climbing onto the lap of a mall Santa. "Hey, Bob, it's me Dave. How you doing? I'm doing just fine. Yeah, still with the Bureau for a few more. How're Marcie and the kids? Good, good. Hey, the reason I'm calling is, I have a State Detective here who's working a missing person's case and a psychic is involved. Yeah, yeah, I know what you think about psychics. Anyway, this detective..." Hartley put a hand over the phone and leaned forward. "What's your name again?"

He gnashed his teeth. "Willard."

Hartley gave him thumbs up. "Detective Willard believes you may have interviewed this psychic and he'd like to ask a few questions. Is that all right? Great, great, I'm going to put you on the speaker." Hartley pressed a button on the phone base and hung up the receiver. "Go ahead, kid."

Willard cringed at being called kid, but tried not to show his frustration. "Mr. Janssen, this is—"

"What's this Mr. Janssen crap?" a gruff voice said. "Call me Bob."

Willard cleared his throat. Normally he liked to keep things formal and businesslike, but this wasn't a normal situation. "Bob, my name is—"

"I know your name, Willard, Hartley already told me. Look, I'm running late to play a round of golf, so can we get things moving here?"

I'm looking for a missing girl and the son of a bitch is worried about playing golf. Glad to see he has his priorities in order.

"I'm working a missing persons case involving a—"

"I know that too, Detective. Can we cut to the relevant information?"

Willard straightened in his chair. Now his blood was up. "All right. A psychic named Mr. Howard is involved in the case. I hear he did some work for you back in—"

"Whoa, partner. The FBI doesn't work with psychics."

"Yeah, yeah, right. That's a load of crap. Off the record, you pompous ass—you interviewed Mr. Howard for several hours at the Behavioral Science office. I want to know your impression of him."

There was a long pause before Janssen said, "Dave, I like this boy, he's got brass ones. You're right, Willard, I did interview your Mr. Howard, if we're talking about the same fella. College professor, early sixties, long hair, has some kind of skin condition that prevents him from going out during the day."

Willard closed his eyes and massaged his temples. "Yeah, that's the guy, but you said he was in his sixties. That can't be right."

"Why not?"

"You interviewed him back in the 80s."

"Yeah, so what's your point?"

"He's in his sixties now. Is it possible you're mistaken about his age?"

"Hold on, I keep a copy of all my notes. Be right back." Over two minutes passed before Janssen returned. "According to my records, Mr. Howard was 63 back in 1986."

Willard opened his eyes. "Why did you interview Mr. Howard?"

"He assisted Baltimore homicide on a number of cases we became involved in. I was interested in learning his *modus operandi*."

"That makes him sound like a suspect."

"Come now, Willard, I'm sure you've been a cop long enough to know everyone is a suspect. Hell, I started every homicide investigation with my wife at the top of my suspect list, and she had one hell of a time coming up with an alibi in a few of the cases."

Willard tapped a finger against his chin. He'd never considered Mr. Howard a suspect and still didn't, but the idea proved interesting. "What did you find out?"

"Mr. Howard is one cool customer. He sat in my office for hours without eating or drinking, calmly answering every question. Didn't even flinch when I read him Miranda."

"Did you learn anything to figure him for the murders?"

"No, but you must understand these cases had practically no physical evidence to go on and no witnesses. Most of the girls were prostitutes. No one misses a whore except her pimp. Unless they were talented, and then a few customers shed a tear or two."

"You said practically no physical evidence."

"All of the bodies were recovered in such a state of decomposition the M.E. couldn't glean anything from the autopsy... however, one of them, woman named Cynthia Rhodes, was recovered after less than a month in the ground. Autopsy showed she died by strangulation."

"How could they tell?"

"As I recall, the hyoid bone was fractured and the blood vessels in her eyes were ruptured. Hmm..."

"What is it?"

"It says here Mr. Howard didn't help investigators locate Rhode's body."

"That's odd," Willard said.

"Not necessarily. No one understands how the mind of a psychic works."

"So y'all didn't come up with any ideas on how Mr. Howard obtains the information?"

"No, but he did know a lot of personal things about the victims, that I do remember. More than other psychics who've assisted in homicide cases."

"I thought the FBI didn't work with psychics."

Janssen laughed. "You're pretty damn sharp, Willard."

"Did anyone make a connection between the murders Mr. Howard assisted you with?"

"There were similarities. The victims were all about the same age and we didn't find their bodies for several months."

"Until Mr. Howard told you where to look?"

"That's right. Except, of course, for the one body."

"How did you find her?"

"The killer buried her too close to the Monocacy River. Spring rains caused the river to rise and uncover her body."

"I talked to a Detective Hollingsworth from Baltimore. He told me all of the bodies decomposed to skeletons by the time they were recovered."

"He probably wasn't aware of Rhodes. She disappeared from Anne Arundel county and not Baltimore. Remember, these cases were never officially linked."

"If one killer committed all of the murders, what would your profile look like?"

"Well, some of it would be easy," Janssen said. "The killer is obviously intelligent and organized to pull this off without leaving clues. Because he's so organized, I would guess him to be an older man, thirties or forties. Young men tend to rush and be sloppy. Also, he's someone who doesn't attract attention."

"Do you think he engages in sexual acts with the victim prior to killing her?"

"Normally, I would say yes, but the evidence we recovered on Rhode's body didn't support that. It did tell us the killer kept her alive for about a week before he killed her."

Willard turned from Hartley as he blew smoke rings his direction. "How do you know that?"

"Based on the insect evidence, the M.E. determined she'd been dead approximately three to four weeks. She'd been missing five weeks at the time her body was discovered. One more thing. The M.E. found several small puncture marks on her left arm."

"Puncture marks?"

"Yes, as if from a needle."

"Was Rhodes a junkie?"

"No evidence of that."

"That's odd," Willard said. "Why'd he kept Rhodes a week if he didn't rape her?"

"With psychopaths, there's no telling."

"You say that as if he's insane and that's obviously not the case."

"You're right, Willard. He's not insane. I suppose thinking that makes it easier to swallow."

"Sounds as if you believed one man was responsible for all of the crimes."

"Didn't matter we couldn't prove it."

Hartley held out the joint and Willard waved him off. "Did the killer take trophies?"

"Let me check my notes." There was a moment of silence before Janssen said, "A few of the girls were missing jewelry, but that in and of itself proves nothing."

"How about their clothes? Did he bury them naked?"

"Always naked... probably kept their clothes as a souvenir."

"Or buried them nude to help speed up decomposition."

"That's right," Janssen said. "Clothing can prevent some kinds of insects from reaching the body."

"This guy," Hartley said, slipping on a pair of headphones, "would have a normal or high IQ. He most likely would be socially adequate. Might be married, or at least date some. If he has kids, he's probably a good father. By all accounts, DeSalvo did all right by his kids."

"Yes," Janssen said, "but he probably suffered harsh physical abuse as a child. Something drove him to strangle all those women in Boston."

"Did the Maryland killer leave bodies all over the state?" Hartley asked.

"He did," Janssen said, "which means he's geographically or occupationally mobile."

Hartley pulled an iPod from his desk. "He probably drives a flashy car."

"And keeps himself and his house clean."

Willard smiled as he listened to the profilers exchange theories.

"I'll bet he contacts the cops to play mind games," Hartley said.

"Or fantasies about being a cop. Based on the lack of evidence, I'd say he kills in one place and disposes in another."

"He probably uses seduction to help restrain his victims. This one sounds like a talker."

Their conversation faded to silence as Hartley fiddled with his iPod. Soon the music of Pink Floyd leaked from the headphones.

Willard saw this as an opportunity to jump back in. "There's something about Mr. Howard that's been driving me nuts, I can't—"

"Find out anything about him?" Janssen asked.

"When I talked to Hollingsworth, he said they couldn't get any information on the guy."

Janssen laughed softly. "Yeah, the same thing happened to me. All I can tell you is he's originally from Vienna and he goes by Mr. Howard."

"Doesn't the bastard have a first name?"

"Of course he does," Janssen answered. "It's Satan. Look, you're wasting your time investigating Mr. Howard. As much as I hate to say it, there are psychics who seem to be legitimate, and who've helped various departments solve murders. A woman named Deborah Heinecker helped the Maryland State Police solve the Louise Williams case in the early nineties. The case had gone cold, and the detectives wouldn't follow up on the information Heinecker provided. They thought the victim had run away with some guy, but Heinecker insisted that Williams' son-in-law killed her. Guess who they ended up arresting for her murder."

"Yes, but Mr. Howard has never provided information that led to an arrest."

"He worked on difficult cases."

Willard gripped the arms on the chair. "Now you're making excuses for him."

"I already told you, I never made Mr. Howard for the killings. I investigated him to find out if he was a fraud, but I couldn't prove it. My advice is to stick to the facts. If your missing person is dead, Mr. Howard may be the only way you find her. Anything else before I hit the fairway?"

"Appreciate your time," Willard said.

"Glad to be of assistance. Talk to you later, Dave."

Hartley didn't answer. He was too busy leaning back in his chair singing, obscured by a cloud of smoke. "I… I have become comfortably numb."

Willard shook his head and left the office.

Chapter 14

The box dropped onto Killgood's desk with a thud. Willard retreated to a nearby chair and sat. "There you go."

Killgood stood and peered inside. "What's this?"

"Your friend Mr. Howard asked for more of Stephanie Coldstone's personals, remember? You can't imagine how humiliating it was to go to the Coldstones and ask for this crap."

"Comes with the job," Killgood said, sinking into his chair. He stared out the window.

Willard squinted as he watched the detective. It was obvious his thoughts were somewhere else. "I went to see the FBI profiler."

"How'd that go?" Killgood asked without looking.

"He wasn't able to give me anything useful."

"Not surprising considering the little evidence we have."

Willard debated whether to mention he had discussed Mr. Howard with the FBI. Sunlight streamed through the window and glistened upon the glass cubicle walls. Beyond the glass, cops went about their business as if they were the sole survivors of their own personal apocalypses. He could strip naked and dance around with a Roman candle shoved up his ass and no one would probably notice.

He reached into his coat for a cigarette but stopped, his attention drawn to the Killgood family photos on the detective's desk. Damn, Killgood's daughter was a looker. He'd love to bend her over his desk. "How many homicides has Mr. Howard helped you investigate?"

Killgood's attention came to him. He sighed heavily and shook his head. "If this is about his credibility, I'll—"

"No, I'm interested in the cases themselves. What transpired, what evidence you obtained, did you have any good suspects, that sort of thing."

Killgood leaned forward and picked up the photograph of his daughter. He stared at it several seconds before sitting the picture down. "You believe all the cases are connected."

Willard sniffed the air and wrinkled his nose at the strong smell of bleach.

Killgood smiled. "The janitors are cleaning the bathrooms downstairs. The stench rises through the vents."

Willard hurriedly lit a cigarette to mask the odor. "I take it your investigators never came to that conclusion?"

"We considered the possibility, but the evidence didn't support a continuing event."

"Were the victims all female?"

Killgood frowned. "Don't waste my time asking questions you already have the answers to."

The retort was a kick in the ass. Willard squirmed in his chair. "Let me guess—young, late teens, early twenties, most of them prostitutes, or pole riders. All vanished without anyone witnessing the crime. Missing for several months until Mr. Howard became involved in the case and helped you locate their bodies or rather, their bones. I'm guessing the coroner couldn't determine a cause of death, but if he did, the evidence confirmed it was strangulation. Does all of this sound about right?"

"And your point is?"

"I'd say there's enough supporting evidence to suggest a single perpetrator committed these murders."

"Could be more than one like the Hillside Stranglers."

Willard fought off a smile. "So you'll admit these homicides are connected?"

"No," Killgood said. "I'll admit there are similarities. Several of the women were either prostitutes or strippers, but two of the victims, Cara Mattingly and Hannah Leeds, were students."

"College?"

"Only Leeds. Mattingly was still in high school."

"What does your gut tell you?" Willard asked.

"My gut tells me it's time for lunch."

Willard took a long pull on his cigarette and blew smoke across the desk. "Anything new from Mr. Howard?"

Killgood waved a hand in front of his nose. "There's a no smoking sign in my office for a reason. Mr. Howard was kind enough to just take your cigarette away. I'm not that nice."

The seriousness of his tone made Willard nervous, but he hid his worry with a casual shrug. "About Mr. Howard?"

Killgood glared at him. "He called me earlier."

"Oh?"

"Said he had a vision of Stephanie Coldstone."

Willard sat up straight. "This should be good."

"Why are you so skeptical?"

"Why are you so gullible?"

Killgood tapped the pistol in his shoulder holster. "First you come into my office and ignore my no smoking sign. Now you accuse me of being gullible. That's two strikes, Detective. One more and you'll get a death sentence."

Willard pulled the cigarette from his mouth and looked for somewhere to put it out. "All right, all right, don't be pitchin' a hissy fit. I apologize for questioning your competence. Please continue."

Killgood handed him an empty soda can and Willard tossed the cigarette inside where it died with a hiss. "As I was saying," Killgood continued, "Mr. Howard called and said he had a vision of Stephanie with a man. Someone he hasn't seen before."

"Good, because I wasted four hours of my life yesterday interviewing her boyfriend because of Mr. Howard's previous vision."

"This man is older, middle-aged, with short brown hair and a thin face."

"Hell of a description. Only fits half the men in the state. Anything else?"

"In his vision Stephanie was crying and appeared to be in pain. Do you think the man might be her father?"

Willard snatched the soda can off the desk and heaved it into a nearby trash can with a bang. "I've got a mind to light up another cigarette despite your threat, just to get back at you for coming at me with that bullshit."

"I never said her father is a suspect."

"No, but I could see it in your eyes. Now I'm supposed to go after Mr. Coldstone because Mr. Howard had a vision. Glory hallelujah, praise God, the case is solved."

Killgood picked up a pen and pointed it at him. "You know, somewhere inside you, there's probably a decent person disguised as an asshole."

"My wife tells me that all the time."

"There's no reason for us to butt heads," Killgood said. "This is your investigation. Believe in Mr. Howard, don't believe, that's up to you."

"At this point, I've no choice but to work with him." Willard glanced at his watch. "Anything else?"

"Nope."

"All right. Call me if Mr. Howard comes up with something after pawing through this new collection of Stephanie's things."

He walked to the door and paused. "In the cases Mr. Howard worked in Maryland, the victims were all young women, most of them prostitutes or students. By the time he supplied investigators with enough information to locate their bodies, they'd decomposed into skeletons, and the M.E. couldn't determine the cause of death. Is it just me or do you find it odd that the murders in Maryland and the ones Mr. Howard has assisted with here are so similar?" He smiled at the stone-faced detective. "Oh well, I guess I'm being too skeptical. Call when you have something."

Willard closed the door, pleased for having put Killgood in his place.

Chapter 15

Mr. Howard removed the cork from the small glass vile and poured the blood inside into a glass containing Romane Conti. After mixing the contents, he walked into the family room and sank into a leather recliner. As he sipped the drink, savoring the burst of energy provided by Stephanie's blood, he listened to Handel's *Giulio Cesare* and imagined himself in the palace of Pharaoh, entangled in the arms of Cleopatra. Theirs would be a love affair beyond all others—including her time with Mark Antony. The sun would rise and fall at their command, in harmonized rhythm to the movement of their bodies. And the moon would take them in its embrace and rock them to sleep.

His introspection turned to Sophie. He remembered the first time they made love on a soft bed of grass in a mountain meadow. She considered him with wide, searching eyes as they joined in body and spirit, the ancient song of Eve passing from her lips to rise above the wind that stirred the spring gentian and delicate meadow clary. What he wouldn't give to be with her now. If Lenhard hadn't turned him, and he died during the plague as intended, would he be with Sophie in Heaven? Or would his murderous past damn him to Satan's lair? To be with Sophie for eternity was a dream that had haunted him for over three hundred years.

A bell chimed to announce a visitor outside the gate. He strolled to the intercom near the front door and pushed the button to speak. "How may I help you?"

"Mr. Howard, it's Chandler. Can I come up to the house?"

A quick inspection of the room confirmed he'd left nothing incriminating lying about. "I will buzz you in."

He pressed another button that unlocked the gate and waited near the door for the detective. A minute passed and the sound of gravel crunching under car tires grew louder until coming to a stop near the front door. A door slammed. Shoes scraped over the sidewalk. He opened the door before Killgood could ring the bell. The detective pulled back with a startled look on his face. "I'm sorry to show up unannounced."

"I am sure you have a good reason for coming. What have you brought me?"

Killgood held a cardboard box. "More of Stephanie Coldstone's things."

"Ah, so Detective Willard came through after all. He is most surprising, yes?"

Killgood motioned with his chin. "Where do you want this?"

"Please, set the box anywhere." He waited for Killgood to put down the box. "You appear exhausted, my friend. Would you care for a drink?"

"Water."

"No wine?" he asked, walking toward the kitchen.

"Not this time." Killgood strolled into the family room and sat on the couch. He stared at the cabinet holding Mr. Howard's collection of antique swords and daggers. "You own some unique weapons."

"Thank you. Most are from India, thirteenth through seventeenth centuries."

"What good is a weapon if you don't know how to use it?"

He filled a glass with ice water and brought it to the detective who took it with a nod. "Ah, but I do know how to use them. So," he said returning to his chair, "how is your investigation coming along? Did you tell Willard about my last vision?"

Killgood sipped his water. "He wasn't impressed."

"Oh?"

"Willard believes it would be a waste of time to investigate Stephanie's father. I agree."

He was surprised and dismayed to hear Killgood agreed with Willard, having counted on his latest false clue to delay the investigation by a week or more. Still, Willard had nothing to go on without a body, and they wouldn't find Stephanie until he was ready to reveal her location. "Perhaps Willard is right not to pursue that line of inquiry. He must know what kind of people the Coldstones are by now."

Killgood stared into space. He wrung his hands on his lap. Mr. Howard felt certain he was distracted by the trouble with Reann's boyfriend and wondered if he and Susan had made a decision regarding his offer to let Reann and her daughter stay with him. An offer he now regretted. When Killgood looked back at him, his stare was harsh and judgmental, as if they were sitting in an interrogation room. "We've never really talked about the cases you worked on in Maryland."

He took a sip of his drink and smiled. "Has Willard been checking up on me? Did he talk with the FBI? He should speak with a profiler named Bob Janssen. I spent many hours with Mr. Janssen as he tried to find evidence to discredit my work."

"I believe he's already spoken to the profilers."

"And he has told you what they talked about, yes? Tell me, Chandler, what is troubling you?"

Killgood put down his glass and cleared his throat. "According to Willard, the cases in Maryland are similar to the ones you've helped with here."

"Yes, in all the cases a murder was involved, what else?"

"All of the victims were young women. The majority of them prostitutes."

"You don't need me to tell you prostitutes are often the victims of violent crime. I believe most if not all of Gary Ridgway's victims were prostitutes."

"Each body you've helped recover was found in a state of advanced decomposition."

"Yes, but—"

"Except one," Killgood continued.

The memory of digging her grave under a full moon came to him. The dark water of the Monocacy River bubbled against the bank as it pushed to the sea. She had light red hair the color of a good zinfandel and freckles under her eyes. Yes, she was beautiful, as were all the others. "Her name was Cynthia Rhodes. As I recall, her body washed up in a flood or something."

"That's right. The water uncovered her before you could lead investigators to her grave. She's the only one they recovered evidence from."

"Ah, yes, I remember, she died from strangulation, which I believe is the preferred method of killing for sexual deviants."

"According to the autopsy she hadn't been raped."

"Did Willard tell you that?"

"I reviewed the case file."

His apprehension grew stronger by the second. It was one thing to have Willard investigating his past and quite another to have a man he considered his friend doing it. "It is true I was not able to help the authorities in Maryland locate the victims' bodies until they had rotted to bones. I have no control over my visions. Do you not believe I wanted to find them sooner?"

"And you never furnished information that led to an arrest."

"Yes, that is also true, but I did provide leads on possible suspects. The fact they were cleared in the investigation does not mean they were innocent."

Killgood looked away. He chewed his bottom lip as he appeared to think. "I've never questioned your ability in the past and I see no reason to do so now. Some cops would never believe you can do the things you do. They have too much pride to admit that someone without investigative training can solve their cases, but pride can be a loaded gun to the temple. I've always trusted you to help me in the past and you've never let me down. I see no reason to stop trusting you now, Willard be damned."

Mr. Howard fought off a smile. "Willard is under tremendous stress, I can see that. I do my best to help him, but as I've often said, there are no guarantees. Perhaps, I will come up with something after examining the things you have brought me. When do you need them returned?"

"No rush, just call when you're finished with them." His chin sank toward his chest. "I talked to Susan about your offer to let Reann and Gail stay with you."

"And she said no."

Killgood raised his head. "Susan thinks Reann would be safer in the nest."

"Ah, yes, she is a good mother bird."

"Ryan's a temperamental SOB. I don't trust him not to try something at our house... and then there's the problem with..." His gaze returned to his lap.

Mr. Howard took a drink. He swished the blood-tainted cocktail around his mouth, savoring the pungent flavor, before he swallowed. "You fear that he will do something with Gail?"

"He insists on visitation, which infuriates me. All he does is take her to the sports bar for cheeseburgers and to watch football."

"It is not cheeseburgers and football keeping you up at night."

"You're right. He's a shiftless character with nothing to hold him here. I'm afraid he's going to run off with Gail. He's already threatened Reann a half-dozen times." His right hand curled into a fist. "I can't let that happen. We'd never find her."

Mr. Howard pressed into the soft leather of his chair and massaged his brow. Killgood was right. If Ryan took off with Gail, they'd never see her again.

"When is the next time he has visitation?"

"Thursday evening."

"The day after tomorrow—that is not a long time. What is your plan?"

"Plan?"

"To stop him."

Killgood chuckled softly. "You obviously don't know how the courts work in this country. I can't legally stop Ryan from taking Gail unless he's already done something."

He wanted to tell him what he really thought, that this was the kind of situation best handled outside the courts, but remained silent.

Killgood stood. "I should be going. About those earlier questions."

"No worries. It is your job to ask questions."

"I don't want you to think that—"

"No need to explain, my friend," Mr. Howard, said, pushing out of his chair. He walked to the detective and patted him on the shoulder. "A young girl may be in danger here. We must do all we can to save her, yes? Now go on home and do what you can for Reann."

"Thanks for being so understanding."

He stood at the front door and watched Killgood's car disappear in a cloud of dust. When he drove out of the gate, Mr. Howard went back inside the house. He returned to the family room and took a drink, Stephanie's blood refreshing to his palate.

"A young girl may be in danger here," he said aloud while gazing out the window at the city lights below. "We must do all we can to save her."

Chapter 16

The muscles in Mr. Howard back tightened from sitting inside the hot car for hours, but what choice did he have? The long surveillance outside Jackson's Discount Tires put him in a bad temper. Bundled in a long coat, gloves, and hat to protect him from the sun, he sweated profusely, his throat screaming for a drink. Ryan loafed around the shop. He spent the majority of his time on the side of the building where he smoked cigarettes. A tall, blond woman showed up and they disappeared into the woods behind the shop. When they emerged from the trees, she was wiping something white from her lips. The more he observed Ryan, the more he hated him. He was a piece of human excrement, fresh from the asshole of the world. With Reann, he was a cockroach that had climbed the stem of a lily.

Five o'clock. Rush hour traffic stacked up behind him on College Avenue. Horns blared, brakes squealed, engines roared as suicidal drivers weaved between lanes, and still he waited and watched. It went against his better judgment to take such a chance, but circumstances dictated action.

Ryan strolled out to his rusting pickup truck a few minutes after the store closed, gray coveralls smeared in grease, cigarette dangling from the side of his mouth. When he arrived at a parked Corvette convertible with the top down, he paused, quickly surveyed the scene, and tossed the burning cigarette inside with a laugh. Mr. Howard gnashed his teeth.

He followed Ryan to his house, an older one-story near the university, and was surprised to discover it neat and tidy. He'd been expecting a yard choked with weeds, the rusting hulk of a car sitting on cinder blocks. Ryan parked in the driveway on the side of the house and went inside. Mr. Howard settled in his seat and waited for darkness.

When the sun vanished behind the distant Rockies, he exited his car and strolled to the front door. He hoped Ryan lived alone, but was prepared to deal with whatever obstacles appeared. Ryan answered the door after several knocks, wearing a pair of faded jeans and no shirt. A tattoo of a zombie gnawing on a severed arm covered his chest. He held a can of beer in one hand. "Yeah," he said.

"Do you remember me?"

Ryan leaned forward to consider him through narrowed eyes. "Aren't you the freak who was at the Killgood's house?"

Mr. Howard suppressed a response as he simmered on the word *freak*. "Are you not the scumbag who abuses women and children?"

Ryan pulled back, nostrils flared. "Get out of my house."

"I'm not in your house." Mr. Howard took a step inside the doorway. "Now I am. Care to tell me again?"

"You fucker." Ryan heaved the beer can, which smashed into Mr. Howard's forehead over his left eye. Cold beer splashed over his hair.

Mr. Howard staggered. Pain radiated across his skull. He touched the spot where the can hit him and stared at his red fingertips. "You've cut me."

"You're dead, motherfucker."

"Yes, I know."

Ryan whirled about and ran into a back room. He returned after a few seconds, holding a revolver. "I'm going to bury you in the backyard and shit on your grave."

"I should think not."

Fire spit from the end of the barrel as the gun went off with a boom. A bullet ripped into the right side of his chest. Mr. Howard stayed on his feet. His chest stung as if filled with a hive of angry bees. He glanced down at the hole in his shirt and shook his head. "Look what you have done. I paid several hundred dollars for this shirt."

Ryan's mouth gaped open. He squinted and leaned forward to stare. "What the hell?"

Mr. Howard smiled. "You have had your fun. Now it is my turn." He flew straight to the ceiling, landing upside down, and scurried like a bug toward Ryan, his actions a blur like an arrow splitting the sky.

He flung himself onto the stunned man, fangs tearing into his shoulder.

"Get off me," Ryan screamed. Bone crunched. Blood exploded onto the walls. The gun dropped from Ryan's hand and he sank to his knees, the fight out of him. Mr. Howard slammed an open palm against the side of Ryan's head and he pitched face-first onto the floor. Mr. Howard stood over him. Lips and chin covered in blood. His chest heaved as he struggled to regain his composure. "That will teach you for ruining my shirt."

***

He sat in a folding chair inside his basement, sipping wine when Ryan regained consciousness. Ryan blinked several times and then struggled against the ropes that held him. His bound feet kicked at the plastic spread beneath him. "Where am I?" he snarled. He winced, his attention shifting to the wound in his shoulder, and then looked downward. "And where are my clothes, you pervert?"

Mr. Howard sighed and put down his glass. "Only someone of your limited mental capacity would associate your nude condition with a sexual act." He stood and walked over to a table, where he picked up a pair of scissors.

Ryan's eyes widened and he resumed struggling against the ropes. "What are you doing?"

He approached the young man, his fingers opening and closing the blades with the clicking of steel. "I call them tally whackers." He grabbed Ryan's penis, stretched it, and positioned the open blades around his member.

"Don't do this, please, please. I'll do anything."

"I am afraid you have done quite enough already, which is why you are now in this position. But do not be afraid, this will only hurt... a lot." He snapped the blades together. Blood spurted into the air like steam from a geyser.

Ryan screamed as his feet tap-danced on the plastic. "Fucking shit, it hurts!"

Mr. Howard picked up the severed penis. "A rather poor example of the male anatomy, I must say."

Tears rolled onto Ryan's cheeks. "Don't kill me. Please, please let me go..."

"You do realize doctors can sew them back on, yes? That is what happened with that Bobbitt fellow. As I recall, his wife cut off his penis and drove around with it for a while before tossing the penis out the car window. I believe they found a duck carrying it around. Can you imagine the trauma that poor duck suffered?"

He held the penis against Ryan's forehead. "I have a needle and thread upstairs. Perhaps, I should attach your member to your forehead, yes? Then everyone will know what a dickhead you really are."

"I'm going to kill you, you bastard."

"I should think not." Mr. Howard seized Ryan's jaw and forced his chin down. He shoved the penis into Ryan's mouth and walked away.

Chapter 17

The son of a bitch bleeds a lot. This perception stayed with him as Mr. Howard cleaned the basement. By the time he rolled Ryan's body into the plastic tarp and carried him upstairs into the backyard, dawn was breaking to the east, a golden sliver of light that pulled back the curtain of night. The sun represented life for most except his kind. He hurried to place large stones over Ryan's grave. No telling when Willard might come snooping around. Ten minutes passed. The sun's rays stung the back of his neck, which sizzled like frying bacon. Time to go.

He hawked up phlegm and spit on the grave. It was bad enough he had to kill the bastard, burying him in the backyard was the work of a madman. Still, what choice did he have? Someone would notice the scumbag was missing. They would find blood in Ryan's house and a revolver that had recently been fired. Mr. Howard touched the spot where the bullet tore into his chest. The wound had healed on the outside, but beneath the skin, it continued to ache. Shovel over shoulder, he returned to the house.

A hot shower did wonders for his psyche. Beneath the water, Mr. Howard experienced a rebirth, a baptism of sorts that cleansed his soul. Only once did he wince at the memory of Ryan's agony, and this was followed by a smile, which he couldn't erase, no matter how hard he tried. The man beat women and children. He deserved everything he got. Yes, he must push this lie until it became the truth. With the blood off his hands, he trudged into the master bedroom and collapsed onto the bed.

***

Four o' clock. He was running late. Mr. Howard slipped into his Fioravanti merino wool suit and slicked back his hair. In the kitchen, he opened the sliding glass door and ventured outside, where the afternoon sun hovered like a bomb about to explode across his world. He strolled over to the grave. "So, Ryan, how are you feeling now? Not too good, I would think." He flared open his coat. "I look stylish, yes? I must be leaving. Try to make yourself useful while I'm gone. Fertilize the lawn or something."

***

The parking lot was nearly full by the time he arrived. He recognized the cars that belonged to staff members. An unusually high number of hybrids with a few gas-guzzling SUVs mixed in. Professors Stephenson and Whitmore would ride their bicycles, having long declared cars instruments of the Devil.

After parking, he exited the Mercedes and smoothed his necktie. He hated affairs like this. If the party was for anyone other than Leslie, he would have stayed home. Several students watched him approach the academic center, no doubt wondering why he wore a fedora, long coat, and gloves on such a hot day. He ignored their curious gazes and hurried into the building. Once out of the sun, he took a deep breath and exhaled slowly. He slipped off his gloves, tucked them inside the pocket of his coat, and hung the coat and hat on a rack inside the lobby.

He followed the sound of hideous music to conference room six. Some nit-wit, probably Van Adams, had hired a tone-deaf band to perform at the party. The lead singer sounded like Boy George going through puberty as he struggled to sing "Tie a Yellow Ribbon around the Old Oak Tree," a song known to drive men insane, and make dogs chase their tails.

He stepped through the doors. The folding chairs had been removed from the room, opening it up for the guests who milled about in small groups, sipping wine as they tried to sound brilliant. Several tables pushed close to the walls held a variety of food, mostly salads, and pastas.

Leslie stood in a far corner talking with Gordon Robb and Bill Stanley, wealthy alumni. They were major boosters of the football team, not that it mattered. The team hadn't enjoyed a winning season since Nixon sat in the Oval Office. When she spotted him, a beautiful smile formed on her face. Her reaction made him smile as well. He took a step forward and Professor Whitmore stomped in front of him. "Mr. Howard in the flesh with the sun still out, now I've seen everything."

He resisted a snappy response. The joke around campus was that if the football team ever wanted to win, they should start Professor Whitmore at middle linebacker. Dressed in a ridiculous orange dress, she looked like a pumpkin that needed to be carved. Considering she rode her bicycle everywhere she went, Professor Whitmore should have been in much better condition. He could only imagine the number of Moon Pies she secretly ate. "Melissa, what a surprise."

She folded her fat arms over her chest. "Why haven't you stopped by to see me?"

"You know I cannot tolerate the sun. Would you like me to burn like Joan of Arc?"

"You're such a jokester." She looked at Leslie. "It's a shame about the dean leaving. She hired me, you know."

"Is that right?"

She punched him in the arm and he stumbled backward. "That's why you need to get out more. Sun or no sun, you need to see more of the world. It's not good for you to stay cooped up inside all day. It's not natural."

"Yes, I agree."

Her attention shifted to one of the serving tables. "I'd better grab something to eat before it's gone. I've started a diet. Lost two pounds last month."

"Two pounds you say? Impressive."

"Well too-da-loo," she said in passing. "I've just got to get me some of those little barbecue wieners."

Mr. Howard shook his head as she stormed the food tables like a soldier charging onto a beach. As he headed toward Leslie, someone grabbed his arm.

"Mr. Howard, well... this is a surprise... out in the daylight for everyone to see." Van Adams released him. His head swiveled like a cockatoos as he elevated his chin.

Van Adams had deliberately arranged the event to start during the daytime to prevent him from attending, but Mr. Howard resisted the urge to complain. Instead, he employed a new strategy, hoping to leave Van Adams in a state of confusion for the rest of the evening.

"Luther, it is always a pleasure to see you at one of these events. I heard you organized this one yourself. Excellent job."

Van Adams's eyelids became slits behind his glasses. "You're talking to me, correct? Luther Van Adams, Assistant Dean?"

Mr. Howard patted him on the shoulder. "Yes, of course I am talking to you." He removed his hand from Van Adam's shoulder and took in the activity inside the room. "And how does our new dean like the school?"

Van Adams continued to glare. "She likes it just fine." He pointed a finger. "You're up to something."

"What do you mean?"

"I will be watching you, Mr. Howard."

"Watching me? What on earth for?"

Van Adams backed away slowly. "You heard me, you sneaky bastard. No more of your Jedi mind tricks."

Leave it to Van Adams to use a reference to *Star Wars*. He probably owned the entire collection of *Star Wars* action figures and played with them every day. Kept them on a shelf beside his plastic Jesus, and Ben Wa balls. Mr. Howard continued through the crowd, acknowledging greeters with a smile and a nod. Leslie stepped past her admirers, arms open wide.

"I'm so glad you could come," she said, pressing against him. She leaned close to whisper. "I'm sorry I couldn't get them to change the time until evening."

"No worries."

"I saw you talking to Van Adams."

"He asked me to meet him in the bathroom so he could give me a blow job," he whispered back.

She put a hand over her mouth to hide a grin. "I believe you know Gordon Robb and Bill Stanley."

He shook their hands. "Gentlemen, it is always a pleasure to meet men with such unwavering support for our university football team."

Robb took a drink of punch and licked a stray drop from his top lip. "You're not much of a football fan, are you?"

"I follow the game from time to time."

Robb massaged his chin. "All right, Professor. What organization oversees the division I championship?"

"I believe you are referring to the BCS. But have you forgotten that Division I football has gone to a playoff?"

Robb smiled and nodded. "Not bad. Let me try another one. What conference has won the most BCS championships?"

"That would be the Southeastern Conference."

"Damn," Robb said, "I guess you proved your point."

"What I want to know," Mr. Howard said, "is when this university's football team will win a national championship."

"Ha," Stanley said, "they can't even win a conference championship. Hell, they'd get beat by half the high schools in this town."

"More than half," Robb added, which made everyone laugh.

Leslie touched him on the sleeve. "Gentlemen, if you will excuse us, I must borrow Mr. Howard for a bit."

"Don't keep him too long," Robb said, "I want to hear what he thinks about our new 3-4 defense this year."

She leaned against him as they walked. "I never realized you were such a football fan."

A quiet laugh rose in his throat. "I knew they would be here so I went on the computer and researched some basic facts about college football."

It was her turn to laugh. "I should've known you wouldn't have time for such a thing." She led him to a quiet corner. "It was nice of everyone to show up. Makes me feel good… as if I'll really be missed. But the truth is you're the only one who will truly miss me, and that's only because of the things I can do for you."

"Yes, I will miss those things."

She slipped her hand into his and squeezed. "Have you met the new dean?"

"Not yet."

"Would you like me to introduce you?"

"Sure, why not? What is she going to do, drive a stake through my heart?"

Leslie steered him toward a woman sitting alone, hunched over a notebook. She massaged her brow as if troubled. "Jennifer, there's someone I'd like you to meet."

She looked up from her papers. Red hair framed a face almost as fair as his. He whispered in Leslie's ear. "I thought she had black hair?"

Leslie whispered back. "She used to dye it."

"Is this the famous Mr. Howard?" she said with a pearly white smile.

He bowed. "It is a pleasure to meet you, Dean Tolliver."

"Please, call me Jennifer." She closed her notebook with a sigh.

"Homework already?" he asked.

She shrugged. "Goes with the job. Actually, I'm reviewing budget reports. I know, I should be enjoying myself, but the board of trustees is breathing down my neck to make cuts."

"Now you know why I decided to retire," Leslie said.

He caught her and Jennifer exchanging furtive glances. The kind women made when flush with desire.

Leslie motioned toward the door. "Would you pardon me? I want to catch Victor James before he leaves."

"Go right ahead," Mr. Howard said. He watched her leave and turned to Jennifer, who gestured toward the chair next to her.

"Can we talk a while?" she asked.

"Certainly." He eased onto the chair, his gaze traveling a path from her slender ankles all the way to her lap. The green in her dress brought out the green in her eyes. He found her quite lovely and it was easy to imagine making love to her. He inhaled through his nose. The smell of blood between her legs was strong and he held back a smile.

"I feel as if I've known you for years," she said turning to face him. She crossed her legs and a quiet moan slipped from his throat.

"And why is that?"

"Everyone likes to talk about you."

He folded his hands on his lap. "I hope they are saying good things about me, but I fear not."

Her eyebrows gathered. "Why would you think that? From what I've heard, you're a respected professor who is liked by your colleagues and students. You have a history of helping the police with difficult investigations."

"And still you consider cutting my position."

She leaned toward him and whispered. "I'm afraid there are many jobs that may be cut. Assistant Dean Van Adams has been helping me review each position at the school."

"Do you intend to act on his recommendations?"

Her right hand slid over his and she made eye contact before saying, "I know you and Van Adams don't get along."

The top of his hand tingled where she touched him. He resisted the urge to kiss her. "Dean Tolliver, I—"

"Jennifer."

He cleared his throat. "Jennifer, it is no secret that I do not get along with Van Adams, but I have never let that interfere with my job."

"I'm well aware of that." Her right eyebrow arched. "What is your first name anyway?"

"Mister."

She sighed. "Van Adams said you could be esoteric."

"A big word from such a tiny brain."

She rolled her eyes. "I should lock you both in a room and not let you out until you've made peace."

"Dueling pistols would work better."

"Are you always this way?"

"Irritating, yes?"

"Let me think on that a while." She pulled back her hand. "Our budget problems put me in a tough position. I do believe Dean Harris is leaving at an opportune time. You see, the government is shoving science and math down our throats."

"The world has enough scientists. What it needs are more poets. Scientists create weapons of mass destruction. Poets create beauty in a world that is starved for it."

"Well said. Unfortunately, ancient mythology has nothing to do with poetry and some people consider your class expendable."

"Some people, as in Van Adams." He cupped a hand around the back of his neck and massaged tired muscles. "Perhaps he is right. Perhaps I have no purpose here."

"I didn't say that."

"No," he said, "but as the saying goes, the writing is on the wall, is it not? Van Adams has wanted to get rid of me for years."

Her lips pressed into a flat line as she considered him with a questioning stare. "My evaluation is ongoing. No one, and I mean no one, is going to rush me into making a decision that affects another person's life."

Her words made him smile inwardly. Perhaps there was hope of keeping his job, not that he needed the income. He'd acquired a small fortune over the centuries in a number of lucrative ventures, most of them legal, and invested his profits wisely. He began by importing Tulip bulbs before the craze swept through Western Europe, and moved next to horses and cattle. In America, he dabbled in real estate, bootlegging, and oil. The real trick was keeping the money hidden from the authorities, most notably the IRS.

"You should sit in on my class sometime," he said. "You might enjoy learning about ancient cultures. Then you will see how little humanity has advanced through the years. We have technology, but we also have religious ignorance and intolerance. We can cure deadly diseases, while allowing millions to die from starvation. I sometimes wonder if reverse evolution is taking place and one day we will all wake up as monkeys. Look at poor Van Adams, he is already halfway there."

She chuckled softly and turned to hide the blush in her cheeks. "You are positively awful."

"Yes, I suppose I am."

She touched the base of her throat and took a deep breath that caused her breasts to rise and fall. "I appreciate your candor. Unfortunately, in my position, I cannot afford to reveal too much of myself. Do you understand?"

He wanted her to reveal much more of herself and get her into all kinds of positions, but that was a discussion for another day. "Yes, you must be a diplomat at all times, I understand all too well. I have known many deans in my career and your tasks are always the same. That is why I could never do your job."

"I'm glad you understand."

"So, how long have you been a dean?"

Her fingers smoothed the papers before her. "Five years. Prior to that, I was an assistant dean for two years, and a professor of English for six. I've always wanted to be a teacher, even when I was a little girl. How about you? How long have you been teaching?"

"For a hundred years it seems."

Leslie walked up on their conversation. "So, you two figure out how to solve the university's budget crisis?"

Jennifer slowly rose from her chair, notebook clutched to her chest. "Mr. Howard has invited me to sit in on his class."

"Is that right?" Leslie gave him a hard stare. "You should do it. Mr. Howard is quite entertaining."

"Yes, I can tell. It was a pleasure meeting you," Jennifer said to him before walking away.

He followed her progress to the door and then shifted his attention to Leslie who continued to glare. He couldn't help but grin. "What? Was I not supposed to be social?"

"I know you. You're already imagining yourself rolling in the sheets with our new dean. I haven't even left and you've already replaced me."

"No one could replace you."

"Has anyone told you you've perfected the art of lying?"

He started to smile but stopped upon seeing Killgood enter the room, a panicked expression on his face. Killgood spotted him and marched straight over. He acknowledged Leslie with a nod before turning to Mr. Howard. "We need to talk."

Leslie appeared confused.

"This is Detective Killgood," he explained.

Her lips pursed into an O. "I see. Well, don't let me keep you."

Killgood waited until she was halfway across the room before speaking. "We've got a problem."

"And what would that be?"

"Not here—outside."

A surge of nervousness coursed through his veins. "Very well. I hope nothing is wrong."

"Everything is wrong."

Chapter 18

Killgood hustled across the parking lot to his police car, an unmarked silver sedan. He unlocked the door and motioned for him to sit. Mr. Howard ducked inside and closed the door. A pine tree-shaped air fresher hung from the rearview mirror. Unfortunately, it made the car smell more like dish soap.

Killgood joined him in the car. Sweat glistened on his brow. He stared straight ahead, the knuckles on his right hand whitening around the steering wheel.

"What is it, Chandler?"

Killgood shot him a sideways glance. "Ryan's gone missing."

Mr. Howard hesitated to respond as he absorbed the news. He hadn't expected anyone to notice the scumbag's absence so soon, not that it mattered. No one was going to find him now.

"Since when?"

"Patrol received a call this afternoon from some junkie who went to Ryan's house. He wasn't there, but she noticed a large pool of blood on the floor. When the officers arrived, they found a revolver near the blood with a spent round. Looks like someone wanted to take him out pretty bad."

"Is that not a good thing? I mean, if he is dead, Reann's troubles are over."

Killgood looked down at his lap and shook his head. "Reann's troubles are over, but mine are just starting."

"I do not understand."

He turned toward him and in a flat voice said, "Everyone in the department knows about the problems we're having with Ryan."

Mr. Howard closed his eyes and pinched the bridge of his nose. "They suspect you are involved in his disappearance?"

"That idea's been tossed around like a lame joke; only, I sense in the back of their minds, my partners are wondering if it's true."

Mr. Howard opened his eyes and stared out the passenger side window. On the lawn between the buildings, a group of students stood in a circle kicking a hacky sack. They were hippie wannabes who belonged to an earlier time. Nearby, two girls wearing Daisy Dukes tossed a Frisbee. They moved like dancers, long legs knifing through the air.

"You have done nothing wrong," he said.

"Do you think I'm involved in Ryan's disappearance?"

He looked at the detective and sighed. "No, but it does not matter what I think. What I was going to say is you have done nothing wrong, so you have nothing to fear. Let them investigate. Let them gather their clues. In the end, you will be exonerated."

"Sounds great, but you're not the one being investigated."

But this wasn't the case. Willard was hard at work checking into his past to discover a link between him and Stephanie Coldstone.

"What do you believe happened to Ryan?"

"No telling. Mixed up with the wrong sort of people, I suppose. If I provide you with some of Ryan's things, do you think you could get a psychic reading?"

A sharp pain pulsated across his forehead. He tried to massage away the ache. "You want me to become involved in two missing person cases?"

"I know it's a long shot."

"Must you find Ryan? Aren't you happy he is out of Reann's life?"

"You're assuming he's dead," Killgood said.

"As are you."

Killgood slammed a palm against the steering wheel. "Shit!"

"Listen," Mr. Howard said. "If you become a suspect in Ryan's disappearance, I will do what I can to help you. In the meantime, let your fellow investigators see what they can turn up. Eventually, this will blow over."

"You mean once the case goes cold."

"I have always heard if you do not catch your killer within the first forty-eight hours, the odds go down considerably, yes?"

Killgood stared out the front window in a daze. He did this for several seconds before saying, "As much as I hate to admit it, I'm glad the SOB may be dead. What kind of man does that make me? I'm supposed to be helping people, not wishing them dead."

"I only met Ryan once, so perhaps I am not in a position to properly judge his character, but from what I saw, he was beyond anyone's help, including yours. I recommend focusing your energy on Reann and your granddaughter. Clear your mind of Ryan. Yes, your associates at the department may suspect you in his disappearance, but do not despair. Ryan is a footnote in history soon forgotten."

Killgood nodded. "Fine, but I still may need you to try locating him."

"I would not know where to start, but as the saying goes, I will give it my best shot." He glanced out the window toward the building. "I should get back for the grand finale."

"Are they throwing a going away party for the dean?"

"Do you know Dean Harris?"

"No, not personally, but I've spoken to her before, a few years back, during safety week at the campus."

"I see."

"Will you be all right out here in the sun?"

"If you read in tomorrow's paper about an old man who perishes from spontaneous combustion, you will have your answer."

He exited the car and offered a quick wave to the Detective. Head down, Mr. Howard walked briskly up the steps in search of shadow.

Chapter 19

Willard squirmed on the thinly padded auditorium seat. He might as well have been sitting on a cinder block. Squeezed between Doris and Dave, their fat arms spilling over the arm rests, he struggled to control his claustrophobia. He'd suffered from it most of his life. Ever since his older brother, C.J., locked him inside a toy chest while their parents were away selling chicken eggs in downtown Richton.

No 'count asshole.

He waited nine years to get even. Nine years until he punched C.J. in the mouth, knocking out two teeth. Still, the damage had been done. He couldn't go through an MRI or CT scan if his life depended on it. Crowded elevators made his pulse soar.

He tried to focus on the stage where Margo attempted to perform ballet. She was a pig amongst swans. A beach ball in a tutu. Twice, she knocked over another dancer while attempting to spin. Now, the swans kept their distance. His cheeks burned whenever Margo moved toward the other girls and they hurried away, eyes filled with panic, the audience breaking into laughter. Doris and Dave didn't seem to notice. They were too busy sucking down M&Ms they had smuggled in. Only generous donations to the dance academy kept Margo in school, not that it mattered. Margo was a lost cause. Six years of ballet lessons down the drain.

A few minutes into the second act, right after Margo flattened her third victim, his cell phone vibrated. In the dim light of the auditorium, Doris scowled at him as he dug the phone out of his pocket. He checked the number. *Killgood. I wonder what he wants.* He leaned toward Doris. "I need to take this call. It's business."

She seized his forearm and dug her fingernails into his skin. "You'd better come back soon. Margo's been practicing hard for this."

On stage, Margo bounced off another girl who landed on her butt with a thud. The girl jumped up and ran off in tears. He looked back at Doris. "Yeah, I can tell."

He wiggled out from his chair and hurried down the aisle, glancing over his shoulder in time to see another girl go down like a bowling pin. Inside the lobby, he dialed Killgood's number and waited. An older couple passed by shaking their heads.

"I'm contacting the school," the man said. "They never should let that fat girl dance."

"She ruined the whole performance," the woman added.

He turned his back to the exit, a sharp ache settling across his brow. Killgood answered on the second ring. "Hello."

"Killgood, it's Willard."

"Thanks for returning the call. Hope I'm not catching you at a bad time."

Inside the auditorium, the audience groaned. Willard shielded his face with a hand. "No, I was just watching my daughter's demolition derby."

"I need you to come to the station right away."

In the distance, a siren wailed. "That might be a little difficult. Can't this wait until tomorrow?"

"We may know where to find Stephanie Coldstone's body."

Willard brought down his hand. He stood taller, his mind no longer on the carnage inside the auditorium. "Let me guess, Mr. Howard had a vision."

"No, this has nothing to do with him."

People streamed out the auditorium doors, disgust etched on their faces. *Sweet Jesus, I hope she didn't kill anyone.* Doris would snort like a bull while threatening to crush him when he told her he needed to go. A threat he took most seriously. "All right, give me a few. I'll need to drop my family back home."

"Thanks. I'll be in the office."

He hung up the phone right as someone shrieked behind the closed auditorium doors. The wail of the siren grew louder. His right hand balled into a fist.

After driving his family home, Willard hustled out to his sedan. Eager to escape the nightmare of the recital, he burned rubber backing out of the driveway. On the interstate he weaved in and out of traffic, frustration from living with a bunch of wide-bodied fuckups blinding him to the danger of his actions. He tried to concentrate on what Killgood had told him. They might know where Stephanie Coldstone's body is located.

Hallelujah!

The sooner he put this case behind him, the better. How did they come up with a location to find her remains? Oh well, at least Mr. Howard wasn't involved… that was almost enough to make him forget Doris's reaction when he told her they had to leave. As expected, she bowed her back and flattened her hands on her hips, ignoring the paramedics behind her on the stage treating the last girl Margo plastered.

"You love your damn job more than you love your family."

He responded with silence which was tantamount to agreeing with her. She grabbed Dave and Margo by the hand and stomped down the aisle. On stage someone shouted, "Code blue." Yeah, code blue all right, his entire life flushed down the commode like a giant turd. It didn't help that the girl on stage was the daughter of a personal injury lawyer.

Shit.

He arrived at the police station and parked near the entrance. The sun was almost gone behind the foothills and the parking lot lights emitted a low buzz as they came alive. A cool front blowing in from Wyoming brought the threat of rain. Hands in his pockets, head down, he marched toward the building, ignoring the two uniformed cops who passed.

Willard slowed as he approached Killgood's office. Killgood was sitting behind his desk. A young woman occupied one of the chairs in front of him. Willard guessed her age to be mid-twenties. She had short black hair that contrasted against the paleness of her skin. Her plain white T-shirt squeezed breasts that belonged on a centerfold.

Probably had a boob job.

When he noticed she wasn't wearing a bra, his penis started to tingle. Damn, the last thing he needed was to walk in with a hard on. He retreated to a bench in the hallway and waited until his erection melted away. A single knock announced his arrival. He acknowledged Killgood with a nod and held out a hand to the woman. "Detective Willard, State Police."

She hesitated before offering her own hand. Small fingers, soft warm palm—crap he felt his erection returning. Willard quickly sat and crossed his legs.

"This is Alicia Whitmore," Killgood said. "Alicia thinks she can help us with your investigation."

He considered her through narrowed eyes. She flushed, her chin sinking toward her chest. "Is that so? Did she witness something?"

"I've had dreams," she whispered.

If he didn't find her attractive, he would have groaned, instead, he cleared his throat to indicate his willingness to listen. "What kind of dreams?"

She continued to stare at her lap. "Nightmares really."

"Oh?"

She viewed him from the corner of her eye. "I see a girl, alone and scared. She wants to go home but she can't."

"What's stopping her?"

"She's… in the ground. She doesn't like it there. It's dark and cold."

Willard gave Killgood a hard stare. "Another psychic?"

The girl shook her head. "Both my mother and grandmother were psychics but I've never claimed to be gifted."

He arms folded on his chest. "Until now."

She looked down and chewed her lip. "Maybe I shouldn't have come."

Killgood waved a finger to draw his attention. "Alicia thinks she can lead us to Stephanie."

"Are you certain the girl in your dreams is Stephanie?" Willard asked.

"After one of my dreams, I saw her picture in the newspaper. It was definitely the same girl."

He worked his tongue against the sides of mouth as he pondered his next move. While he'd always considered psychics to be frauds, he recalled Janssen saying that some of them seemed to be genuine. Perhaps this girl was one of the truly gifted. At least she was easier on the eyes than Mr. Howard. He pushed out of the chair and gestured toward the door. "I'm going to talk with Detective Killgood for a moment outside."

She nodded without raising her head.

Killgood joined him in the hallway. "This is your investigation—what do you want to do?"

Willard walked to a window and pressed his forehead against the glass. The top pane stood open and hot summer air swirled inside, carrying the smell of wild barley that grew in an adjacent field. "You have more experience working with these people than I do."

"I've never had two psychics simultaneously assisting in an investigation."

"Does she seem legit to you?"

There was a moment of silence before Killgood answered. "I guess we won't find out unless we let her take us to the body."

He faced Killgood. "Fine, then let's see what she can do."

They returned to the office and sat. She squirmed in her chair, her gaze moving between the two of them. "So?"

"So," Willard said, "we decided to let you help us."

"I won't go to jail if this doesn't work, right?" she asked.

"You won't go to jail," Willard answered looking at Killgood who smiled behind his desk. "But, perhaps we should wait until morning to make it easier for you."

Her head came up and she turned toward him. "No, we should go now."

"Are you sure?"

"I'm sure."

Killgood drove. Willard sat on the front passenger seat with the girl in the back behind Killgood. Willard liked it this way because he could steal glances at her. She had one of those faces that would always look young and he imagined her in a cheerleader uniform without panties, skirt flying up to reveal a triangle of black pubic hair. If he concentrated, he could almost taste her.

Killgood stopped at the intersection with the main road. "Which way?" he said.

She hesitated for a few seconds. "Go left."

"You want me to turn north?"

"Yes, north."

He steered onto Timberline Drive and headed north. When they reached the intersection with Mulberry, she unbuckled her seatbelt, leaned forward between the front seats, and checked both directions. Willard edged close enough to smell her flowery perfume. "Where now?"

"Right... yes... go right."

Killgood headed east on Mulberry, passing warehouses, auto repair shops, and various small businesses. Near the interstate, they drove by motels and pancake houses. Semis filled the parking lot of a truck stop. A cattle truck rumbled onto the road. Beyond the highway, the land flattened. Buildings gave way to farms. Willard continued to watch the woman. She pressed her face against the window as they came to Gillstrap, a small farming community. "He came this way."

Willard exchanged questioning glances with Killgood. "Who came this way?" he said over his shoulder.

"The man... he came this way with Stephanie." She flattened a hand against her chest and took several deep breaths. "He noticed the sky... the stars... and the smell."

"What smell would that be?" Killgood asked.

She waited several seconds. "Manure, yes, he smelled the manure." She lowered her window and thrust her head outside to stare at the night sky. "And the moon... he noticed that too." She sat back in the seat, but left her window open.

"This man," Willard said, "can you see him?"

She grimaced as if suffering a headache. "His hands are..." She began to massage her temples furiously, fingers turning in a tight circle, faster and faster.

Willard sighed. He wanted to believe her, but after experiencing Mr. Howard's performance, found it difficult. "What about his hands?"

She stopped massaging her temples and sat straight up. "Wrinkled... they are wrinkled and pale like new snow."

"Anything else?"

"He loved her," she whispered.

Willard blinked several times as he digested her words. "Loved her?"

"Yes. In his own way, he loved her. And she knew it. She knew he struggled against his conscience. He took no pleasure in the thing he did."

"What did he do?"

She pressed back against the headrest and closed her eyes. "You don't need me to tell you that, Detective. It won't be much longer now."

"What won't be much longer?"

"You'll see."

He looked at Killgood, who shrugged. "Is it like this working with Howard?"

"Well, I'd say—"

"It's not like this with Howard," she said.

They both stared at her. "Do you know Mr. Howard?" Willard asked.

"Mr. Howard," she repeated softly without opening her eyes.

Willard turned around in his seat. "I'll take that as a no." He folded his arms over his chest and grunted softly. He could be home in bed, his head swallowed by a big fat pillow, dreams of... his big fat wife snoring beside him... ugh. Thinking of Doris made him want to puke.

The road belonged to them now. He hadn't seen another car for several miles. If not for the glow of the moon, the surrounding darkness would be complete, and suffocating, like the space inside a locked toy box. Willard clenched his teeth. *Mama, Daddy, someone, please, please let me out of here. Please. I don't want to die here. Someone open this thing. Can't move, can't breathe, this thing's a coffin. Please help me!*

"Stop!"

Killgood slammed on the brakes causing the nose of the car to dive. Willard pitched forward and slammed back into the seat. "Nice stop, ace."

She unbuckled her seat belt, leaned between the seats, and pointed toward a turn off. "This is the place he took her."

"Are you sure?" Willard asked.

She nodded. "He turned off here."

"All right," Killgood said, instinctively checking for traffic before turning north. He drove onto a dirt road. Tires spit gravel while stirring up a gray dust cloud behind the car. He slowed to a stop, the car headlights illuminating an entrance sign for the Grasslands National Park. "He brought her to the park?"

"That's just great," Willard said. "This place belongs to the Feds, which means if she's out here, the FBI will get involved. I hope you've stocked up on your K-Y, Detective."

She massaged her brow, fingers dancing over her flesh like spider legs. "Notebook."

"What about a notebook?" Willard asked.

She pinched her thumb and forefinger together and moved her hand as if writing with a pen. "He wrote something here. Something about the sign."

"The entrance sign?"

She nodded.

He could tell from Killgood's expression that he also wondered why the killer took notes about the sign.

"Go straight," she said.

Killgood let off the brake and the car rolled forward. They crossed a cattle guard, a metallic rumble rising up through the floorboard.

"He wrote something about that too," she said.

"The cattle guard?" Willard asked.

"Yes, he wanted to remember it."

"Perhaps to help him relive the experience," Killgood said.

She reached up to tap Killgood on the shoulder. "It's dark."

"Yes it is."

"No, not that," she said, "cut your headlights."

Willard turned in his seat. "Why?"

"He did it… the man… when he brought her."

Killgood cut the headlights and the world vanished as if someone had dropped a black cloak over the land. Willard squirmed with unease. "Are you sure he cut the lights? How could he see anything?"

"He sees everything," she said, settling back in the seat.

They continued driving, moonlight bringing out the detail of a barb wire fence and an occasional yucca. She drew in a breath, which caused both detectives to turn, and pointed toward a solitary tree on the horizon. "There, that's the spot. He buried her near the tree."

"Are you sure?" Willard asked.

"Yes, this is the place."

When they came parallel to the tree, Killgood stopped the car.

"No, not here."

Killgood glanced at him, his left eyebrow arched, and then at the girl. "I thought you said this was the place?"

"Back up about ten yards," she said.

Killgood sighed as he slipped the car into reverse. He finished backing up. "Is this where you want it?"

"He parked here." She said, opening the door.

She was out the door so fast Willard barely had time to blink. "Maybe she needs to pee."

Killgood grunted. "Hey, I don't know anything about this girl, so don't blame me if this turns out to be a wild goose chase."

"I will most definitely blame you."

They joined her at the back of the car. She faced the trunk, staring straight as if in a trance. Her hands clawed the air. "Her body…"

"What about her body?" Willard asked.

"He… pulled it…"

"What does that mean?"

She grabbed his arm so hard it hurt him. "He pulled her out of his car. Dark… black… maybe blue… with doors at the rear."

Willard gently pried her hand from his arm. "Like a van?"

She closed her eyes and pinched the bridge of her nose. "Yes, I believe it was a van." Her eyes opened wide. "He talked to her."

The detectives exchanged questioning gazes. "I thought she was dead," Killgood said.

"Yes, she was dead." She scurried toward the grassland beyond the road.

"Alicia, wait!" Killgood said and jogged to catch up. "Hasn't anyone warned you about snakes?"

"He buried her on the other side of the fence."

"How did he get her body over the fence?" Willard asked coming alongside Killgood.

She hurried to the fence and rested a hand on top of a post. She looked up and down the fence line and started north. After traveling a few yards, she stopped. "That's how he did it," she said, pointing to a spot where the fence gaped.

Willard switched on his flashlight and tromped to the opening. He touched the wire. "It's been cut."

She brushed past, pushing the wire aside. Her path was direct and without hesitation. She stopped walking and sank to her knees. A long, pitiful moan rose from her chest. The detectives hurried to join her.

"What is it?" Killgood asked. His flashlight cast a circle of soft light on the ground.

She motioned with her chin. "He buried her here. She's alone, so alone, and frightened. Stephanie doesn't like it here."

"Look," Willard said, swinging the beam of his light from side to side, "the ground is sunken over here."

Killgood nodded. "Like on a grave." He started toward the car.

"Where are you going?" Willard asked.

"I've got a shovel in the trunk."

The girl now hugged herself and rocked back and forth, tears glistening on her cheeks. She looked at Willard. "He loved her... like a daughter."

"A loving father doesn't kill their daughter."

"It's his curse. He must kill to live."

"Yeah... well, most serial killers feel that way."

She pushed off the ground and brushed off the front of her skirt. "He doesn't consider himself a killer."

"Neither did Ted Bundy."

"This man... he needs something from his victims...to live. It's not sexual... and he wasn't abused as a child... no, they give him life. He dies without their sacrifice. Do you understand?"

"Yeah, sure," he said, while all the time thinking she was as cuckoo as Mr. Howard. The only thing Killgood would dig up was dirt.

Killgood returned with a shovel. He turned off his flashlight and jammed it into a back pocket. "Mind giving me some light? If there is anything here, I don't want to destroy evidence."

Willard aimed his light at the spot on the ground and Killgood gently sunk the blade of the shovel into the earth.

"The soil is soft beneath the surface as if it's been recently turned," Killgood said over his shoulder. He carefully placed the dirt in a pile and scooped out another spade full.

The girl's breathing became rapid. She worked her fingers through the sides of her hair, over and over. "Hold on, Stephanie. We're almost there."

Killgood continued to work, the pile of dirt growing taller. He paused to wipe off his brow. "Holy shit," he said.

"What is it?" Willard asked.

Killgood gestured toward the hole. "Something pale. I think its skin."

Willard stepped closer and shined the flashlight at the spot. His stomach ached as if he'd been punched. "I see it."

Killgood dropped to his knees. He cautiously moved the tip of the blade around, lifting out small quantities of dirt. Tossing aside the shovel he used his hands to brush away loose soil. He looked up with a stricken expression on his face. "Fingers."

Alicia covered her face and sobbed.

The energy drained out of Willard and his shoulders sagged. "I reckon we'd better call this in."

Killgood stood, hands on his hips, and took a deep breath, which he exhaled with a puff. "Do you still think psychics are full of crap?"

"Not all of them," Willard replied.

Chapter 20

Mr. Howard awoke shortly after noon, long before his usual waking time of four o'clock. Restless, he'd tossed and turned in bed, anxiety nagging at him, flickering through the corridors of his mind like a candle flame inside a dark room. Something was wrong. Could it be the problem with Killgood? Perhaps it was a mistake to kill Ryan. No, he deserved his fate. Even the penis chopping felt like justice. He should have considered the complications for Killgood, who had enough to worry about working with Willard on the Coldstone case. Pushy bastard. Willard was probably the first in line every day at school with an apple in hand to impress the teacher. Make the grade, go to college, and for what, to be a cop?

Ludicrous.

He strolled over to his writing desk and turned on a lamp. He blinked several times while scanning the room. Where was Stephanie? Her spirit typically was there to greet him whenever he awoke. He shrugged off her absence and dialed Killgood's cell phone. Killgood answered after one ring.

"Homicide, Killgood."

He noted stress in the detective's voice and assumed it was due to Ryan's disappearance. "Chandler, I have been thinking about your problem with Ryan, and I was—"

"Mr. Howard, this isn't the best time."

"You sound tired."

"Yeah, well, I've been up all night at a crime scene, getting my blood drained by a bunch of goddamn mosquitoes."

"Has there been a homicide?"

Several seconds passed. "We found Stephanie Coldstone."

The room started to spin. Blood rushed from his head. Mr. Howard grabbed the desk for support and eased onto a chair. "How?"

"Another psychic led us to her body."

"A psychic you say?" The only well-known psychic in town was Susan Tate and having met her, he quickly came to the conclusion she was as phony as he was. "Susan Tate?"

"No, a young woman, her name's Alicia Whitmore. Claims her mother and grandmother were both psychics, but doesn't consider herself one. Guess she'll need to reconsider that now. I'm surprised she found the body before you did. You must be getting rusty."

Mr. Howard massaged his brow as he thought. *Too early, it is way too early for them to find the body.*

"I did have a vision of Stephanie a couple nights ago, but did not consider it useful."

"Oh, what kind of vision?"

"I saw Stephanie in a dark place. The land was flat. There was a tree and a fence near the tree. It is not much."

"All right... well, at least we'll have some evidence this time. Maybe, we'll catch the scumbag who killed her."

In his mind, Mr. Howard envisioned himself racing down a bright tunnel toward a spot of darkness—a reversal of a near-death experience. There wouldn't be a rebirth for his soul when everything was said and done. "Has this psychic provided information about a suspect?"

"Nothing much in the way of a physical description, but she said he drives a dark colored van."

His left hand curled into a fist. "Damn it."

"Something wrong?"

Mr. Howard took a deep breath to calm his nerves. "No, no, I dropped something. That is fantastic news, yes. Perhaps I will get an opportunity to meet Alicia? Who knows, we might even work together on this case." He flattened his hand on the desktop. Under the light, his skin appeared translucent, his veins purple and swollen with blood—Stephanie's blood. If the cops needed evidence all they had to do was draw his blood for DNA testing. "Is Doctor Allen performing the autopsy?"

"No, the state's doctor will be handling it. This entire case is fucked. No one knows who has jurisdiction. The Feds showed up at the crime scene and demanded to be in charge."

"The FBI is involved?" he said, feigning ignorance.

"The grasslands are a national park."

Of course, I knew that, he wanted to say. *The more agencies involved the better.* He envisioned further interrogation from FBI profilers who would try to understand his role in this little drama. He didn't find them particularly intimidating, unlike Willard, who seemed to see beyond his false persona. The FBI would thwart Willard's efforts to find the real killer. With any luck, Willard would be off the case entirely.

"Oh, yes, I seem to remember that. I have never been to the park myself, but several of my students go camping there."

"The son of a bitch drove a long way to get rid of her body."

"He did indeed." He pictured the van in his garage. He'd wisely purchased the van out of state and registered it using false identification; still all it would take is someone like Willard snooping around to confirm it belonged to him. But he would need a warrant for that and what judge in his right mind would issue one with no more evidence than Willard had. But what if this psychic provided information that led to him?

"I'd better let you go. I'm tired as hell and can't wait to get home."

"Yes, I am sure you are. I will call if I come up with anything else."

"You do that."

After hanging up the phone, Mr. Howard sat for a long time staring straight ahead, his mind in a fog. Never before had he felt this vulnerable, not even when the body of Cynthia Rhodes turned up sooner than expected. It was Willard. He didn't like him from the moment he first saw him.

Mr. Howard left the master bedroom and walked into his office. He logged on to his computer, typed the name Alicia Whitmore, and did a search. The picture on her Facebook page showed a young woman with a fair complexion and long black hair. Her dark eyes betrayed sadness. She listed no one as her friends, which made him wonder why she felt the need to create a page on the social network. He studied her profile: single, born and raised in Colorado, college educated, lived in town, only a few miles from him, self-employed as a web designer.

He scrolled down the page to find her interests: favorite bands were 10 Years and Big Country; favorite books *The Grapes of Wrath, To Kill a Mockingbird,* and *Twilight,* favorite movies *Let the Right One In,* Bram Stoker's *Dracula,* and *Twilight.* Mr. Howard sighed. *So, Alicia has a thing for vampires. I wonder if she would like to meet a real one.*

He leaned closer to the screen to study her face in more detail. "I find you somewhat attractive, which is probably most unfortunate for you." He tapped his chin. "Poor, Alicia. Why now of all times did you have to discover your gift? You could have read palms at the fair and made a fortune instead of assisting that bastard Willard. This is not good, Alicia. Definitely not good."

Chapter 21

Doris sat at the kitchen table behind several empty Ding Dong boxes. She'd taken the foil wrappers from the cakes, wadded them into balls, and arranged them to spell out "Fuck You." Willard almost laughed at her ingenuity. She glared at him with tiny pig eyes as he walked to the refrigerator and grabbed a beer. He unscrewed the top and sank onto a chair at the far end of the table. Looking at her made him sick to his stomach. She had always been on the plump side, even when they first met, but back then he considered her ass a nice soft pillow for his thighs. Now every time she sat down, somewhere in the world a tsunami rolled toward shore.

He swigged his beer. "Nice to see you too."

"Do you realize how long it's been since I last heard from you?"

He took another drink. "Should I?"

"Twenty-eight hours."

"Yeah, well, time flies when you're having fun."

She slammed a fist onto the table and the foil balls leaped into the air. "Who is she?"

Someone needs to shove an apple in her mouth and serve her on a big silver platter. He smirked behind the raised bottle. "Stephanie Coldstone."

"That's the bitch you're screwing?"

"She's the girl we just dug out of the ground."

Her expression softened. "She's the one who went missing."

"That's right," he said. "She ain't missing no more."

Several seconds of awkward silence passed between them. "You still should have called. I was worried sick."

"Yeah, well, you had your Ding Dongs to keep you company."

She pushed back her chair, the metal legs screeching over the tile floor, and struggled to stand, her body shaking, and blood rushing into her chubby cheeks. Air whistled from her lungs when she finally straightened. "You're a sorry piece of shit."

"I'll drink to that."

"Aren't you the least bit interested in how your daughter is doing?"

"I'm more interested in the kid she nearly killed. I hope you looked up lawyers in the phone book."

"Fuck you!" She grabbed a loaf of bread off the counter and hurled it at him.

He ducked and waited until she was gone to get up and walk into the office. At his desk, he leaned forward and rested his head in his hands. He should sleep, but there were too many thoughts in his brain to let that happen. An image of Stephanie's corpse appeared. She'd been a looker all right. While staring at her nude body, he became aroused. What it would be like to have sex with the dead? He quickly put this notion out of his mind. Necrophilia was too bizarre even by his standards.

Whoever killed you is a clever SOB. A goddamn phantom that doesn't attract attention.

He recalled his discussion with the FBI profilers and their assessment of the killer. Well organized, older man, not insane, who might have taken jewelry from his victims. Willard tapped his knuckles against his forehead. "What else did they say... think, think." And then it all came back to him, normal or high IQ, socially adequate, possibly married or involved with someone.

What else, what else?

Probably drives a flashy car, keeps himself clean. He opened his briefcase and rifled through the contents for a photograph he'd taken. He placed the picture on the desk in front of him and stared at the smirking face. *You drive a flashy car, don't you? And you're older, well organized, with a high IQ. And as I recall, Hartley said you'd like to contact the police to play mind games. I'd say those things pretty much describe you, Mr. Howard. Don't you agree?*

Could Mr. Howard be a serial killer? Even if he was a killer, how to prove it? Willard's entire body tingled at the idea of going after Mr. Howard, as if he were a hunter venturing into tall grass in pursuit of a lion.

"Let's see what the autopsy reveals," he said, turning his attention to the computer. He opened up Google and typed in Alicia Whitmore. He checked her Facebook page. "I see you've cut your hair." Leaning forward, he gazed into her dark eyes. *Why so sad? Is it because you've listed no one as your friend? You and I could be friends. Very close friends. Let's take a look at your profile. Hmm, you're a college grad, no surprise, and a web designer, good for you.* He checked her interests and groaned upon seeing she had a fascination with vampires. "Why does everyone find vampires so..." He studied Mr. Howard's picture. "...fascinating?" He rolled his tongue against the sides of his mouth.

As I recall, Mr. Howard wrote a book about vampires. I wonder what he has to say about them.

His attention returned to the computer. He quickly found a listing for Mr. Howard's books. "Let's see here, *Sub-Saharan Africa Mythology,* and *Mythology of the European Lowlands.*" He yawned. "Sounds interesting, I should order a copy of both to help with my insomnia." He scrolled down the page. *All right, here are your novels.*

He read the descriptions and rolled his eyes. *A story about a witch who lusts after a boy and something about the Devil finding Eve in Oklahoma... Yeah right, no wonder no one wanted to buy them. But where's the other book?* He leaned toward the screen. "There it is, *The True Story of Vampires.*" The book blurb said *The True Story of Vampires* offered a comprehensive view into the world of vampires that went beyond the common myths created by novelists and screenwriters. A real glimpse into the strange and captivating world of the undead.

And they pay you to write this shit?

A quick search told him a copy was available at the library. He put a hold on the book and planned to pick it up on his way to the autopsy the next morning.

A dull ache traveled through his brain in waves as he relived the day's events. He never believed psychics were real before, but even he couldn't deny Alicia Whitmore had a gift. She led them straight to Stephanie's body, without bullshit clues about obscure visions. Her success made Willard question the sincerity of Mr. Howard, and yet, he couldn't dismiss Howard's history of helping law enforcement agencies. Still, there was something about him that didn't seem right. Willard felt it in his gut. Unfortunately, now his case belonged to the FB-fucking-I. Sorry bastards, they'd never find Stephanie's killer. But he could still investigate on his own. At least until Captain Tate gave him another assignment. Jesus H. Christ. Why did the killer have to bury her in the grasslands?

Doris snored inside the master bedroom. He cringed as the wet sound carried throughout the house. Leaving the office, he collected a blanket from the hall closet and shuffled to the couch. Stretched out beneath the cover, he closed his eyes and tried to sleep, but a vision of stampeding elephants popped into his head as he listened to Doris. He growled softly and tried to think of something more pleasing. He remembered Alicia Whitmore squirming on the backseat of Killgood's car. She'd be a good fuck, he had no doubt. Picturing her naked, arms open to welcome him, he drifted off to sleep.

Chapter 22

Willard loosened his necktie as he marched toward the entrance to the medical examiner's office, a nondescript building constructed from mustard colored bricks. It was only ten in the morning and already sweat bubbled across his brow. At least it was a dry heat, not like the humid crap in Mississippi. His shirt never stayed dry during a Gulf Coast summer. He hated autopsies about as much as he hated his yearly prostrate exam. With both, he came out feeling violated. This one promised to be a three-ring circus now that the Feds were involved.

A blonde greeted him with a wide smile. "Can I help you?" she asked in a sickly sweet voice. Someone needed to remind her she worked at the morgue and not an amusement park.

He flashed his badge. "Detective Willard, I'm here for the—"

"I know why you're here, Detective." She handed him a pen and pointed at a paper attached to a clipboard. "Sign in please."

He scribbled his name and tossed down the pen.

She continued to smile like one of those Japanese sex robots. "Take the hall to your left. Go through the double doors and take the first door on your right. You'll find coveralls and a mask inside your locker along with a key lock. Don't forget to leave it when you're finished."

Inside the changing room, he held up the coveralls and laughed. He'd just spent eighteen hours beside a rotting corpse and now they were worried he might catch something or contaminate the evidence. He slipped the white coveralls over his clothes and zipped them in front of the mirror. He looked like the white rabbit from Wonderland. A door opened and another rabbit entered the room. "There you are. You'd better hurry up. I think they're about to start."

"What are you doing here?" Willard said pulling his cap over his hair.

Killgood shrugged. "I wanted to see where this thing's headed."

"I don't imagine either of us will be there at the end." Willard followed him through a door that led into a short hallway. Killgood paused outside a door marked Autopsy Room.

"I hope you ate a big breakfast. We'll probably be here a while."

Willard shivered as he entered the examining area. The air conditioner roared as it pumped out cold air.

Why do they keep the room so damn cold? She's been lying in a hole for a month.

A group of four men stood in a ragged circle at the far side of the room. Even with their bunny suits and masks, Willard recognized them as the FBI agents who worked the crime scene. The lead agent was a former football player from CU. A big bastard with sloped shoulders, who spoke in a low voice, words struggling off his tongue as if his mouth were full of peanut butter. His partner was the complete opposite, a little guy who rushed his words. The other two agents were green, having recently graduated from the Academy. The big agent had a Polish surname Willard couldn't pronounce, so in his mind, he called him Agent Yogi and the little guy Agent Boo Boo.

At the burial site, Agent Yogi talked into his cell phone while Agent Boo Boo ordered the supporting cast to do an outward spiral of the area for evidence. One of the agents discovered a shoe print that ended up belonging to Killgood. Other than that, all the uppity agents managed to do was stir up dust. The crime scene guys came in next. They took photographs of the scene, the grave, and Stephanie's body. They even had someone taking pictures from a helicopter. The crime scene was clean, much to their chagrin. No trace evidence, no impressions, no obvious body fluids or hair and fibers. She didn't appear to have been shot or stabbed so there was no weapons and firearms evidence. Two of the crime scene investigators discussed the bruising on her neck and decided she'd been strangled. A five-year-old would have come to that conclusion.

A forensic entomologist, Dr. Aaron Marquart, was called to collect bug evidence. Willard had worked with Marquart before and respected him. He was about what one would expect of a guy who loved bugs, with a deep tan from spending his time outside in pursuit of specimens, bald head, and long sideburns that made him look like a werewolf. He always wore shorts, even during the coldest winters. Bug tattoos covered his arms and legs. Marquart stood over the grave, shaking his head as he slipped on latex gloves. "What a waste," he said, digging into his toolbox. He took out a pair of forceps and a killing jar.

"Do you think you'll have any trouble establishing the PMI?" Killgood had asked.

"I don't establish the post mortem interval," Marquart said, kneeling beside the grave, "but I should be able to tell you how long she's been exposed to the environment. I'll need to check with the weather station in Nunn to see what the temperature's been for the past month. I'm surprised coyotes didn't get to her, but I can already see that Calliphora vicina, what you would call Blow Flies, have been here."

He worked a hand under the corpse and examined the area beneath with a flashlight. "This is interesting. The maggot activity is below normal. Heavy rainfall can slow fly activity. As I recall, this area had a period of heavy rain that lasted for several days approximately three weeks ago. Based on what I'm seeing, I would say she's been in the ground no more than three weeks." Several beetles scampered out of the hole. Marquart had smiled as he watched. "They like to eat the dry skin. It's kind of like going to a buffet for them."

Inside the examining room, Killgood gestured toward the agents. "The big cocksucker told me I didn't need to be here."

"What did you say?"

"I politely reminded him that you and I discovered the body, then told him to go fuck himself."

Willard smiled behind his mask. "I'm sure that went over well."

A set of double doors banged open and the diener strolled in, pushing a body bag on a gurney. One of the gurney wheels wobbled and made a god-awful squeaking sound that bounced off the walls. Two men walked in behind the morgue attendant. One of them was the crime scene investigator who was at the gravesite. He assumed the other man was the doctor who would perform the autopsy. The diener rolled the gurney over to the steel examining table. All three men put on latex gloves, and the assistant unzipped the body bag. With the help of the crime scene specialist, he lifted what remained of Stephanie Coldstone onto the table. The diener went to work removing plastic covers tied around her hands to preserve fingernail samples.

"You may take fingerprints now, Agent Powers," the doctor said to the crime scene investigator.

He lifted Stephanie's right hand. "Her fingers are bent toward the palm."

"Will you need to cut the tendons?"

Agent Powers grunted as he worked to straighten a finger. "I don't think so, but with her body in such a dehydrated state, I'll need to inject glycerin in order to get a print." He walked to a small table and returned with a syringe filled with clear liquid. Carefully inserting the needle into a finger, he slowly pushed fluid into the skin. He paused several seconds before massaging the fingertip. "A few more injections and I'll be good to go."

The doctor waited for him to finish with the fingerprints and then approached the officers who had gathered to watch. "Good morning, gentlemen. I am Dr. Moore. I will be conducting the autopsy. Please feel free to step closer and ask questions. No question is too dumb… well, that's not entirely true. Recently a sheriff asked me why a deceased transvestite was missing his vagina. Apparently, he believed all transvestites were hermaphrodites."

Agent Yogi raised a hand. "The girl you're looking at today isn't a transvestite, is she?"

Dr. Moore blinked several times and turned to the diener. "Thomas, it seems we have another Einstein in our midst."

The tall, blond assistant chuckled. "Another junior G-man."

The doctor joined the assistant at the table. "Did you take the X-ray?"

"Yes. Nothing unusual showed up as you expected."

Killgood gestured toward the doctor. "Come on, let's get closer." Willard followed him to the table. They took a position a few feet behind Dr. Moore, who watched their approach with a gleam in his eyes.

"Ah, two fellows who are not afraid of the dead. Have you witnessed an autopsy before?"

They both nodded. "Very good," Dr. Moore said.

Thomas squeezed a rubber body block under Stephanie's back, causing her chest to protrude forward while her arms and neck fell back. Dr. Moore clicked on the microphone of a small handheld recorder. He slowly walked around the table. "August second, ten twenty-two AM, examination number four two three. White female, shoulder-length reddish-brown hair." He leaned over her face and feathered back an eyelid. "Green eyes. Approximate age, seventeen. The blood vessels in the eyes are ruptured. Any identifying features?" His head swiveled as he looked over the body.

"Three moles on her left side near the breast."

Dr. Moore walked around the table and joined Thomas. "Yes, they almost form a triangular pattern. I don't see anything else of significance." He looked up and waved someone over to the table. "Agent Powers, will you join us?"

The crime scene investigator walked over to Dr. Moore and stood near Stephanie's head.

"As I'm sure you are aware, Agent Powers, the fine-textured, alkaline soil of the eastern plain absorbs fluid from a corpse. That combined with the hot, dry weather explains why the remains are in a dry decay stage. Therefore, I will attempt to draw blood directly from the victim's heart rather than a vein. With this in mind, I will start with the rape examination."

Willard leaned toward Killgood to whisper. "She wasn't raped."

Killgood's eyebrows pulled inward. "Why do you say that?"

"I'm not sure... just a feeling. This guy... he needed her for something more than sex."

Dr. Moore strode to a table and picked up a box that held the rape kit. He placed the kit on a tray positioned over the body. The doctor went to work combing through Stephanie's pubic hairs in the hope of capturing a hair left by her killer. He did this for several minutes and looked up. "I don't seem to be finding anything." Following procedure, he used a larger comb to check the hair on her scalp. Next he took a pair of tweezers and pulled over twenty hairs from the root in both the pubic region and the scalp. He placed these in a special envelope, which he sealed and marked with his name and the date to establish the chain of custody. He next used swabs in and around the vagina, the anus, and body checking for semen and saliva.

"I find no evidence of rape," Dr. Moore said.

Killgood turned to Willard. "Good call."

Willard remained quiet, but a warm feeling of satisfaction spread in his chest.

While Dr. Moore performed the examination, the crime scene investigator edged around the table taking photographs. Bursts of white light exploded with a click of the shutter. "Let us move on to the wounds," Dr. Moore said. He focused on the neck and pressed a hand against her throat. "There's bruising on the neck and the hyoid bone is crushed. This evidence along with the condition of the blood vessels in her eyes leads me to believe the cause of death is strangulation."

Willard wasn't surprised by the news, having recognized the tell-tell signs of strangulation back at the gravesite, furthermore, strangulation was often preferred by serial killers such as Buono and Bianchi who liked to be close to their victims and for most of them there was a sexual component to the killing. However, he sensed this wasn't the case here. "Dr. Moore?"

The doctor looked over his shoulder. "Yes... Investigator?"

"If her body had remained underground for say, a few months, would you have been able to determine she had been strangled?"

"Doubtful. Her skin would be gone and the bones scattered. I'm surprised scavengers didn't find her before you did." Dr. Moore raised Stephanie's left arm. "This is interesting."

"What?" Killgood asked.

Dr. Moore pointed to several small discolored spots on the arm near the elbow joint. "These are needle marks. Did this girl have a history of drug usage?"

A sudden pain shot through Willard's skull and he grimaced.

Dr. Moore stared at him. "Do the needle marks mean something to you?"

Willard massaged his temples as he thought.

Needle marks, where have I heard about needle marks?

"I'm not sure. I seem to recall hearing something about needles, but I'll need to check my notes. As far as drug usage, the girl has no history of it."

Dr. Moore turned to Thomas. "Perhaps the killer drugged her in order to make her relax. It wouldn't be the first time. The toxicology report will tell us."

"He didn't drug her," Willard said.

Everyone glared at him. "Why do you say that?" Agent Powers asked.

"I'm not sure... but, I don't think he wanted her drugged. The ligature marks prove he kept her tied up. And since he chose such a remote spot for the burial, I'm guessing the killer lives someplace isolated. Someplace he can come and go from at all hours without arousing suspicion."

"Perhaps your deductive reasoning is correct, Detective," Dr. Moore said. "Only time will tell." Doctor Moore motioned Thomas forward. "Now, let us move our examination inward and see what clues the internal organs hold."

Thomas leaned over the body. He used a large scalpel to make a Y-shaped incision in the trunk, curving the cut beneath the breasts as was custom with female corpses rather than the straight cut done on men. The tail of the Y extended to the pubic bone, deviating slightly to avoid the navel. When he finished making the cut, Thomas went to work peeling the skin, muscle, and soft tissues off the chest wall.

Willard pressed his hand under his nose and turned away as the smell of the rotting muscles washed over him. The stench reminded him of raw lamb and it took him several seconds to acclimate to it. The high-pitched whirl of an electric saw filled the room as Thomas opened the rib cage. Willard was amazed at the speed with which the doctor and his assistant removed the organs to the dissecting table.

"Interesting," Dr. Moore said as he drew a blood sample from the heart. "She has suffered considerable blood loss." Thomas used a scalpel to make an incision around the crown of the head. He divided the skin and soft tissues and with a grunt, pulled the front flap of skin over Stephanie's face, her identity buried beneath a mask of red meat.

Thomas went to work cutting around the equator of the cranium with a Stryker saw, the blade whining as it sliced, puffs of white rising from the incision. After removing the skull cap, he used a scalpel to sever the spinal cord and Dural reflections, and lifted out the brain. He joined Dr. Moore and together they weighed and dissected various organs. When Dr. Moore opened the stomach, a stench that reminded Willard of a Mississippi outhouse in July flooded the air.

"Look here," the doctor said, pointing with a scalpel toward the stomach, "there is still food. Do you understand what this means? The suspect fed her and then immediately killed her. That's why the pyloric valve between the stomach and the small intestine snapped shut."

Willard took a deep breath through his mouth and forced himself to step closer. He stared at the contents of the dissected stomach and saw gray and tan crumbles, mixed with small pieces of a dark reddish material. "What is that?"

"Some kind of meat and fruit."

"Looks like Weiner Schnitzel and plum cake," Thomas said.

Killgood stepped next to Willard. "I thought Weiner Schnitzel was a hot dog."

A deep chuckle rolled from Thomas's gut. "Everyone thinks that. Weiner Schnitzel is veal, covered in batter and fried. My grandmother was from Vienna. She used to make us Weiner schnitzel and Viennese plum cake all the time."

Willard's headache intensified. "I'm going to take off." He turned from the table and walked toward the dressing room. Inside, he sat on a bench, peeled off his mask, and took several deep breaths, reveling in the air that didn't smell like shit. The door opened and Killgood entered. He removed his mask and hair cover.

"Why'd you leave?"

"No reason to stay. We already know how he killed her. The question now is why?" Willard pulled off his hair cover and unzipped his bunny suit. "And why did he need to keep her alive for a week? That's taking a big risk and this guy doesn't strike me as a risk taker."

Killgood sat on the opposite bench. "Yeah, I'm struggling with that too. I can understand why he'd keep her if he wanted to rape her or torture her, but there's nothing to indicate torture except for those needle marks."

"Which neither one of us believes were the result of torture."

Killgood nodded. "You're right. Those marks are too precise to have been caused by torture. They appeared to line up perfectly with her veins. Maybe he kept her doped."

"I don't think so," Willard said.

Killgood unzipped his protective coveralls. "He did take her clothes and a locket."

"Everything he does, he does for a reason. I'm not convinced he wanted her clothes or that locket for trophies."

Killgood slipped out of his covering. "What's the deal about the needle marks?"

Willard leaned onto his thighs and rested his head in his hands. "I remember something about needle marks. I'm sure I have it in my notes." He stood and ran a hand through his hair, damp with sweat despite the cold air in the autopsy room. "Do you figure this case is connected to the disappearance of Ryan Gabbert?"

Killgood's cheeks flushed. "The cases aren't related."

Willard slipped into his jacket. "I know all about your connection to Ryan. Put your mind at ease. I don't think you had anything to do with his disappearance."

Killgood sighed heavily. "We should contact Alicia Whitmore to see if she can come up with anything else."

Willard nodded. "What about Mr. Howard? He's been unusually silent."

"When I told him we'd discovered Stephanie's body, he said that he had a recent vision about her, but didn't contact me because he didn't think the information was useful."

Willard's right hand balled into a fist. "You told him we recovered the body?"

"Why not?" Killgood's eyes narrowed. "You still don't think he's involved in this, do you?"

"What did Mr. Howard tell you?"

"He said he saw Stephanie in a dark place and something about the land being flat and a tree, and a fence."

"Which pretty much describes the crime scene." Willard massaged his eyes. "I find his timing somewhat odd, don't you?"

"What now?"

He went to Killgood. "I've got reading to do. Call me when you've set something up with Alicia."

Willard drove three blocks to find a shady place to park. He opened Mr. Howard's book on vampires. "Let's see what you have to say." He turned to the first chapter, *A Brief History of Vampires*.

Vampires are said to be mythological or folkloric beings that subsist by feeding on the blood or life essence of living humans. They are recorded in various cultures throughout the world and go back to prehistoric times. In the early 18th Century, the term "vampire" became popularized as an influx of vampire superstition spread from areas such as the Balkans and Eastern Europe in Western Europe.

"Interesting stuff, Professor, but not what I'm looking for." He flipped the pages, quickly scanning the contents, until stopping on a page that talked about the appearance of vampires.

Vampires are, by nature, creatures of the night. Due in part to the death of their own cells at the time of transformation and their reliance on fresh blood from an outside source, a vampire's skin is typically ashen in appearance. Vampires are sensitive to sunlight, like a human that suffers from Polymorphic Light Eruption or PMLE. Because of this, they must take precautions to protect their skin from direct sunlight. Prolonged exposure to sunlight is fatal to vampires.

Willard looked up from the book. "Son of a bitch. Mr. Howard said he had PMLE." He fanned through the pages until coming to a section about vampire feeding.

On average, a vampire must replenish the blood within their body approximately once a year. Because a vampire draws energy from the blood source, it is best for them to choose a younger victim in good health, rather than an older adult. A common myth surrounding vampires is the taking of blood by biting the jugular vein of its victim. Real vampires grow fangs for the purpose of self-defense, not for the taking of blood. If fangs were used to extract blood from the victim's neck as portrayed in popular books and movies, the bite to the jugular vein would produce far more blood than a vampire could ingest during a single feeding. Additionally, a bite that opened the jugular vein would almost always prove fatal. An actual vampire typically relies on either a small dagger to open a vein in the victim's arm or more commonly a needle. This allows the vampire to control the output of blood and only take as much blood is required to restore the vampire's energy. It is not necessary for the vampire to kill their victim at the time of feeding; however, newly turned vampires have been known to kill in a feeding frenzy. Because vampirism is taboo in modern society, and because the vampire has a difficult time finding a willing partner in the giving of blood, they may turn to murder as a way to conceal their activities.

A stabbing pain spread through his stomach as if a hand grabbed hold of his guts and twisted. *That's where I've heard of a needle before. When they recovered Cynthia Rhodes body in Maryland, the ME found needle marks in her arm, just like Stephanie Coldstone.* He scanned through the book until coming to a section titled, Avoiding Detection.

It is imperative for a vampire to fit into modern society without drawing attention. A vampire will find an occupation that does not produce suspicion, while allowing the vampire to work at night. The average vampire lives alone, in a home away from the general public that provides the privacy needed for hunting. They have few friends, although the vampire may become involved in a sexual relationship with a living human. A vampire must choose their victims with care, focusing on individuals who live on the fringe of society such as prostitutes, and avoid anyone whose disappearance would bring unwanted attention from the media or the police. A vampire will seek to gain the trust of law enforcement officers through cooperation and assistance. Because vampires are closer to the realm of spirits than the living, they are prone to see the spirits of their victims. This can prove unsettling for a vampire that has formed an emotional attachment with a person prior to killing them. With this in mind, vampires typically find ways to reunite the body of their victim with the victim's family rather than risk continued visits from the spirit of their victim who is seeking peace.

Willard stared out the window. The afternoon sun beamed through the glass and perspiration dotted his brow. Heat rising like in the Eastern Mississippi woods, a flame that consumed the energy and hope of people with none to spare. He tried not to think about baking in his car as he considered what Mr. Howard had written. He snapped the book closed and tossed it on the seat. With a flick of the wrist he started the car and drove out of the parking lot. "You're not writing about mythical vampires you no 'count son of a bitch, you're writing about yourself."

Chapter 23

Mr. Howard stood with his back to the class, staring at the floor. The top of his shoulders ached as if supporting a heavy weight. His students whispered, no doubt wondering what was wrong with him. All the while an expectation repeated inside his head. *Alicia Whitmore is going to lead the cops straight to me.*

He recalled everyone he'd killed throughout the ages. Most of them were young women. Beautiful roses that withered at his touch.

Perhaps it is my time. I have been cruel and evil and must pay the price.

He'd never survive in prison. Where would he obtain the fresh blood his body required? There was an alternative. A stake to the heart and his problems were over, unless of course, the Devil had other ideas. Whatever the course, it ended with him burning.

It didn't help his sullen mood that Ryan's spirit appeared earlier inside the bathroom as Mr. Howard showered. Ryan whined and moaned about living in a hole in Mr. Howard's backyard, and complained nonstop about his penis amputation. He continued to grumble even after Mr. Howard explained to Ryan that he didn't need a penis in the spirit world. Getting rid of most spirits proved easy enough—once their bodies were reunited with their families they vanished like smoke in the wind. There were, however, exceptions. The ghost of Molly O'Neal haunted him for over five decades until he left Europe for America. She used to wake him from his dreams and follow him everywhere he went, singing:

Goosey goosey gander,
Whither shall I wander?
Upstairs and downstairs
And in my lady's chamber.
There I met an old man
Who wouldn't say his prayers,
So I took him by his left leg
And threw him down the stairs

If there was a way to murder a ghost, he would have killed her long before he moved.

"Mr. Howard, are you all right?"

Jennifer Tolliver stood nearby, eyebrows gathered as she considered him with a concerned gaze. The overhead lights cast a warm glow across her pale skin. Her beauty would have inspired the ancient poets. She was Helen standing on the wall of Troy, watching with trepidation as her beloved Paris battled Menelaus in a failed effort to end the war. A weak smile quivered on his lips. "I apologize. I did not hear you come into the room. Are you here to sit in on my class?"

"You invited me, remember?" Now her eyes held a wounded look.

"Yes, yes. Please, have a seat." He motioned toward an empty spot on the front row next to Karen. Jennifer took a deep breath and exhaled with a soft puff before walking to the chair and easing onto the seat. Her gaze traveled to the short skirt riding up Karen's thighs and she cleared her throat. Mr. Howard fought back a laugh as he strolled to the podium. Reaching into his pocket, he began to pull out his eyeglasses, and stopped upon seeing Jennifer watching him. He peered down at the open book, grateful he'd memorized nearly everything on the page.

"In African voodoo," he began, "the sky serpent Damballa makes all of the water on the planet. Furthermore, the movement of his coils creates mountains and valleys, so in essence, he has replaced the Christian God as the creator. The waters of the world were released after Damballa shed his skin in the heat of the sun, and when combined with the sun, formed a rainbow. Damballa fell in love with the rainbow and made her his wife."

"I could fall in love with a snake," Karen said, batting her long eyelashes.

"You've probably fallen in love with lots of snakes," Brian Spriggs said, producing laughter in the room.

Karen flushed. Her chin sank toward her chest. Jennifer eyed her for a moment as the laughter faded. She twisted around in her seat to face the students. "Throughout history, serpents often stood as symbols of fertility or a creative life force in part because they are seen as representations of the male sex organ."

Several students giggled like kindergartners. She looked back at Mr. Howard and rolled her eyes. "Think about it," she continued. "There's a reason sexy pop stars and actresses pose nude in photographs with large snakes coiled around their bodies."

"Just imagine what they do when the cameras are gone," Spriggs said.

Mr. Howard left the podium and strolled over to Jennifer. His gaze swept the room. "I would like to introduce you to your new dean."

The air seemed to leave the classroom as students stared at her with open mouths. Mr. Howard walked back to Spriggs and rested a hand on his shoulder. "Dean Tolliver, I would like to introduce you to Brian Spriggs... a legend in his own mind."

The tension vanished and laughter returned to the room. Spriggs slumped in his seat under Jennifer's withering gaze. Mr. Howard returned to the podium where he finished his lecture on African voodoo. If someone later asked what he had said, he wouldn't have been able to respond because he'd spent the entire lecture making love to Jennifer in his mind. When the bell rang, they shared knowing glances as the students filed out of the room. As the last student walked through the door, she wiggled off the seat and stood. Her silk blouse fluttered against the contour of her breasts. "Are all your classes so interesting?" she asked.

"Not all of them have a sexual connotation."

She brushed past with the scent of strawberries and boosted herself onto his desk. He was surprised by her action, which he found somewhat childish and utterly stimulating. Her skirt wrapped tightly across her legs. He longed to lift the skirt and explore the soft flesh of her thighs. She sighed, her playful countenance suddenly serious. "Van Adams is pushing the Board to let you go."

He shrugged off the news. "It is not the first time."

"But it may be the last."

The heavy weight returned to his shoulders. "You think he will succeed?"

"I'm trying to save your position," she said, "but I don't—"

"I understand." He picked up his textbook and stashed it inside his attaché. "You will give me a good reference, won't you?"

"Let's hope it doesn't come to that."

He put on a false smile. "There have been greater tragedies in the world, yes."

"I heard the police found Stephanie Coldstone's body. Did you help them?"

The last thing he wanted was to talk about Stephanie Coldstone and the police, but knew a response was expected. "No, they managed that on their own this time."

"I'm sure you're glad they've found her."

He forced another smile. "Yes, I was relieved by the news. Tell me, how do you like your job so far?"

She shifted on the desk and he swore that her legs spread just enough to make him consider the action a subliminal message. "Perhaps we can discuss that over—"

"Mr. Howard." Willard stood in the doorway with a cat-that-ate-the-canary look on his face.

Jennifer slid off the desk and stood. She smoothed the front of her skirt, her focus never leaving the smirking detective. Mr. Howard resisted the sudden urge to kill Willard. Why had the detective come to see him without Killgood? It was only a matter of time before Willard connected the dots that revealed Mr. Howard as the murderer.

He gestured toward Jennifer. "Detective, this is Jennifer Tolliver, our new dean."

She held out her hand and Willard stepped forward to shake it. "You must be here on official business."

He nodded. "Detective Willard, State Police."

Jennifer turned to Mr. Howard. "We will continue our discussion another time." She faced Willard, dipped her head, and hurried from the room. Willard watched her go, his left eyebrow arched.

"Nice lady."

Mr. Howard ignored him and walked behind his desk. He sat and gathered loose papers into a pile. "I understand you've located Stephanie Coldstone. That is good news, yes?"

Willard took a seat across from him. "Good news for some people. Not so good for others."

Mr. Howard looked up from the papers and stared straight into Willard's eyes. "Do you have a suspect?"

"I was hoping you could help me with that."

Several seconds passed. "You are wondering if I had more visions."

"Killgood told me about your most recent vision. Pretty damn accurate description of the burial site." Willard drummed his fingers on the tabletop. "Has anyone ever tested your psychic ability?" He stopped drumming and reached inside a coat pocket.

"Who would want to test me?"

Willard opened a small box and took out what appeared to be a deck of playing cards. "I don't know, maybe your colleagues who study such things, or perhaps the FBI."

So, Detective, it has come to this at last. You think it will be easy to drop the noose around my neck. We will see about that. "You brought Zener cards?"

Willard nodded. "Very good, Professor. I take it you've seen them before?"

"There are psychologists at this university who dabble in the paranormal."

"Then you know how they're used." Willard shuffled the cards. When he finished, he placed the deck face down and lifted the top card turned toward him. "I'm going to concentrate on the symbol and send you the answer using my mind. Are you ready?"

"What is the purpose of this experiment?"

"I'm going to send you the answer now." Willard focused on the card before him for several seconds and looked up. "What symbol is on the card?"

"I have no idea."

"You weren't able to read the psychic message I transmitted?"

"Is that what you were doing, Detective?"

Willard slipped the card into the bottom of the deck and drew another one. "Let's try again." He stared at the card for several seconds. "All right, what symbol am I looking at?"

"If I knew, I would not tell you."

"Because you're not a psychic."

"I do not believe you can test my type of psychic ability."

"Bullshit."

Mr. Howard leaned back in his chair. "Do you only have faith in what your eyes can see?"

"I know what I'm not seeing in you."

He raised his right hand, thumb and index finger pressed together as if holding something. "Tell me, Detective. What symbol is on the card I am holding?"

Willard's lips flattened into a grimace. "You're not holding anything."

"Because that is what your eyes tell you. Do you believe in God, Detective?"

"What?"

"It is a simple question. Do you believe in God?"

Willard shrugged. "Yeah, I suppose so."

"Why? Have you ever seen Him?"

"No."

"And yet you have faith in His existence. But you have no faith in my ability, and why? Because I failed to provide the answer you sought in your little card game? I have proven myself for many years, Detective. Who are you to question my ability?"

"You didn't lead us to Stephanie Coldstone."

"That is true, however, if I—"

"You didn't lead us to Stephanie Coldstone," Willard repeated, his voice louder and filled with indignation.

Mr. Howard pushed out of his chair. He shoved the loose papers into his attaché case. "It is late and I am tired."

Willard returned the Zener cards to their box and stood. "They found needle marks in Stephanie Coldstone's arm at the autopsy."

"Did she use drugs?"

Willard smiled. "They found needle marks in Cynthia Rhode's arm too."

"Implying what?"

"I read one of your books, Professor."

"Oh, which one?"

"The True Story of Vampires."

Of all the investigators who pursued me, it is the one who listens to Johnny Cash that discovers my secret. Go figure. I should have been more careful when I wrote that damn book. I should have anticipated something like this. But how could I have foreseen the rise of a river or the coming of Alicia Whitmore? Perhaps my story is meant to end this way. Perhaps I wrote those things, provided detailed clues to my existence because I want to be stopped. I am tired of killing. I am tired of almost everything, but if the game has lasted for three hundred years, please do not mind, Detective, if it lasts a bit longer.

"The only book of mine that made any money. People are enraptured with vampires, yes?"

"According to your book, vampires suffer a skin condition such as yours."

"That is the legend, Detective. I have never found a real vampire to verify it."

Willard withdrew a pack of cigarettes from his jacket. He considered them for a moment before putting the cigarettes away. "What I found interesting is the part about a vampire using a needle to draw blood from its victim. I never would have thought of that."

"Another legend that needs to be authenticated."

"Maybe it will be." Willard smirked again as if enjoying a game he knew he would win. "I also enjoyed the part about vampires turning to murder in order to conceal their activities. I was... how did you put it... oh yes, enraptured by it all."

Mr. Howard took a step toward Willard, who backed away. Mr. Howard stopped. He stared into the detective's wide eyes. "I do believe we are finished here."

Willard nodded. "I'll be in touch, Professor."

Mr. Howard walked to the door and turned out the light. *You have taken the match in a direction I failed to anticipate. The next move belongs to me, Detective Willard. I trust you are ready for it.*

Chapter 24

Mr. Howard sat inside his dark bedroom, hands gripping the arms of his wing-backed chair so tightly his fingers ached. Fear coursed through his brain. The hunter had become the hunted, and a cage awaited him.

Willard.

Damn him.

Think, think, there must be something I can do.

Murder was not an option. For all he knew, Willard had already shared his suspicions with his supervisors. No, the man was too arrogant for that. Willard had to come by the classroom and proclaim victory in person before telling anyone else. Still, it was only a matter of time before he talked. Would they believe him? Would they believe a kindly old professor who had helped the police in numerous investigations could be a serial killer? And a vampire at that? It would take more than words in a book and a few needle marks to make the case. Their skepticism wouldn't deter Willard, who'd become Mr. Howard's Javert. But to kill a cop was madness. Even Killgood would turn on him if he did such a thing. If he couldn't kill Willard, perhaps he could discredit him somehow. Yes, damage his reputation and everything ended. But how? Even a cop like Willard must have secrets.

Inside his office, he searched the Internet for information on Willard. After several minutes he found Willard on the State Police website. A photograph taken at some kind of awards banquet showed the grimacing detective standing beside a heavyset woman identified as Doris Willard. His wife perhaps? Mr. Howard shifted his attention to her. It was much easier finding information on Doris Willard than her police officer husband. No surprise. A visit to Doris Willard's Facebook page shocked him. In the photographs, she'd put on a lot of weight, probably due to stress from living with such an asshole. His children favored their mother. Willard was grimacing in every photograph taken with his family.

So, Detective, your lovely bride is a bit on the plus side. I bet her weight is a source of discord between you. You are ashamed to be seen with her and so you avoid social functions. Making love to her disgusts you. Do you fantasize of having sex with a woman who is firm and small? Is that your great secret? A couple of minutes later he had Willard's home address. Mr. Howard smiled at the screen.

Now I have you.

Mr. Howard retrieved a slip of paper from his desk. The phone number of a Jason Stanis was scribbled on the paper. A former cop fired for theft of city property, Stanis now worked as an unlicensed private investigator. He'd never used Stanis before, but he came highly recommended by several professors who'd used his services to avoid being blackmailed by female students. Stanis was the just the kind of guy to dig up something on Willard.

An out-of-breath Stanis answered after the fifth ring. "Yeah," he said, the word stretched like taffy as it slipped off his tongue.

"Is this Jason Stanis?"

"Fucking-a. Who's this?"

"My name is not important. What is important is the job I am about to offer you. A job that you will accept."

"What's in it for me?"

"I will pay you fifty thousand dollars up front and fifty more when the job is finished."

A long silence followed before Stanis spoke again. "Is this for real?"

"Yes, Mr. Stanis, the offer is most definitely real. Are you interested?"

"Listen, I ain't whacking anyone. That ain't my thing, understand?"

"I do not want you to kill anyone."

"Yeah, good, so, what am I supposed to do?"

"I need you to follow someone. I need whatever information you can obtain about this man. Photographs, video, anything I can use against him."

"He really pissed you off, huh? Following him and taking pictures ain't going to be a problem."

"One more thing," Mr. Howard said, "the man is a police detective."

"Damn. I knew there had to be a catch. You want me back in the pen?"

"If you do your job properly, he will never learn of your involvement."

"I don't know... sounds risky."

"One hundred and fifty thousand."

"Fuck... a hundred and fifty thousand. Yeah, I'm in. When do I get the money?"

"I have your address. I will send you the half of the money along with further instructions in the morning. Lose the money and you will suffer most grievously."

"I get it," Stanis said. "How long do I have to come up with something?"

"The sooner the better."

"How do I reach you?"

"You'll have that information in the morning. Good night, Mr. Stanis." Mr. Howard hung up the phone, a satisfied smile on his face. "Now onto the psychic." As he pondered what to do about Alicia Whitmore, the telephone rang.

It was Leslie. "I hope I'm not catching you at a bad time."

"You could never do that."

A long silence followed before she spoke again. "Are you still helping the police now that they've recovered the body?"

Ryan's spirit floated into the room. He pointed at his crotch and then at Mr. Howard. Ryan shook his fist and vanished. Mr. Howard sighed. He would need to do something about that bastard and soon. "They might still need my help, but a new psychic is involved in the case."

"How do you feel about that?"

"Fantastic. Now I can concentrate on more important things."

"Like keeping your job?"

He recalled Jennifer coming to him with news about Van Adams latest effort to get him fired.

I will need to thank her properly one day.

"My job belongs to the university. They can do what they will with it. But I must admit the idea of that skirt-chasing moron forcing me out is…" A sudden idea made Mr. Howard sit up straight.

"What are you thinking?"

"Nothing."

"Liar."

"I am the king of liars, yes. Lucifer holds nothing over me in that department."

She chuckled. "Well, Lucifer, the reason I'm calling is to see if you can drive me out to the airport on Friday."

A smile formed on his lips at the possibility of her taking a night flight just to see him one final time. "When would we be leaving?"

"My flight's at eleven thirty. I'll take a cab to your house around eight."

"I can pick you up at your place."

"No," she said with a touch of sadness, "my place is empty and cold. Besides, I'll have made my peace with this by then and don't want to hang around here any longer than necessary."

"I understand. I have moved a few times myself and not always under the best of circumstances." Mr. Howard opened Van Adam's Facebook page on his computer. He glared at a photograph of the pompous Assistant Dean surrounded by several smiling young women wearing short shorts and T-shirts that showed their midriffs. *The fool is not afraid to reveal his true nature. This will be his undoing.* "I will be delighted to drive you to the airport."

"You say it as if you're glad I'm leaving. Are you already making plans to get into Jennifer Tolliver's pants?"

Her intuitiveness made him chuckle. "I do not believe Dean Tolliver's pants would fit me."

"I noticed you checking her out at my farewell party."

"I believe you were also checking her out," he said.

"She is a beautiful woman."

"Yes, she is beautiful like you."

"Stop trying to cheer me up."

He tracked a fly that buzzed around the computer monitor. His right hand shot forward and plucked the fly from the air. If Bram

Stoker were writing his story, this would be the part where he found someone named Renfield to eat the fly. Instead, he crushed the bug between his thumb and forefinger.

"Have you given anymore thought to moving?"

Mr. Howard wiped what remained of the fly on a tissue. "To Florida?"

"We did discuss it remember?"

"I remember. I am still thinking."

He wanted to tell her that with everything going on, and the strong possibility he could be arrested for murder, a move to Florida might be in his best interest, but the less a woman knew about a man, the better off they both were. Especially if he wasn't a man at all.

"Trust me, I have not ruled out a move to Florida. What will I do here if Van Adams succeeds in getting me fired? Become a night watchman?"

"Move to Florida and you can watch over me."

"You are a sly temptress."

"I will see you on Friday."

"Yes, on Friday," he said.

They hung up and he returned to Van Adam's online profile. Mr. Howard scrolled through his photo wall, astonished by the number of pictures featuring Van Adams with scantily clad women. Despite his Harvard education, it was obvious which head he reasoned with most of the time. Mr. Howard tapped the screen. "An old legend says that whenever a bell rings, an angel gets its wings. But what about us poor devils? Should we not be rewarded whenever someone screams? I say it is time to find out, my friend. Yes, it is most certainly time."

Chapter 25

Willard pulled back from the computer screen and rubbed his eyes. After researching vampires for three hours, he felt no closer to understanding them. Why would Mr. Howard believe he was a vampire? Did he have a blood fetish or perhaps Haematodipsia? Is that the reason Stephanie Coldstone wasn't raped, the act of drinking her blood satisfied his sexual thirst? The son of a bitch was no psychic, which was why he had to go see Mr. Howard and test his so-called psychic skills. As expected, the professor failed and then offered some psychobabble bullshit about having faith in what cannot be seen. *He can spew that nonsense to the other prisoners while they're fucking him in the ass. Murdering sack of shit.*

Willard tapped his chin while plotting his next step. In the morning, he'd talk with Captain Tate and lay out his entire case. With any luck, they'd be serving a search warrant at Mr. Howard's house in the afternoon. He considered calling Killgood. Bad idea. Killgood and Mr. Howard had been friends for a number of years, and the risk that Killgood might tip him off was too great.

He forced down his now warm beer. Cheap crap Doris bought for him. Couldn't she do anything right? Thank God she was already asleep when he arrived; otherwise he'd be forced to listen to her whine about her stressful day. As if running out of Ding Dongs were really a big deal.

"A vampire," he said to the ceiling, "why in the hell does he think he's a vampire?" He was struck by an idea. Women had a hankering for vampires now, especially young women who read that crap in books. Did Mr. Howard pretend to be a vampire to lure them to their doom? But if this was the case, why not rape them? The bastard was probably telling the truth about needing Viagra.

I'll bet he hasn't had a stiff one in years… no, centuries. He is a vampire after all.

Willard laughed. He often laughed at his own jokes, even when no one else found them funny.

I wonder if a lot of women get off on vampire role playing.

He opened up the Swingers Just Wanna Have Fun website and clicked on women seeking men for casual encounters, followed by the term vampire. His jaw dropped as the screen filled with names.

"Damn. I got a mind to get in on this vampire shit." He clicked on the top profile, a twenty-something chick from Boulder, nearly as round as Doris. In her photograph she wore a G-string, pasties on her sagging breasts, and pair of black wings. The women in the first six profiles all looked similar.

These are the right women for vampires. A guy would have to be dead to want sex with one of these bimbos.

As he moved down the list, he came across sexier women, thinner, but with curves, the majority shaved and showing off their bat caves. When he opened the profile of Lusty Lady, he choked on his beer. The skinny nude girl staring back at him was his sixteen-year-old neighbor Lorraine.

I should tell her parents about this. Bill and Martha would be pissed. But how could I explain why I was on the website?

He leaned toward the screen for a better look. Lorraine had slim hips and small breasts, not like the other so-called vamps that looked like they'd been beat with an ugly stick. Still there was something about her that made him go, "ah." Did she undress with her bedroom curtains open? If he was going to investigate the situation properly, he should verify that before contacting Bill and Martha. He closed his eyes and imagined himself inside Lorraine's bedroom, lifting her nightgown over her head. She moaned like a coyote seduced by the moon. His breathing became rapid as he massaged his crotch. What a great fantasy. It was perfect, just him, Lorraine, and…

"When did you get home?"

Doris. Shit. He sat up straight. "A couple of hours ago. This case is a bitch."

She shambled into the room wrapped inside a pink fuzzy robe. He groaned. *Now I'm seeing pink elephants.*

Doris started behind the desk. He shot forward, fingers pounding on keys to close the website.

"What are you looking at? Nude women?"

"Yeah right."

"You sure didn't want me to see whatever it was."

"I didn't know you had a thing for dead bodies."

She blinked several times. "What are you talking about?"

"Crime scene photos, Doris. Murder victims. I'm a cop, remember?"

"How could I forget?" She moved behind him and dug her fat fingers into his shoulders. They stabbed like daggers as she attempted to give him a massage. Unfortunately, she massaged like a Viking woman on steroids.

He grunted and winced as pain shot down his spine. "Damn, Doris," he said, wiggling out of her grasp, "you got a mind to kill me?"

Her bottom lip protruded and quivered. "Everything I do for you is wrong. But I'm trying, damn it!" A tear rolled onto her cheek.

For a moment he felt sorry for her. Somewhere beneath that whale blubber was the woman he'd fallen in love with. But he would never want to be with her again. Her body had become too strange, too odd to hold his interest. He wanted a woman he could make love to without feeling like he was fucking a bean-bag chair.

Her tears rained harder now and glistened on her swollen cheeks. He longed to find someplace nice and safe for Doris to live. Ah, ha, the zoo! It would be perfect. She could even take the kids with her. He'd save a fortune in lawyer fees and groceries with them gone. On weekends he could visit and toss pork chops into their cage. "I think you're trying too hard."

She wiped her eyes on the back of her hand. "Meaning what? Are you going to divorce me?"

"What?" He stammered as if the notion had never crossed his mind. "Why would you think that?"

"You don't love me," she whined, the word me stretching out forever. "You think I'm fat."

"Have you seen yourself in the mirror recently? Does more than half your body even fit inside the mirror?"

The sad, child-like expression on her face vanished, replaced by a fierce mask that would frighten the bravest of souls. Her face became bright red and her eyes held a predator's hunger. Her right hand balled into a fist, and for a moment, he feared she would unleash her wrath with a roundhouse punch requiring him to respond with deadly force.

"If I didn't love you, I'd probably—"

"Why do you love me?" he asked.

"God, I hate you." She turned and stomped away like an angry dinosaur.

"But you said you loved me," he called to mock her. The door slammed and he let out a breath. "Crazy bitch doesn't know what she wants." A smile curled his lips.

That's not right, she knows what she wants. Doris wants to cast a spell and turn me into a giant Ding Dong. She'd have an orgasm as she sucked down the cream.

A chuckle rose from his chest as he checked his emails. His laughter died when he saw an email from the woman on the swinger's website. Nervous energy raced through his veins as he clicked on the message.

Jesus H. Christ, she wants to get together right away.

He continued to read.

Holy shit, I've never done this before. Is it possible?

At the bottom of the message, she'd pasted in a nude photograph of herself. He leaned toward the screen, eyes bulging like a space alien. She was small, firm, someone he could actually wrap his arms around. He forgot about everything going on in his life: his problems with Doris, his kids, Stephanie Coldstone, and Mr. Howard. A calendar popped up inside his mind. He worked through the dates. Saturday, he could meet her on Saturday. Shit, he'd promised to take Margo to the mall with her friends. To Hell with that. He'd end up at the food court for hours watching the little hogs stuff their faces.

He quickly typed in a reply with a time for Saturday and the address of his secret love shack. After hitting the send button, he sat back, hands interlaced behind his head, and a big smile on his lips. Saturday couldn't come soon enough.

The sound of Doris wailing carried through the closed office door. He closed his eyes and listened, her suffering sweet music to his ears.

Chapter 26

Willard slammed the door behind him and tramped over to the desk. He plopped onto his chair and let out a sigh. The meeting with Captain Tate had been a disaster. Tate sat quietly with his arms folded over his chest, listening as he laid out his case against Mr. Howard. When he finished, Tate informed him that the case now belonged to the FBI, and he was to stop investigating Mr. Howard immediately.

Goddamn it, he didn't listen to a single thing I said about Mr. Howard. Why won't anyone believe me? We've got the bastard by the short hairs and nobody's going to do a damn thing about it.

The office door squeaked open.

"Willard." Detective Sanderson stood in the doorway with a look of distress on his face.

"What is it?"

"Your wife's been taken to Riverside Hospital with chest pains. Sorry." Sanderson turned and walked away.

***

As he drove to the hospital, his mind replayed the fiasco inside Captain Tate's office. He knew he should be worried about Doris, but after spending the last fifteen years in a nightmare she created, he found it difficult.

"Chest pains," he grumbled, "she gives me ass pains every goddamn day. The doctor's should pump her stomach. They'd probably find a hundred Ding Dongs."

Confusion set in. It came from being a cop. Certain situations dictated he must act in a way that went against human nature. Looking down at the body of a murdered child, he should express outrage or sadness. Instead, he stood like stone, his chest as hollow as a Tin Man's. Doris was his wife and the mother of his children. Didn't she deserve his compassion? He took out his wallet and stared at a photograph taken on their wedding day. "Hell no," he said and slipped the wallet back inside his pocket.

The six-story hospital appeared in the distance like a giant tombstone against the bright blue sky. He pulled into a parking spot reserved for police vehicles and shut off the engine.

"I was already having a crappy day, now you had to go and make it worse with this little drama of yours," he said, climbing out of the car.

Inside the crowded waiting room, a woman behind the counter, who reminded him of Margo's pet stick bug, greeted him with a doleful expression.

"Can I help you sir?"

He leaned over the counter to whisper. "I'm here about my wife, Doris Willard."

"You don't have to whisper, sir."

If you knew my wife, you'd understand why I'm whispering.

She typed in Doris Willard on her computer keyboard and read the information on the screen. "Please take a seat in the waiting room and I will have someone come out to see you."

"Can't I just go back and visit her?" He looked at his watch. "I should get her home before *Judge Judy* comes on. She loves that show."

The woman glared at him through her eyelashes. "Please have a seat, sir."

He grunted softly and dragged himself toward the waiting room like a prisoner on his way to the death chamber. The idea of sitting with a bunch of lowlifes made him want to shoot someone. He walked over to the chairs, dodging a plastic block thrown by a toddler wearing only a diaper, and squeezed between two women the size of Doris. One of them smiled and winked. A soap opera played on the television. He closed his eyes and shook his head.

I'm in Hell.

By the time a nurse came out to see him, he'd read ten magazines, watched four soap operas that flashed just enough skin to make them interesting, ate a bag of potato chips, and drank two cups of coffee. The nurse's nametag said Bethany. She had a cute smile with dimples and when she bent over to talk to him, he imagined standing behind her, pressed against her ass. "Mr. Willard?"

He tossed down the *Redbook Magazine* in his hands. "Yeah?"

"Your wife is in surgery."

The word surgery slammed into his brain like a pile driver. "What on earth for?"

"Emergency bypass. She's a lucky woman, a few more hours and she wouldn't have survived."

He should be celebrating Doris's apparent victory over death, but the thought of living with her as she recovered made him want to hit something. Would her mother, Paula, come to stay with them? Christ, their grocery bill would double. Paula ate as much as Doris and bitched twice as loud. A few weeks with her and he'd be breaking out handcuffs and duct tape.

"How much longer will she be in surgery?"

Bethany looked at her Hello Kitty watch. "I can't say for certain, but I'd guess another four or five hours."

Christ. What was he going to do at the hospital for four or five hours?

"I can take you up to the surgery waiting room."

If she looked anything like Doris, he'd decline her offer, but the idea of walking behind Bethany brought a smile to his lips. "Appreciate that."

***

Seven hours without a word. He sprang out of the chair in the surgery waiting room and stood with his hands on his hips. A stinging pain shot through his kidneys and the throbbing in his knees made him dread growing old. Thankfully, he'd called their neighbors Tom and Janice and arranged for them to pick up the kids and let them sleepover. Maybe their mother's brush with death might persuade them to stop mimicking her eating habits. *Nah, the little shits could never give up their junk food.* When they kicked off, he'd paint little golden arches on their coffins.

He sank back into the chair and sighed. The air smelled like pine cleaner, an improvement over the stench inside the emergency room. Through the windows afternoon shadows lengthened. Parking lot lights flickered to life and cast a pale glow. A tall man with dark skin emerged through a set of double doors. He wore a white lab coat and green scrubs. Willard didn't need anyone to tell him this was the surgeon. He walked straight over and held out a hand.

"Mr. Willard?"

"Yes."

"I'm Doctor Kapoor." He took a seat.

"Kapoor, that's Indian right?"

"Yes."

"Been in the States long?"

Kapoor blinked several times. "My family came to America years ago."

"So, what's happening with Doris?"

"Doris suffered a heart attack at work. The paramedics arrived within minutes and gave her Nitroglycerin. When she arrived here, we did an EKG. Doris had an abnormal heartbeat, and inadequate blood flow. Based on the EKG, the ER doctors ordered a nuclear scan that revealed severe blockage to the right coronary artery, left anterior descending artery, and the left main coronary artery. At that point, I was contacted and made the decision to perform an emergency coronary artery bypass. I used a blood vessel from Doris' leg to create an alternate pathway of blood. The surgery required that we…"

Blah, blah, blah was all Willard heard as he pretended to be interested. When the he finished explaining the procedure, the doctor asked, "Do you have any questions?"

"Doris is too fat."

Doctor Kapoor appeared uncomfortable as he massaged the front of his neck. "She is obese. Perhaps she suffers from Genetic Susceptibility. Are her parents also obese?"

"I never met her father, but Doris's mama is a heifer." He reached up to scratch where the shoulder holster had been rubbing all day. "Doris eats like a hog. Watch her stuff her pie hole and you'll never want to touch food again."

"Doris needs to incorporate diet and exercise into her daily routine. With support, she has an opportunity to lose weight and regain much of her health."

"Oh, I get it. Everything is my fault. I'm the one force-feeding her junk food."

"I didn't say that, Mr. Willard."

"You implied it." He stood and stared at his watch. "How long will she be in the hospital?"

Doctor Kapoor regarded him for several seconds. "Two days in ICU, followed by three or four on the floor unless there are complications."

"I'd best see her before I go."

The doctor rose from the chair. "A recovery nurse will come get you." He held out his hand.

Willard pulled his phone from his coat. He stared at the doctor's hand hanging in space, offered a quick nod, and punched in the numbers for Dave's cell phone. Doctor Kapoor shook his head as he strolled toward a set of double doors. Dave answered his cell phone with urgency in his voice.

"Dad, how's Mom?"

"Still fat."

"What?"

"She had a heart attack."

"Oh my God, is she going to be all right?"

He wanted to reach through the phone, grab Dave by the neck, and slap him. "You know why she's here, don't you? It's all that goddamn junk food she eats. The body can only take so many Ding Dongs until it explodes."

"She's sick, Dad."

"Yeah, she's sick, and she won't get better unless she stops eating all that crap and joins a gym. And the way I figure, the same thing is going to happen to you and your sister one day if you don't stop stuffing your faces all the time."

A long silence followed before Dave said, "How long is Mom going to be in the hospital?"

"Well, she had to have surgery, so if we're lucky, at least a couple of weeks."

"What kind of surgery?"

"Bypass surgery. That's what happens to fat people, son. They get sick and die."

"Don't you care about Mom at all?"

"Hey, I'm here, aren't I? Listen, you and Margo stay with the Masons tonight."

"When can we see Mom?" Dave sounded as if he were about to cry.

"Man up, boy. Your mom's going to be all right. I'll talk to you and Margo after school tomorrow. Good night."

"I love you, Dad."

"Good night, Dave."

Jesus H. Christ, what a pansy. Maybe trying out for wrestling will be good for him.

He rifled through a stack of women's magazines before settling on a *National Geographic*. Skimming over articles about Global Warming and oil exploration at the North Pole, he settled on a story about the Mazooba Tribe of Central Africa. The photographs showed half-naked tribal women dancing in a fertility ceremony.

"Mr. Willard?"

A nurse stood before him. Her gaze traveled to the magazine and he snapped it closed. "Yes."

"You can see your wife now."

"Uh, yeah, reckon I'd best do that."

She led him to the ICU unit. He remembered visiting the ICU when his mother died. He hated it. The place smelled strange, a combination of iodine and death. Behind the tiny glass-walled rooms, life support machines beeped in rhythm with the wet ragged breaths of the patients. During the day, the sobbing of visiting relatives added to the depressing cacophony.

"This way," she said, leading him past the nurse's station. She stopped outside a room. "She's still groggy from the anesthetic and has a breathing tube, so don't expect much. Try to keep the visit short."

"No problem."

He stepped into the room and his mouth fell open at the sight of Doris on the bed. Her skin was the color of fresh cream. A plastic tube red with blood and what appeared to be guts snaked out from beneath the covers near her chest. Two IV lines pumped medicine into her veins. A breathing tube dangled from the side of her mouth. He shivered as he pressed against the side of the bed. Why did they keep the place so damn cold? It was as if they were preparing the soon-to-be dead for their trip to the morgue. Her eyes opened, her gaze coming straight to him. He reached for her hand and pulled back. It didn't feel right. He wasn't in the mood to play the part of loving husband. "Fine mess you've gotten yourself into."

He clutched a handful of the bed sheet. "What's happened to you, Doris? What's happened to us? We used to love each other. You used to care about me. Now all you care about is stuffing your face. Look what all that eating has done to you and the kids. Is this how you want to live? You make it so hard for me to love you. Is that your plan, to drive me away?"

She blinked several times, her chest rising and falling. A tear rolled onto her cheek.

He shook his head. "Don't take on like that, Doris. I'm not leaving you. A divorce is too damn expensive." At the nurse's station, the nurse who guided him to the room watched with a stern expression. He looked back at Doris. "It's going to be okay. Maybe I'll bring you some flowers tomorrow. Well, got to go home and get some rest. Take care of yourself."

He hurried from the room without a second glance.

Chapter 27

Mr. Howard sat in the living room grinding knuckles against his temples. The stress building inside his head made his skull feel like it had been cleaved with an ax. What was happening with Willard? Should he call the PI for a progress report? Damn it, he hated when events spiraled beyond his control. In the past, killing was easy. If a village girl disappeared in the night, her neighbors hid behind locked doors and prayed for salvation. The local population never took action until several girls had vanished and by then, he was well on his way to a new killing ground. Now he must be sneaky and clever, and worry about detectives like Willard.

He put on Brahms *Sonata No. 3 in F Minor*, the somber piano matching his mood, and poured a glass of Chateau Petrus in which he mixed a small vile of Stephanie's blood. The music and wine did little to cheer his mood. The buzzer near the front door went off. Someone waited outside the gate. He finished the wine in his glass before walking over to answer.

Probably Willard wanting to ask more questions. If he wasn't a cop, he would soon find himself in a grave.

He pushed the button to respond. "May I help you?"

"Professor Howard."

The soft voice belonged to Dean Tolliver. A smile crept up his face. "Jennifer, is that you?"

"May I come inside? We need to talk."

"Yes, of course," he answered. "I will unlock the gate. Please come up." A warm feeling spread from his chest at the thought of seeing Jennifer again. He opened the door and stood outside. She navigated her black BMW sedan up the road to his house and pulled into the driveway. The engine went quiet and Jennifer emerged, a hand raised in greeting.

"Thanks for seeing me."

"My pleasure."

The skirt she wore revealed her narrow hips. Teenage hips. Mr. Howard waved for her to enter. "Come inside, I will fix you a drink. You like wine, yes?"

A playful grin formed on her cherry lips as she breezed past. "Wine would be delightful." Her head swiveled as she took in the house, and the shining hardwood floor, the spotless white leather furniture, the impressionist paintings that adorned the walls, and the Steinway grand piano in the foyer. "Your home is beautiful."

"Thank you," he answered, closing the door.

"Your books must have sold well."

He lightly pressed a hand against her back to steer her toward the living room. "No, not at all. There does not seem to be much interest in ancient mythology outside of my classroom, and even there, I am afraid that most of the interest belongs to me."

She continued to look around as she eased onto the sofa. "Your house is so—"

"Large. Yes, everyone who visits wonders how a professor can afford such a place." He went into the kitchen. "The truth is I brought money over from the old world."

"Your family is wealthy?"

"That depends on how you define wealthy. We were not the Rockefellers, no, but we lived comfortably." He poured a glass of wine. "Here you go."

She reached for the glass, her sexy smile returning. "Thank you."

He started to turn to walk back to his chair. "Wait," she said, and patted the couch. "Sit with me."

Blood surged through his veins at the prospect of being near her. Taking a deep breath, he strolled to the couch and sat beside her, so close their kneecaps brushed. He was struck by the paleness of her skin and her hair the color of an autumn sunrise through the leaves of a red maple. Surely Lefebvre would have loved to replicate her beauty on canvas. She could have been his new Chloe. Typically, he gravitated to women with darker skin that contrasted against his, but with Jennifer, he would make an exception. She sipped the wine and ran her tongue over her upper lip to capture a stray drop. "Very nice."

He crossed his legs to conceal his growing arousal. "So, why did you need to see me?"

She took another sip and set her glass on the end table. "Van Adams has gone behind my back to the Board of Trustees."

"As I expected."

A series of wrinkles formed on her brow as her eyes narrowed. "They are going to cut your position."

One of the buttons on her blouse had worked loose and she wasn't wearing a bra. Tiny freckles decorated her breast like points of interest on a map. He longed to travel the road that led to her soul. To know her completely, every inch of softness, and every secret taste her body concealed. *This is madness. She is not here for that. No, she came as a friend.*

He forced himself to sigh, believing some kind of response was in order. "I knew this day would come."

She leaned forward and placed a hand over his. "Aren't you upset?"

He stared at her hand, reveling in the warmth she gave, and then into her eyes. "Perhaps it is time I move on."

She blinked several times. "My God," she said, the words passing like a gust of wind. She flattened a hand against her chest. "What's happening to me?"

Most traits associated with vampires were pure myth, the product of overactive imaginations, but the power of seduction was in fact a skill shared by nearly every vampire, whether male or female. If a woman maintained eye contact with him, she soon would be under his control as if hypnotized. He glanced past her toward the front door.

I should make her leave before it is too late for both of us. She deserves more than I can give her.

She lunged forward and kissed him. Pulling back, she swallowed hard. "I can't believe I did that."

He looked at the door once more, his mind telling him to make her leave while he unbuttoned her blouse. He worked his hands inside the silky material and feathered the blouse back and off her sloping shoulders. She trembled as he brought his mouth to her breast, his lips and tongue tasting with gentle urgency. His hands unfastened her skirt. Pulling back, he brought her skirt and panties with him. He spread her legs and worked his way upward, fingers exploring the softness of her flesh. Eyes closed, she arched her head and moaned.

As his tongue traveled a path along her thigh like a serpent homing in on its prey, a single thought repeated in his mind. *I should have taken a Viagra.* He longed for the days when he was young and physically fit, with everything in good working order. At his age he found moving his tired old bones around a confined space taxing.

As if sensing his discomfort, she asked, "Should we go to the bedroom?"

Sweet Mother of God, I'm about to fuck a saint. He stood and held out a hand.

Inside his room, he gestured toward the bed. "Make yourself comfortable." She stretched out on the mattress with a purr. He dashed off to the bathroom. *This is madness.* His hands trembled as he opened the pill bottle. After swallowing the Viagra, he felt renewed and hopeful. If he could just engage her in a half hour of foreplay everything should work as required.

He returned carrying a lit candle, which cast a flickering glow over the darkness. She waited with open arms. A quiver of doubt tingled down his spine. Thirty minutes, he reminded himself, in thirty minutes, everything will be fine.

"You seem nervous," she said.

He pretended to dismiss her with a chuckle as he placed the candle on the headboard. "Are you not nervous the first time with someone new?"

"Not really." She wiggled up against him. "I can't wait to feel you inside me."

And you will in twenty-nine minutes.

"We are not teenagers. We should take our time."

"Maybe we should hurry through the first round."

I am about to step into the ring with Ali and my pill is guaranteed for one round only. "We have all the time in the world," he said, stroking her face. A tiny grimace revealed her frustration.

"Then let's start making good use of it."

Sex with Jennifer was like trying to fuck a lascivious tiger. It was all he could do to hang on as she rolled him around the bed. "Jennifer," he said, glancing at the clock and noting he still had twenty minutes until the pill kicked in, "if you do not slow down, my heart will explode."

"Don't worry, Professor. You'll do fine." She winked and slid down his stomach. The tiger latched on as if lunging for a steak.

He suppressed a scream as she went to work, and melted into the sheets as his resistance faded. She was a magician with her tongue. If she were a prostitute, he would double her fare because she made him feel that good. She suddenly sat up and raised her hips. Before he could protest, she took hold of him and positioned herself for entry. He glanced at the clock. *Damn, fifteen more minutes to go.*

Too late.

He slid inside her with a soft "oh Lord" whispering from his lips.

"That's right," she said, her hips grinding around and around like a machine that couldn't be turned off.

Blood surged into his member and he thanked God for the miracle workers at Pfizer. This was one old vampire who would last through the first round. After that, he could promise nothing.

He grabbed hold of her buttocks, silky soft and firm. Something caught his eye. He squinted. Leslie stood at the foot of the bed, arms folded over her chest, staring at him with an exasperated look.

Am I hallucinating? What is in that pill?

Then it hit him. He grabbed the tiger by her waist and tossed her onto her back.

"Hey," Jennifer said and punched his arm. "What was that for?" She followed his gaze to the end of the bed. "Oh shit."

"You were supposed to drive me to the airport," Leslie said, her voice hollow and without emotion.

He rolled off the bed and hurried to her. Taking her elbow, he steered Leslie away from the bed. "This looks bad, yes?"

Her gaze traveled to his erection. "Not to Jennifer."

He massaged the back of his neck, his attention shifting between the two women. Jennifer sat up on the bed, the sheet pulled only to her waist, her breasts exposed and inviting.

She is doing that on purpose.

The women maintained eye contact. Any second, he expected them to be at each other's throats. "I am sorry, Leslie."

"Liar."

He reached out to touch her cheek and she pulled back. "Please, listen."

"Hey, you don't owe me a damn thing."

He grabbed her arm and turned her away from the bed. "I will not apologize for doing what comes naturally to me. I am a man who likes to make love to women. Jennifer showed up to tell me the board is going to let me go. After that, human nature kicked in and here we are."

"You couldn't even wait until I was gone to replace me in your bed."

"Never replace."

She raised her face to the ceiling, hands raised, as if seeking divine intervention. "Spare me the bullshit."

"Every woman brings a unique talent to the bed. Some, like Jennifer are wild and impulsive. You on the other hand knew how to find pleasure and make it last. I say this with complete honesty. You are the best lover I have ever had."

"And you probably told her the same thing right before I walked in."

Jennifer slid off the bed and approached with an exotic sway of her hips. Leslie's eyes widened as Jennifer's naked body pressed against her. "What are you doing?"

Jennifer laid a finger against Leslie's lips. "No words."

Leslie blinked several times. "What?"

The tiger moved with lightning reflexes, arms encircling its prey, mouth pressed against the mouth of its victim. Leslie pulled back and blinked several times. "Wait a second."

"We both know you want this," Jennifer said, her words drawn out in a sexy whisper.

Leslie twisted against the tiger's hold, a mumbled protest squeaking from her throat, then relaxed. The tiger and its prey joined in a flurry of kisses and probing hands. They stumbled toward the bed, Leslie's clothes flying off like a kite with a broken string. He strolled over to his chair and sat, not that they noticed. As he watched them entwine, he couldn't help but think God was a ninny hammer to believe Eve needed Adam for anything more than his semen. If Lilith had wandered back into the picture, she and Eve would have managed quite nicely without Adam around.

The tiger rolled and fought for position, only to surrender to the will of its new master. They merged and flowed like lacey curtains swimming in a summer breeze. Hands brought pleasure to places only a woman could understand, tongues massaged flesh and produced quivers and sighs. He looked past them to the clock. His thirty minutes had long expired. Soon, he'd be as worthless as an abandoned dream. But wait... the activity on the bed stopped and the women considered him with hunger in their eyes. Jennifer slid off the bed with a grin. "Come along, Professor, we haven't forgotten about you."

She took his hand and pulled him to his feet. His penis wavered between erection and total melt down.

I could take another pill. It's not like it is going to kill me. "I should use the restroom first."

"No, you're not getting away from us." The tiger's paw took hold of him and his blood surged.

She brought him to the bed where Leslie waited with open arms.

The weaker sex indeed.

He closed his eyes and surrendered to their will. They poured over him like the waves of a warm sea and he floated into a state of euphoria.

***

They drove in silence. Leslie stared out her window, a smile on her face. The night fell hard about them, darkness spreading like spilled ink over the passing scenery. In the glow of approaching headlights she appeared younger.

"What are you thinking?"

She turned toward him, her smile remaining. "You and Jennifer aren't going to miss me."

He would miss her, but the thought of Jennifer in his bed did soften the blow. "You enjoyed yourself, did you not?"

She looked down at her lap and nodded. "That wasn't my first time with another woman."

"I know."

Her left eyebrow arched. "How?"

"You talk in your sleep."

She settled against the seat with a sigh. "What are you going to do if the college lets you go?"

He tried to forget about the situation with Van Adams by thinking of dark jungles and mating tigers and secrets carried to the grave. The secrets that made a person what they were, the interesting side of a personality kept out of view, locked away for the private pleasure or pain of their owner. To Hell with Van Adams and the Board of Trustees. He weaved around a slow moving car. A sign announced the exit to the airport in one mile. "I will find a way to pass the time."

"With Jennifer."

"Perhaps."

She chewed her bottom lip as she thought. "You can still move to Florida."

He offered a smile. "I am still invited after tonight?"

"We have a history."

"You want me for more than sex?"

She chuckled softly. "Honestly, you are more interesting out of bed than in it."

He was no Casanova, but he wasn't prepared to hear her say it.

"Oh don't pout," she said. "You're not half-bad for a man your age."

"Your words are so comforting."

She laughed again. "Yeah, well, after tonight I might expect more from you in the future."

Did they have a future together? He'd never settled down with a woman longer than a couple of years after Sophie died. How could anyone compete with a wife who greeted him each morning with a cup of steaming coffee and raised skirt? Still, of all the women he'd known, Leslie was the only one he would consider joining in a serious relationship. The sex was nice, but he loved her for her mind. She somehow managed to stay ahead of him most of the time. She was a Rubik's Cube whose colors never matched no matter how hard he tried to make it happen.

"I have charged windmills my entire life. Perhaps this knight needs to retire."

"I can't imagine you retiring."

"That is why I said perhaps."

He pulled up in front of the terminal. "I can park and walk in with you."

"I'm not one for good-byes." She opened the glove box and pushed the button for the trunk. After retrieving her bags, she leaned inside the car. "I probably should hate you for what just transpired, but I can't."

"You can thank Jennifer for that."

"No, I can thank you." She gave him a peck on the cheek and pulled away.

When she disappeared through the terminal doors, a familiar ache settled into his heart.

Chapter 28

Willard awoke with a headache, which was still better than waking up next to Doris. After popping two aspirin, he shuffled into the bathroom to take a shower. The warm water cleared his mind and he went through his schedule for the day. He'd need to pick up the kids after school. They'd probably want to visit their mom in the hospital, unless he came up with a good excuse for them not to go. He could say she was too weak and looked so bad after surgery he didn't want them to be scared by her appearance. That wouldn't be a lie. She *always* looked bad.

As he slipped on his shoulder holster, he almost wished someone would give him the excuse to use his gun. A piece of dry toast washed down with lukewarm coffee and he was out the door. He stared across the street at the Mason's house and then at his watch. It was still early. He could drop by and check on the kids. "Nah," he said, unlocking the car.

His cell phone rang before he was out of the driveway. "This is Willard."

"Willard, it's Killgood."

Margo stood in the front window of the Mason's house waving. He slouched and turned away to avoid eye contact. "What do you need?"

"Alicia Whitmore called."

His headache suddenly intensified. "Did she find Jimmy Hoffa this time?"

Killgood grunted. "She says she has information about the case."

"It's not my case anymore. Have her contact the FBI. I'm sure those Hoover boys would love to talk to her. They're always looking for a headline."

"Fuck the FBI."

Killgood's proclamation brought a smile to his face. "All right, Killgood, you've got my attention."

"She's on her way to the station. Can you drive up?"

"I'll have to come up with some bullshit excuse for my boss but I'm sure I can think of..." He snapped his fingers. "I got it. Doris had a heart attack yesterday. The doctors did an emergency bypass. I'll just tell them I need the day off to be with her. No one will miss me."

"I can believe that. Who's Doris?"

"My wife."

There was a long pause. "Your wife had a heart attack and you're going to work? That's cold."

"No, that's reality. See you in a few." Willard hung up and called the office. As expected, no one cared if he took the day off. When he retired, there'd be no going away party. No gold watch. No slaps on the back or well-wishes, and he didn't really give a shit. He tossed the phone onto the car seat and raced toward the highway. For once, having Doris as his wife would pay off.

***

He knocked once and didn't wait for a response before stepping inside Killgood's office. Killgood sat behind his desk. Alicia Whitmore occupied one of the two chairs in front of the desk. She sat cross-legged, her skirt rising past her knees. One look at her tall black boots and that annoying Nancy Sinatra song jumped into his head.

He gave a quick nod to Killgood and offered his hand to Alicia. She hesitated before taking it. "It's good to see you again," he said, smoothing his necktie while sinking onto the chair.

"I've had a vision," she said. "It came to me this morning while I was stepping out of the shower."

Why couldn't I have been there to see that?

He cleared his throat, his gaze journeying to Killgood and back to her. "Is that normal?"

Her left eyebrow arched. "What?"

"Having visions in the shower?"

"A vision can come anytime."

Yeah, and so could you.

He folded his arms over his chest. "All right, why don't you tell us about your vision?"

"Well, like I said, I was stepping out of the shower when I saw it."

"Saw *what*?" Killgood asked.

She stared at her lap. "Stephanie Coldstone."

"Where did you see her?"

"She was in a dark place. Standing. Arms and legs tied. There were tears on her face."

Killgood flipped open a small notebook and scribbled something. "Anything else?"

"I heard music. Classical music. Rachmaninoff."

"How do you know it was Rachmaninoff?" Willard asked.

She turned to glare at him. "I majored in music. I know Rachmaninoff."

"All right," Willard said, "go on."

"Then I saw someone. An older man."

Killgood glanced up from his notebook. "With Stephanie?"

She nodded. "He was dancing."

"Dancing how?" Willard said.

"A Viennese Waltz."

"Let me guess," Willard said, "you minored in dance."

Killgood shifted in his chair. "You said this was an older man. Are you certain? Did you get a good look at him?"

"I saw his hair."

Willard leaned forward and considered her with a critical eye. "That's it?"

"He had long, silver hair," Alicia said with a trace of anger in her voice.

Willard straightened. He massaged his brow, a sudden brainstorm driving away his headache. "Did you see where he lived?"

She looked at Killgood who stopped writing and then at him. "A big house. Modern style, like a Frank Lloyd—"

"Wright," Willard finished for her.

She nodded. "Built against the side of a mountain."

"Hey," Killgood said, "I don't like where you're going with this."

"It makes sense," Willard said. "How many homicide investigations has he assisted on? A dozen or more?"

Blood painted Killgood's cheeks a deep red. "Just because you don't like the man, doesn't mean he's a killer. I've known him for years. He's been to my house for dinner."

"Proving what? Ann Rule used to work with Ted Bundy and let him drive her daughter home." Willard turned to Alicia. "What else did you see in your vision?"

"Blood."

"What does that mean?" Killgood asked.

"He needed her blood," she said.

Willard sat up straight, spine pressed against the hard wooden slats of the chair. "The book, the son of a bitch's book."

"Would you mind translating?" Killgood asked.

Willard ignored him, his attention focused on Alicia. "In your vision, was this man drinking Stephanie's blood?"

"Yes."

"Where did he take it from?"

"A wound on her arm."

"Did you see how he made the wound?"

Her attention moved between the detectives. "He used a needle."

His right hand clenched and unclenched.

I knew it. I knew that bastard was the killer.

He needed to talk with Killgood now. Someone had to believe him. "Anything else you can tell us?"

Alicia touched the base of her throat and massaged the skin as she thought. "I can't think of anything."

"Did you hear any conversation in your vision?"

"Nothing I could make out. Sorry."

"Don't be sorry," Willard said. "You've been most helpful. You will contact us if you have another vision?"

She stood and smoothed her skirt. "I'll be sure to do that. Anything else?"

Willard stood and opened the door. "You're free to go." As he watched her walk away, he imagined bending her over a table.

"What in the hell just happened?" Killgood asked. Willard reached for a cigarette while dropping onto his chair. "Hey, I told you no smoking in here."

"Yeah, I remember." He lit the cigarette and took a long pull. Killgood scowled behind his desk. "I know Mr. Howard's your friend, but he warrants further investigation."

"Aren't you the guy who doesn't believe in psychics?"

"There's something about Alicia that makes me think she's the real deal."

Killgood leaned back in his chair, hands behind his head. "All right, let's hear it."

He took a quick pull on the cigarette and turned to blow a little cloud of smoke over his shoulder. "Did you ever read Mr. Howard's book about vampires?"

"Can't say I have."

"All right. Let's start with what we know to be true, agreed?"

Killgood nodded.

"Mr. Howard is approximately sixty years old. He speaks with an accent, possibly Austrian."

"Can we please skip all the minor details and get to the important stuff?"

Willard took another pull on the cigarette and searched for a place to toss it. *If I couldn't convince Captain Tate of Mr. Howard's guilt, how in the hell am I going to make his friend believe it?*

Killgood grumbled under his breath and handed him a coffee mug.

"Thanks," Willard said, crushing the cigarette inside the mug. "I read Mr. Howard's book on vampires. According to the book, vampires use a needle to draw the blood of their victim. The same way Alicia saw the killer taking Stephanie Coldstone's blood."

Killgood leaned forward to rest his elbows on his desk. "The ME found needle marks on one of her arms."

"Needle marks were found on one of the victims back in Maryland."

"Was Mr. Howard involved in that investigation?"

"That's right," Willard said, "but he didn't help police locate her body. A flood uncovered her grave before she decomposed. Not only that, she'd been strangled."

"Just like Stephanie Coldstone."

He leaped out of his chair, coming face to face with Killgood. "Damn it, man, you heard her, he lives in a mansion in the foothills, has long, silver hair. And don't forget what the morgue assistant said about Stephanie's stomach contents."

"It reminded him of Austrian food and Mr. Howard is from Austria." Killgood closed his eyes and pinched the bridge of his nose. "So you believe Mr. Howard is a vampire who pretends to be a psychic to throw us off?"

"No, I don't think vampires are real, but Mr. Howard does, and apparently he believes himself to be one."

Killgood opened his eyes. "You'd never get a grand jury to return an indictment against him based on anything you've said." He picked up his pen and pointed it toward Willard. "Your supervisor told you the same thing, right?"

Willard slouched in his chair. For a moment he thought he'd turned Killgood against Mr. Howard. Now that support slipped away. "Aren't you the least bit suspicious of him?"

Killgood picked up the photograph of his kids and stared at the image. "You've laid out some interesting facts, but they don't add up to

Mr. Howard being a serial killer. The way I see it, you've never liked him and your personal prejudice is clouding your judgment."

Willard jumped out of his chair again. "You contrary asshole. Prejudice has nothing to do with it. The facts are there if you'll open your eyes. You're letting your friendship with Mr. Howard blind you to the truth."

Killgood gently set the frame down and looked up with a blank expression on his face. He seemed to be staring past Willard, his mind somewhere other than in the room. After several seconds of silence he calmly said, "You're right, he has been my friend, but that's not why I won't investigate him."

"What is it then?"

"Doesn't matter. This case belongs to the FBI now."

"If that's how you feel, why'd you call me to come up here?"

Killgood stood. "I'm not sure. I thought Alicia might give us something we could use to find Stephanie Coldstone's killer. I was wrong. Now if you will please excuse me, I have work."

Willard glared at him. "How many women must die before anyone will listen?"

"When you have something worth hearing, we will listen. Give my best to your wife. I do wish her a speedy recovery."

Willard hustled from the office and stormed out of the station, head down, his headache returning with a vengeance. Inside his car, he slammed a fist against the dashboard. "Stupid son of a bitch. I hope Mr. Howard rips your heart out, asshole."

Chapter 29

Willard smirked on the inside while taking in the stunned expressions on Dave and Margo's faces as they stared at their plates filled with steaming vegetables.

"What's this?" Dave asked, poking at the broccoli.

"Dinner."

"You've got to be kidding," Margo said.

"Look at yourselves," he said. "You could rent your bellies as trampolines." Dave and Margo exchanged wounded glances. So their feelings were hurt, boo-fucking-hoo. They needed to hear the truth, and he wasn't in the mood for their nonsense after getting shot down by Killgood. Nothing grated on a cop's nerves more than knowing a suspect was guilty and not being able to do anything about it. "You'll get used to eating healthier. You don't want to end up like your mom, do you?"

Dave's fork dropped on his plate with a clang. "Speaking of Mom, when are we going to see her?"

"Yeah," Margo said, "I miss Mom."

"You miss the piles of crap she serves you. The way I figure, from now on, things will be different. No more candy, no more cookies, forget those late-night snacks. You both will eat healthy foods, and get some exercise."

"Why would I want to do that?" Margo asked.

"Because you're big and fat, and no boy is going to want to take you to the prom."

She pushed out of her chair, tears in her eyes. "Oh, Dad, how could you say such a thing?" She spun around and waddled out of the kitchen like a hungry penguin.

Willard took a bite of his hamburger. Dave shook his head. "What?" Willard asked. "You think I was mean to your sister? You both need to hear the truth. You're a couple of oinkers, real Porky Pigs, and quite frankly, you embarrass me."

Dave sipped his water and wiped his lips onto the back of his hand. If his words had hurt him, Dave refused to show it. "We're going to see Mom tomorrow, with or without you. I can't believe you haven't gone to see her today."

"I already told you, something big came up at work."

"Bigger than our mother's health?"

Willard snickered softly. "Honestly, is there anything bigger than your mother?"

Dave scowled. "You can be a real jerk sometimes." He stood and walked away.

For a brief second, Willard fantasized about shooting his son in the back, the insolent little bastard, but decided it would be too messy. Besides, Margo would hear the shot and come out to investigate, and he'd be forced to waste a bullet on her as well. One day, after his Cabbage Patch Kids lost some weight, they might actually appreciate the hard line he took.

He tossed the half-eaten hamburger down, his appetite gone, grabbed a beer from the fridge, and retreated to the office. Settling in front of the computer, the day's tension eased as reread the email from the woman on the swinger's website. Tomorrow, he would entertain the first of many women at his secret love nest.

"Dad?"

Margo stood in the doorway with a sad puppy face.

Jesus H. Christ, I didn't even hear her open the door. I need to be more careful.

He closed the email. "Knock next time."

"Do you hate Mom because she's fat?"

"I hate that she's fat. Look what it's done to her."

She chewed her lip as she thought. "Do you hate me and Dave?"

Her question caught him off guard and it took him a moment to come up with an answer. "I don't want you to follow in your mom's footsteps. I don't want people laughing at you behind your backs."

"Is that what they do?"

If he was a tactful person, this would have been an opportune time to lie, but instead he said, "People who watched you dancing the other day were laughing at you. They said you're a hippo and had no business being on the stage."

She blinked several times, her eyes glassy with tears. "Is that what you think?"

"Do you want the truth?"

Her gaze went to the floor. "I wish you wouldn't hurt us all the time."

"Is that what I do?"

She looked up with determination in her eyes. "Take us to see Mom tomorrow."

He stared at the computer monitor. How long would it take to fuck the shit out of the woman from the swinger's website? One hour, two hours? With any luck, she'd be worth an entire afternoon, but he'd never met a woman that good in his entire life. He looked back at Margo. "I need to do something in the morning, but when I return we can go."

"You're lying."

"Hey, I've got a pretty important job or haven't you noticed?"

"Tomorrow's your day off."

"Yeah, well, cops don't get a day off. When I'm finished with my job, I'll take you kids up to the hospital. In the meantime, I suggest you get your butt to bed."

"It's not even eight o 'clock," she protested.

"Then you should get plenty of sleep."

"Asshole."

"What'd you say?"

"You heard me."

No twelve-year-old was going to talk to him that way. "Get back here!" He leaped to his feet, fingers working loose the buckle on his belt. Her eyes widened and she fled into the hall. He tore after her and caught up outside her bedroom. Seizing a wrist, he twisted one of her arms behind her.

"Daddy, you're hurting me!"

Dave peeked out of his bedroom. "What's going on?"

"Stay out of this!"

"Dave, help!" Margo called.

He glared at his son. "You heard me, boy. Go to bed."

Dave hesitated before ducking into his room. Willard forced her arm higher.

"Daddy, please no!"

"You think you can sass me? I'll show you what my daddy did if I got smart with him. I'm going to tan your hide." He threw his chest against her and drove her inside her room. A hard shove sent her reeling. She crashed against a dresser and folded onto the carpet. He locked the door and finished removing his belt. "Get up, damn it."

Her cheeks glistened with tears. "No, Daddy, no!"

"Get up!"

She threw out her hands. He swung wildly, the belt striking her palms with a whack. "Ahhhh," she cried, pulling her hands against her chest.

"That's what you get for fighting me. Now stretch out on the bed."

She shook her head. "Please, you're hurting me."

He rushed toward her, belt flashing through the air, "I don't... give a shit..." —*whack, whack,* the belt ripped over her thighs— "...if I'm hurting you. Get on that bed."

"Daddy, please!"

He grabbed one of her arms and dragged her toward the bed. "Get up there and take it!"

Deep, wailing cries rose from her chest as she scooted on her knees to the mattress and lay down. "Please, Daddy." Her voice trembled. "Don't hurt me anymore please."

There was a knock on the door. "Dad, what's going on?"

"Get out of here, Dave. This is none of your goddamn business," he said over his shoulder.

"Is Margo all right?"

"Get out of here, boy, or you're next!" He waited to hear Dave's door close before turning his attention back to Margo on the bed. "You damn kids show me no respect. You think I treated your grandpa like that? Hell no, he'd wear me out, just like I'm going to wear you out."

He swung the belt with all his strength. *Whack, whack, whack,* leather popping against flesh. At first, she howled, her body quivering under the assault, but then she fell silent and stopped moving. He gasped for air, his face speckled with sweat. He looked down at her, suddenly small and insignificant in his eyes, and felt pity. Damn Doris, it was all her fault. She fattened the kids up. She tricked them into believing she was the one who loved them best. One day they would understand. One day they would realize he had their best interests at heart. "Don't you ever talk back to me again, you hear me?"

She said nothing, the only sound her soft whimpering.

He brought his face close to hers. "Did you hear me?"

"Yes."

"Get your ass in bed and don't get up. If you're good, just maybe, I'll take you brats up to the hospital to see your mom. Got it?"

"Yes, sir." She slowly climbed onto the bed, wincing as she swung her legs upward. She curled into a ball, her back toward him. He brought her covers up to her shoulders and leaned down to kiss her wet cheek.

"Good night. I love you."

No response.

He raised the belt and smacked her again. "I said I love you!"

"I love you," she whispered.

He slammed her door closed. Outside Dave's room, he leaned close to shout. "If I hear you coming out of this room, I'll beat your butt." He continued to the office where he slumped in his chair. "Fucking kids. Fucking wife. My world is goddamn cesspool and I'm drowning in it."

Chapter 30

Mr. Howard stood on the front porch staring down at the city lights. A warm breeze swirled from the southwest, caressing the back of his neck. The sound of Ravel's *Bolero* drifted from inside the house. He swayed in rhythm with the melody, the memory of floating like a wayward cloud between Leslie and Jennifer vivid in his mind. Why couldn't it always be like that? Why couldn't his life be simple and beautiful, the way it had been before his transformation? Sophie's soft fingers interlaced with his. The sound of children laughing filling the rooms of his home. A golden sunset reflected on the surface of the Danube.

He walked to a lawn chair and sat. Head in his hands, he thought of future events sure to pass. Why were his actions ruled by death? And then he remembered the line from the Heurigen song, *Der Tod, das muss ein Wiener Sien*—Death himself has got to be a Viennese.

"Don't pity yourself. You don't deserve pity." Ryan's ghost floated nearby. Mr. Howard couldn't wait to get rid of Ryan's corpse and free himself from this torment. Day and night, Ryan crawled like a spider into his brain and spun a web of guilt and accusations.

"You are right, of course, and perhaps my rage went unchecked with you. To cut off your penis was a most unpleasant thing to do, yes. But you played your part in our little drama, did you not? Your abuse of Reann and Gail forced my hand. How can a man with a moral conscience stand by and do nothing in the face of such charges?"

"You plan to kill again."

Mr. Howard winced as a sharp pain stabbed his right temple. "Why do you always show up to ruin my mood?"

"Who will you kill this time?"

"I plan to kill no one."

"You are a killer and a liar."

"And you are dead, which means I may choose to ignore you. Go back to your grave and leave me in peace."

"The way you left me in peace?"

He whirled toward the spirit and shook his fist. "Go now or I swear, I will never return you to your family."

Ryan's ghost faded like a mirage swallowed by the desert sun. Mr. Howard stood. He returned to the balcony railing and leaned forward, the lights of the city a white sea across the darkness before him. He hated specters—everything about them. They typically displayed foresight and the ability to predict parts of his future long before he had a chance to plan it. Ryan was an idiot in life. No surprise he remained an idiot in his afterlife. If Mr. Howard were going to kill anyone, it would be Detective Willard, but that would only complicate an already complicated situation. No, the best way to handle this predicament was to maneuver the pieces on the board to his advantage. He must capture the queen and neutralize the king before they could place him in checkmate.

With this in mind, he wondered why he hadn't heard back from the PI. Surely, he could dig up dirt on a man like Willard, a miserable civil servant who resented his lot in life. The man must have secrets. Everyone had secrets.

No matter, he could only control certain things, and so he focused his attention on Alicia Whitmore, psychic extraordinaire.

When he first moved to town, Mr. Howard marveled at how empty the streets became at night. Some evenings he drove through the entire city without seeing another car. But then, someone had the bright idea to list the town on one of those ten best lists. A few years later, the town ranked as the best place to live in the entire country. After that, people poured in by the thousands. The crime rate shot up, school testing scores tanked, and the roads became clogged at all hours. At least one good thing came out of the process; the town no longer ranked in the top ten on any of the lists. Being a Friday night, the streets were crowded with late-night traffic, mostly bored college students looking for a party because they were too young to drink in the Old Town bars. If he drove the Mercedes, he risked being spotted by one of his students. Who would recognize him through the dark tinted windows of the panel van?

It took him fifteen minutes to drive to Alicia Whitmore's house, a small Craftsman-style home, probably built after the Second World War. A high-intensity bulb burned at the front porch casting a wide circle of light across a tidy yard enclosed by a picket fence. Insects flew in and out of the light in a frenzied dance. Several houses down, a group of five or six teenage boys gathered around a car. Offensively loud music spoiled what would be a peaceful night. The boys laughed and whooped while drinking something in shiny silver cans, which he assumed was beer. One boy pissed into the gas tank of a nearby car. Two more wrestled on a lawn, either combatants or lovers in need of a hotel. The scene before him was perfect. No one would notice him. Not that he worried. Vampires could move about without drawing attention, as if invisible to the world. Perhaps the world didn't want to acknowledge the presence of something so terrible and vile, and so chose to ignore it, the way the British and French ignored Hitler until it was too late. But he wasn't Hitler with the goal of wiping out a class of people he loathed. Mr. Howard was an equal opportunity killer. If a person possessed what he needed, they could have purple skin and pray to Rafekee the monkey god for all he cared.

He slipped out of the van and walked straight to Alicia's gate. As suspected, the drunken boys were too busy with their self-indulgence to pay attention to an old man. He didn't bother unlatching the gate, but instead floated over the fence. Among his many powers, levitation was perhaps his favorite. Countless lovers, their minds clouded by wine, had watched with amazement as he circled above the bed. For an unfortunate few, they soon discovered the graceful eagle was in fact a vulture, but he made certain to keep their suffering at a minimum. And then there was Alexandra, beautiful pale princess of the Russian winter, whose green eyes still haunted his dreams. Unable to bring himself to end her life, in a moment of madness, he transformed her into a vampire. His plan was for them to continue as a couple, traveling the continent while dining on the blood of the rich. How could he foresee she would hate being a vampire almost as much as she came to hate him? She vowed revenge against the one who gave her eternal life, while seeking out the companionship of younger vampires. He had but one choice, and so he fled westward on a moonless night, never returning to Russia's icy steppes.

He swept into the shadows surrounding Alicia's house, moving like a breeze that stirred autumn leaves, and made them sound like falling rain. As stealthy as a black cat, he crept from window to window, his predator eyes in search of a prize. There, at last, he found her, asleep in a back room with a light on.

She is afraid of the dark, and rightfully so, but the light will not save her. Evil can be found in the brightest of lights.

He focused his energy, the way a spirit does to move objects, and manipulated the locking mechanism on the back door. A tiny click of steel announced his arrival.

Inside the house, he tip-toed along a wall—as quiet as the Grim Reaper coming to steal away a soul. When he arrived at her bedroom, he found the door closed. A gentle push caused the hinges to squeal and she stirred on the bed. Four steps in, she sat up, eyes bulging, chin toward her chest, fear and resignation in her expression.

"I knew you'd come for me," she said in a calm voice.

He glanced around the room. "Where is your holy water? Your cross? Your garlic?"

"Would they have done any good?" she asked.

"I would drink the water, kiss the cross, and eat the garlic. Then my breath would kill you."

Mr. Howard walked to the bed and sat beside her. Her Facebook picture failed to capture her true beauty. She was a harvest moon in the light of stars, casting a warm glow upon a frost covered field. She was the palette that held all the bright hues demanded by a master artist. He could never kill her, despite the threat she represented to him. Fortunately, he didn't have to. "You saw me in your visions."

"Yes," she whispered and looked straight into his eyes. "They call you Mr. Howard. You teach at the university."

"You are correct. Why did you not share this information with the police?"

"The one policeman, Killgood, is your friend. He would never believe you capable of murder unless he caught you in the act, and even then, he'd have a hard time trusting what he saw."

"Is that the only reason?"

She wrung her hands on her lap. "I knew the police could never protect me from you, and so, I started to think that maybe if I didn't reveal your identity, you would grant me a small mercy."

"You consider sparing your life a small mercy?"

She stopped moving her hands. "I know what you are."

This brought a smile to his face. "Is it that difficult to say the word?"

"I just never imagined I'd come in contact with a real… vampire." She grasped his hand. The act surprised him, but he made no attempt to pull back. "For someone who's dead, you seem so full of life."

"Do not believe everything you read in books, including mine. When it comes to vampires, most authors are clueless."

A chuckle passed from her lips before she turned serious again. "You mean to kill me. Promise to make it quick and as painless as possible."

He placed his free hand over hers and patted. "I am here to take you with me. I will not kill you. This is comforting, is it not?"

"Are you going to turn me into a vampire?"

"I believe one psychic vampire is enough, yes?"

"But you're not a real psychic."

She was clever and intuitive, and maddeningly sexy. Without a doubt, excellent vampire material, but she would leave him just like Alexandra. Even in the world of the undead, a man could not escape the limitations imposed by age. A thousand blue pills couldn't make him the lover he once was. "You are correct. I am not a psychic and you will never be a vampire."

"You pretend to be a psychic to fool the police." She shook her head. "Cops are so stupid."

"You met Detective Willard?"

"Oh yeah, my skin crawls at the mention of his name. I swear he'd screw a rabid dog if he knew he wouldn't get bitten."

"Ah, that explains why the scent of a canine was on his clothes the last time we met." He patted her hand again. "Willard is not to be underestimated. What he lacks in morals, he makes up for in fortitude. The man cannot be easily tricked or manipulated. Willard is the shrewdest investigator I have ever known."

She pulled her hand free, but made no attempt to flee. "There's more."

"What do you mean?"

"You don't pretend to be a psychic only to mislead the cops."

"Why would you say that?"

"You always lead them to the bodies of your victims."

He massaged the hairs on his chin as he considered his response. There was no fooling this woman. She saw through his lies as fast as he spun them.

"It's their ghosts, right?" Alicia asked. "You're haunted by the spirits of your victims."

"Do you see ghosts?"

Alicia nodded toward a far corner. "My dead mother is watching us now. She doesn't approve of your behavior, but finds you kind of sexy." Alicia rolled her eyes. "All right, Mom." Her attention came back to him. "She's not happy with me for telling you that last part."

He stared into the corner. "I do not see anyone."

"You're not a psychic, remember?"

"I only can see the specters I am meant to see."

"So, am I right about your ghosts?"

He took a deep breath, which squared his shoulders, then slowly released it. "Yes, the spirits of my victims haunt me until their bodies are reunited with their families. They torment me, night and day, popping up when I least expect it, whining and begging me to take them home."

"You're burdened with guilt for what you do."

"Did you believe all vampires are mindless killers? I am no Dahmer or Chikatilo. I take no pleasure in causing pain or taking lives."

She dipped her head to look at him through her eyelashes. "That's not totally true, is it?"

"Of course it is."

"Are you forgetting the poor man who had the misfortune of riding out in front of you on his bicycle or Ryan, who wanders the spirit world without his penis? Killing them came easily for you."

Although he found Alicia's psychic abilities admirable, he didn't need her to remind him of his shortcomings. Yes, he had a temper, and yes, it sometimes got the better of him and drove him into a homicidal rage, but he could control it, most of the time. The people he killed for blood were not victims of rage or hate. They represented opportunities to satisfy his hunger, and maintain his life force. They deserved empathy. A crazy bicyclist and a wife-beater deserved what they got.

Okay, maybe Harvey didn't deserve to die for threatening to sue him, but Ryan got what was coming to him.

"Only God can sit in judgment and you are not God."

"I might be, you never know," she said.

"No offense, but if you are God, I am disappointed you let me walk so easily into your dreams."

She raised a finger. "Ah, but as God, I made the decision to let you in."

"No. Every decision made on this night has been mine. You no longer enjoy freewill. You are a little butterfly fluttering inside my jar. Your wings can pound in desperation, but you will never escape."

"Then you do intend to kill me."

He reached inside his coat for a tin box. Removing the lid, he pinched some of the blue powder inside. He placed the powder on his palm. "I already told you I will not take your life and yet you continue to doubt me."

"You don't have a great history for telling the truth."

"I tell you the truth in the way I want you to understand it." He gestured toward the powder. This was ground from a Peruvian mummy by a shaman. "It will make you sleep. When you awaken, you will belong to me."

"That's not exactly what I wanted to hear. Can't you come up with something better?"

"Very well, this is all part of a bad dream and when you wake up, I will be gone forever and your life will go on as if I never existed."

"You could make that lie the truth."

"Unfortunately, lies are the truth of my life." He leaned forward and blew the powder into her face.

***

She awoke with a start, her arms battling the ropes that secured her. After a few seconds, she calmed, her gaze traveling to him in his chair. "This is the place you held Stephanie."

He stood and strolled to the record player. "Do you like Gorecki's *Symphony No. 3*? His *Symphony of Sorrowful Songs*."

Somber music filled the basement. He turned to face her. "The soprano is Zofia Kilanowics. She sings each of three movements in a different Polish text. The first, an old Polish lament of the Virgin Mary, followed by a message written on the wall of a Gestapo cell during the Second World War, and lastly, a Silesian folk song about a mother who is searching for her son killed in the Silesian uprising."

He returned to his chair positioned a few feet in front of her and sat. "Some people say this piece represents the suffering of millions in World War Two. Perhaps, or perhaps Gorecki sought to represent sorrow and pain on a more universal level."

"Like the sorrow and pain inflicted by a vampire."

"I did not choose to be as I am, any more than you chose to be my guest. Fate has a way of making our decisions for us, yes?"

Her eyes betrayed pity, as if she found within herself, even at her moment of suffering, the capacity to forgive. He shuddered at the power she held over him. "One day," she said, her voice firm, but lacking emotion, "you will die, and when that happens, I pray your soul can find peace."

"I do not deserve peace." He pushed out of his chair, holding her in his gaze, and started up the stairs, his footfalls heavy and slow. Pausing at the top, he stared back into her newfound prison. This was one of those moments when he filled with self-hate. He sighed and turned off the light.

Chapter 31

Willard had three things on his mind as he drove toward his love shack—sex, Johnny Cash, and vampires. He imagined himself the Marquis de Sade, surrounded by naked women who were chained to beds, waiting eagerly for him to satisfy their desires. The voice of Johnny Cash singing "Ring of Fire" filled the chamber as he moved to the first woman. She arched her back, tongue flicking in and out of her mouth, lips working like a fish out of water. And he was ready to take her when Mr. Howard stepped before him, joined by Doris in her hospital gown, dragging along an IV stand. "What are you doing here?" he asked them. Doris turned to Mr. Howard and said, "I told you he was a rotten bastard," to which Mr. Howard replied, "Yes, I know." The image vanished from his mind and he slapped the steering wheel. Sharing his life with Doris and Mr. Howard was bad enough. To have them invade his fantasies was simply too much.

Johnny's gravelly voice continued to fill the car as Willard turned into Kane Estates. Outside the trailer park sat a neighborhood of older middle-class homes. Most of the houses belonged to recent college graduates and retirees. His duplex sat in the middle of the block. At the time he bought it, the homes were maintained and neat. Now, most stood vacant with dust-covered windows and foreclosure signs. He parked in the drive and shut off the engine. A white pickup passed slowly by, but kept on going. He glanced at his watch. She would arrive in less than an hour.

Once inside, he went straight to the bedroom to check on his device. The idea for it came to him while watching Margo perform in a school production of *Peter Pan*. At first, his attention was drawn to the girl playing Tinker Bell, a cute blonde with a big toothy grin. When impure thoughts of plugging the green fairy in the ass filled his mind, he drove them out by concentrating on the boy playing Peter. As the boy flew over the stage suspended by a cable, it hit him. A pulley, some kind of rope, and a harness. When put together, he had his device. It would be perfect.

Shadows filled the bedroom. Even with the light turned on, the room appeared dim. This wouldn't do. He wanted to see everything clearly. Willard opened the blinds. Slats of sunlight filtered inside. He glanced around the fenced backyard. "Fuck it," he said, and raised the blinds several inches. Opening the blinds seemed stupid and daring, like having sex inside a crowded movie theater, but who was going to be watching? And even if someone happened upon them, who cared? He wasn't ashamed of what he was about to do. Hell, whatever pride he had disappeared the first time he climbed upon Doris for another round of "is it in yet?"

He picked up the leather harness lying on the bed and smiled. It took him a week to put the device together. Doris kept interrupting his work, poking her cow face inside the garage to moo, "What are you working on?" After he told her it was none of her goddamn business, she continued to stare at him with a dumb expression. "Do you want to come inside and watch *American Idol* with me?" Hell no, he had said. I would rather pour gasoline over myself and swim in a lake of fire. She retreated with her lips pulled down in a pout as if learning the Ding Dong factory had blown up and she'd never get another one. Her sadness made him chuckle and motivated him to finish.

Willard tossed the harness down and ventured into the kitchen. The refrigerator stood empty except for three bottles of beer. Inside the family room, he sank into the big leather recliner he bought on Craigslist and drank his beer. Eyes closed, he pictured Doris lying inside the hospital. *I'd love to see her fat ass on a treadmill. Wait, what am I saying? No one in their right mind would want to see her fat ass on a treadmill.* He yawned. The mess with Doris and the Coldstone investigation had worn him down.

Rapping on the front door stirred him awake. He took in the room, his mind clouded until remembering the reason he was there, and then a big grin settled on his face. "She's here. Hot damn."

He opened the front door. Bright sunlight made him wince and he blinked several times. His gaze traveled down to the woman standing before him. The top of her head came to his waist. Flaming red hair framed a pale, freckled face. Dark brown eyes looked up at him. Her small lips, garishly painted bright red, pursed into a bow as she considered him. "Are you Swinging Dick?"

It took him a moment to remember his user name on the website. "Are you Ride Me Like a Shetland Pony?"

"That'd be me." She leaned to peer around him. "So, do you plan on inviting me in or what?"

"Oh, sorry." He stepped aside for her to pass, his gaze fixed on her tiny ass.

"Nice place," she said, while looking around.

He closed and locked the door. His heart quaked. Sweat appeared on his brow. "Care for a drink? I've got beer."

"Nah, I'm here for fucking not drinking."

His heart beat faster. "Reckon so."

She glanced over her shoulder, eyelids drawn down. "You still want to do this, right?"

"Why wouldn't I?"

She shrugged. "Some guys fantasize about sex with a dwarf but when presented with the real thing, retreat faster than a dickless man in a pissing contest."

Retreat? Hell no.

"No, I want to do this," he said.

"Are you sure?"

He nodded. "Let me show you the bedroom." He gestured toward the room on his right.

"Now we're talking," she said, tottering past him. She entered the room and paused at the end of the bed. Her gaze moved from the pulley and rope hanging overhead to the leather harness on the mattress. "You've got to be shitting me."

He swallowed hard. Pushing past her, he picked up the harness. "It'll be great."

"Yeah, right. You expect me to wear that thing?"

"I made it myself."

She looked back at the pulley. "Attached to that?"

He stroked the soft harness leather. "The harness won't be uncomfortable."

"And you're going to—"

"Lift you with the pulley." He flexed to show off a bulging bicep. "I've been working out."

"Hey, I ain't putting on no goddamn freak show."

She didn't realize she was born a freak show, just like The Human Snake he'd seen in the carnival tent as a boy. A midget woman without arms or legs, she wiggled around in a cage wearing only a diaper. He remembered finding her attractive. He longed to touch her, to hold her in his arms and feel her settle against him. Over the years, his fantasy of having The Human Snake grew. One day, he would have a woman like her.

"It won't be like that," he said. "Trust me, this will be fun." He reached into his back pocket for his wallet. "I can pay you."

She snarled and her face screwed up into a ball of fine wrinkles. "I ain't no whore." She turned to leave.

He grabbed her arm. "Please don't go. I wasn't trying to pick at you. I'm sorry, I meant nothing by it. I want to be with you, that's all."

She yanked her arm free, her gaze returning to the harness. "If I don't like it, you'll—"

"Stop right away. I swear."

A deep sigh rose from her chest. "I must be out of mind." She snatched the harness from him. "Tell me what to do."

"You'll have to get naked."

"What a shock."

His face burned as if he were an inexperienced teenager having sex for the first time. She went to work on her clothes, stubby fingers unfastening buttons on her blouse. When she was down to her bra and panties, his throat went dry. She had a sack-of-potatoes body, little pockets of fat appearing in places he never imagined possible. He figured he was an expert on body fat after having the misfortune of seeing Doris naked, but this was something different. Something alien to his eyes. The bra came off and tiny breasts sagged toward her stomach. Her panties slid down her cottage cheese thighs revealing her clean-shaven vagina. A tattoo on her hip said, *top, bottom, behind, just give it to me.*

"What now?" she asked, hands on her hips.

He opened the harness. "Put this on."

"I'll need your help."

His neck tingled and the feeling spread across his shoulders. "Here," he said, pressing the harness against her belly. "Hold it for me."

Soft warm hands brushed over his as she held the harness. He moved behind her. Five moles on her right shoulder formed a ragged question mark. What was there to question? Everything about her felt so right. He couldn't wait to be inside her. His hands trembled as he fastened the hooks.

"Does it fit all right? Is it comfortable?" He stood before her. The harness pushed her breasts up and tiny purple veins around her nipples swelled with blood. His hands thrust forward and seized her breasts. He squeezed and released her skin, over and over, a muted coo escaping her throat. He took a breast in his mouth, tongue dancing about her firm nipple. Her cooing became a moan. Tiny fingers weaved into his hair. She yanked back his head.

"Get out of your clothes and show me how this thing works."

He was Superman getting ready to fuck Lois Lane, his clothes flying off as fast as he could remove them. Her left eyebrow arched at the sight of his erect penis. "What?" he asked, sensing disappointment in her eyes.

"Nothing," she said. "We can make this work." She climbed onto the bed and tugged on the rope attached to the pulley. "Want to hook me up, lover boy?"

He joined her on the bed, a shiver racing through him as his penis brushed against her thigh. After attaching the harness to the hook on the rope, he brought his mouth to hers. She pushed him away. "Don't."

Head down, he scooted away from her. For the second time, heat spread through his cheeks.

"Maybe later," she said, brushing a hand over his arm. "What's next?"

He grabbed a handle at the end of the rope and pulled hard.

"Whoa!" she squealed, her body lifting off the bed. He moved the handle from side to side and she flew like an acrobat across the big top. Willard stretched out on the bed, tugging on the rope to make her soar above him. Her stubby arms and legs clawed at the air. He slapped her on the hip, which sent her spinning. "I'm gonna be sick," she said.

Sitting up, he put out an arm to stop her. They came face to face and she pressed her hands against his cheeks and kissed him. A mischievous grin appeared on her lips. "What else can you do with this thing?"

He lay back down and wiggled around until their hips aligned. Taking his erect penis in his left hand, he positioned it for entry, while his right hand lowered her body over him. She spread her legs and he brought her down on top of him. It took several tries for everything to mesh, but once he figured out where to guide her, he slid inside her easily. He used the rope to lift and lower her, up and down, up and down, like a carousel horse riding a pole. Her mouth hung open as she groaned. His left hand flattened against her lower back to keep her in position, while his right worked the rope to move her. Up and down, up and down, in and out, in and out, her body was trembling and his penis throbbed with the arrival of new blood. A deep ache formed in his right forearm and bicep. He sweated heavily, the bed beneath him wet and cool. Still, he pulled on the rope, blinding hot pain spreading across his brain. And then he came. Tension fled tired muscles and his body relaxed. He let the slack out of the rope slowly. She settled against him, a smile on her bright red lips, sweat glistening on her brow.

"Wow. That was better than I expected."

"I told you," he said, feeling proud. She leaned forward to rest her head against his stomach. He raised his chin to look down at her. The sight of her small lumpy body repulsed him, as if she had suddenly transformed into a hideous beast. Everything felt out of kilter. He closed his eyes and gnashed his teeth to fight off the negative feeling taking root in his brain.

"I can't wait to try it again," she said, the fingers on her right hand probing his chest.

He continued to clench his teeth as her creepy crawler fingers moved over him. His breathing became rapid. The world closed in around him and he was buried by it.

"Are you all right?"

He forced himself to nod. "Yeah, just give me a minute." Three quick breaths. Eyes open, he stared at her oversized head, like a jack-o-lantern smiling at the person who carved it. He had in fact created her from the depths of his desire, from the part of him that lived in the shadowed corridors of a dream. He was Frankenstein; only Frankenstein didn't screw his monster. "I'm feeling better, thanks."

She pushed onto her elbows to stare into his eyes. "For a second there, I thought you were having a heart attack. I know I'm a good fuck, but come on."

A good fuck? Ha, I'd rather stick my dick in a toaster and watch it fry than fuck you again. "Yeah, you're something special."

She smiled at his words.

"My daddy used to say I was special." She rested her head on his stomach and sighed. "He said I was his little princess."

Little all right, not sure about the princess part.

"Daddy worked as a clown for the Magnus Brothers Circus."

What a surprise.

"Mama was part of the horse act. Sometimes she joined the clowns. Circus life was fun when I was young. I'd go and visit The Amazing Armando in his trailer. He swallowed swords and breathed fire. Armando used to poke marshmallows on a stick and breathe fire to roast them for me."

I'll bet he poked more than marshmallows.

She sighed again. "As I got older, the circus became boring. I'd stare at the kids in the crowd and wanted to be like them, with a regular home, and friends who weren't adults. Daddy and Mama tried to give me a normal life, but there's nothing normal about a circus. I was the typical teenager, rebellious as hell. I discovered at thirteen I could make more money in a week giving blow jobs than my parents earned in a month. I really earned big bucks when I let men screw me. Why do guys find dwarfs so attractive?"

I'm not the one to be asking that question.

"When Daddy found out about my evil ways, he beat me real good in the name of Jesus, so I ran away on my sixteenth birthday. Seemed like the thing to do at the time. Life on the road for a runaway dwarf ain't easy. I learned to use my condition to my advantage, like I had at the circus. It hurts to be laughed at. I mean, I have feelings too, they're just inside a really small body. I fell in love with the same boys the normal girls liked, only, I didn't have a chance in Hell of them falling in love with me. Oh, they loved banging me just fine, or tossing me to their drunken friends like I was a beach ball. But that was all I was good for. A dwarf's life is lonely. Even if we hook up with other dwarfs, there seems to be something missing. It's as if God wanted us punished for some unaccountable sin."

She pulled at his chest hairs. "I considered being a nun, but I like sex too much. Maybe that's my sin. Anyway, I took some classes at the community college, learned how to use a computer. Things are a little better now. I met a dwarf who says he loves me. Larry is all right, I suppose, but he's not very exciting. He's one hundred percent dwarf if you know what I mean. So, I posted my ad on the swinger's website looking for adventure, and boy, did I ever find it with you. This crazy thing of yours is kind of fun." She pulled one of his hairs hard.

"Ouch, that hurt."

"Sorry," she said, letting go. "Had to make sure you were still alive. You sure are a quiet one. Here, I've gone and told you my life story, and I don't know anything about you."

His entire body tensed. "What did you say?"

Her eyebrows pushed inward to form a V. "I said I've told you my life story, but I don't know anything about you."

He grabbed her waist and tossed her aside. "Son of a bitch."

"Hey," she said, pushing onto her knees. "What was that for?"

Willard rolled off the bed and stood. "He keeps them for a week before killing them in order to get information."

"What are you talking about?"

He pounded a fist against his forehead. "Mr. Howard. He kidnaps the girls and holds them at his house because he needs time to learn about their lives. He needs to know everything about them in order to make us think he's a real psychic. He could lead us to their bodies, but not to a killer, because he is the killer."

"Are you some kind of cop?"

He climbed onto the bed and clutched her shoulders, squeezing so hard, she winced. "The forensic entomologist said she'd been dead three weeks. I never could figure out why he kept her alive for a week until now. I know your life story because you're here to tell me. I know about life in the circus and how you gave men blow jobs, and took a beating for Christ. Son of a bitch, I can't believe I didn't see it until now, and the sad part is no one will listen to me."

He released his hold and massaged his brow. "The bastard is going to kill again unless someone stops him, and with his history of assisting us, he knows he'll never get arrested. There must be some way to prove he killed Stephanie Coldstone. I have to think."

"While you're thinking, would you mind unhooking me? It's time for me to go."

"Yeah, yeah, you're right," he said and went to work unfastening the harness. He quickly popped open the hooks. She took a deep breath when the harness came off.

"Thanks for whatever," she said, gathering her clothes. "Maybe we can get... no, I don't think so." When dressed, she gave him a quick peck on the cheek.

He gestured toward the door with his chin. "Bye."

She huffed and stomped from the room. The front door slammed and he stretched out on the damp bed. The shadow of the rope swayed across the ceiling like a cobra responding to the hypnotic call of a snake charmer's pungi.

Fucking a dwarf, I must be out of my mind. Next time, I'll do Siamese twins. Can Siamese twins even fuck? I guess it depends on where they're attached. But first, I've got to do something about Mr. Howard. Maybe, I'll drive a wooden stake through the bastard's heart. Then I can find those twins.

***

It was nearly five o 'clock when he arrived home to a dark house. After unlocking the front door, he poked his head inside and gave a hearty, "Hello, anyone home?"

No response.

"Where are those little shits?" he said, walking to the kitchen. He prepared a turkey sandwich, grabbed a bag of chips, a diet soda, and headed to his office. Inside, he sat the plate on his desk, an uneasy feeling in his gut as he pondered the silent house. Dave and Margo hadn't made plans to visit friends and it wasn't like them to go behind his back on anything. He left the office and walked down the hallway to check their rooms. Empty. "This is so weird," he said, returning to the office.

As he ate the sandwich, he mused over Mr. Howard. There must be a way to prove the son of a bitch killed Stephanie Coldstone.

How?

He needed evidence. Of course he needed evidence.

Stupid.

But where to find it? The professor's house? That's where he would have held Stephanie. That's where he drew her blood. There had to be something. Bodily fluids? The needle he used on her arm? Wait a minute, he took her necklace. Yes, that's what he would find if he could get inside Mr. Howard's mansion. Wouldn't work though. No judge was going to give him a search warrant based on a hunch.

Damn.

To put Mr. Howard out of his mind, he remembered his encounter with the dwarf. Time had softened his opinion of her and her lumpy little body. Truth was she could ride his cock anytime she wanted. Not that she would want to after the way he treated her. He went on the swinger's website and stared at her profile for a long time. What was her name? He never bothered asking. He had a mind to email her an apology. Beg her to give him another chance. Or should he…?

Wait, what was this, real Siamese twins, and they were from Siam no less. Glory to God and praise Jesus. He'd hit the jackpot. Two heads, one body. Perfect for what he needed. Maybe he could build a bigger harness. Shit, he'd need to really work out to hoist their weight. To hell with that, he'd be happy just to tag em on the bed. Talk about multiple orgasms. He went to work typing a message. Halfway through, the phone rang.

"How could you?" a tearful voice asked.

"Doris?"

"Hell yes it's me. Who where you expecting?"

"Obviously, not you," he said.

"Why didn't you come to see me?"

He groaned, already tired of this conversation. "I saw you last night."

"Why didn't you come today? Don't you care about me?"

He opened his mouth to speak but nothing came out.

"Didn't you hear me?"

"Now don't take on like that, Doris. It can't be good for your heart. Truth is I had to work today."

"On Saturday?"

"Yeah, important case."

The sound of her sniffling came through the receiver. "You shouldn't beat Margo."

He pushed forward in the chair. "Who told you that?"

"Who do you think?"

"The kids came to see you? I told them to wait, the little brats."

"They were concerned about their mama."

"Yeah, right. They're just pissed because I told 'em to go on a diet. Fat little monsters. You want 'em to end up in the hospital like you? Can't you see what you're doing to them with all the sweets and junk food? Jesus Christ, Doris, can't you see what you were doing to yourself? Don't tell me you couldn't see your reflection in the mirror, or are you too damn embarrassed to look at yourself?"

"Dad, stop being so mean!"

A low growl escaped his throat. "Get off the phone, Margo."

"Why wouldn't you bring us to see Mom?"

"Put your mother back on the line or I'm going to whip your butt so hard you won't be able to sit down for a week."

"Dad says he's going to beat me again," Margo said, her voice distant.

"Hand me that phone," Doris said. "Don't you dare talk to our daughter that way. Now she's crying again."

"Good. I meant every word I said." He looked at the clock. "I'll be at the hospital in twenty minutes to pick up the kids. Tell them to be waiting at the entrance."

"They're spending the night at the Spencers' house."

"Hell no."

"Hell yes. We already made arrangements. Tomorrow, I expect you to come see me. Bring flowers and a nice card. And plan to stay all afternoon."

"How about a triple meat burger and a large order of fries with a chocolate shake to wash it all down?"

"You be here."

He slammed down the phone. "Damn bitch. I've treated her like a queen for years and this is the thanks I get? No more Mr. Nice Guy. No more compassionate, loving husband. I'll toss her fat ass out on the street and then we'll see who'll want her."

Chapter 32

Inside the basement, Mr. Howard held the fork toward Alicia, still tied against the wall. She opened her mouth to accept the Wiener Schnitzel and he carefully placed a bite between her lips. "What do you think?"

"Good," she mumbled while chewing. "You made this?"

He beamed at her approval. "My mother taught me to cook when I was a boy. At the time, I hated her for it. You see, I wanted to be off with my friends creating mischief, but now I am grateful to her and sometimes wish I had not killed her."

Alicia's eyes opened wide. "You murdered your mother?"

"It is true, I am afraid. A part of me cannot be controlled, much like the legend of the wolf man during a full moon. Most of the time, I can suppress the homicidal rage that lives within me, but from time to time, it escapes to cause havoc." He offered another bite of the food.

"Is that why you killed Stephanie Coldstone?"

He glanced over his shoulder. "We should enjoy music with our dinner." He set down the plate and thumbed through his record albums. "Rachmaninoff will do. Stephanie loved Rachmaninoff."

He placed the record on the turntable. The soothing sound of a piano filled the basement. Mr. Howard returned to Alicia with the food. "You already know the answer to your question because you know what I am. That part of me, the vampire, has more humanity and compassion than my human side I believe. But should that be a surprise given the sad state of human history? Vampires have been around nearly as long as humans, and yet, we do not kill indiscriminately on a mass scale, nor do we target our victims based on their race or religion. We do not seek their land or treasure, no. We take what we must to survive. What human should sit in judgment when you consider the nature of the species?"

"I don't judge you as a vampire but as someone who kills. You claim your motive is need, but that's a failed argument. A sexual deviant kills to satisfy their desire. A psychopath kills to quiet the demons of their souls. Every killer claims to have a reason for their action, but in the end, there's no justification for murder."

This girl is too smart for her own good.

He smiled as he offered another bite of Wiener Schnitzel. "Vampires have not always killed their victims, and if the ignorance of the Church had not driven us underground and turned us into evil creatures to be feared, we would not kill today. Vampire bats do not kill their prey, but take only what they need. It should be the same for us."

She finished her last bite and he carried the plate over to the table and returned with a glass of water. She drank the entire glass in five long swallows. He used a handkerchief to wipe a drop from her upper lip. "Better, yes?"

"Thank you," she said and smiled.

After taking the glass to the table, he pulled a chair in front of her and sat. "I do regret that you must be restrained this way. It is not done to humiliate or make you feel vulnerable. We both know you would try to escape if presented the opportunity, and this will not do."

"How much longer do I have?"

He considered her with a narrowed gaze. "I do not understand your question."

"Until you kill me," she said.

"I am not going to kill you. I already explained this."

"Why should I believe you?"

"You will not die by my hand, I swear."

She struggled against her restraints. "Then why am I here?"

He closed his eyes and concentrated on the music. The melody brought him peace, something he longed for, but never seemed to find. He looked back at Alicia, inquisitive, brilliant, and frightened. She would have been a good wife for the right man. "I cannot have you leading the police to me, therefore, I need time to think, to make a plan."

"Then you must kill me to guarantee my silence."

He stood and paced. "You come from a long line of psychics, yes?"

"My mother and grandmother were both gifted."

He stopped pacing. "In what way?"

She shrugged. "The usual, I guess, seeing spirits and talking with them, visions of future events, and past events, things like that."

"You say it as if those gifts are normal. I do not see the future and my visions of the past rest only in my memory. As for ghosts, the only ones I see are the spirits of those I have killed. Your family is unique. I have seen gifted people before. Grigori had visions of the future. He foresaw the murder of Nicholas and his family."

"Grigori?"

"Better known by his last name, Rasputin."

She blinked several times. "You knew Rasputin?"

"I have known many famous people."

"What was Rasputin like?"

"A drunkard who smelled like moldy cheese, but he had a way with women, yes, they loved him. He suffered from hypersexuality. Grigori never met a woman he would not fuck. Pardon my vulgarity."

Alicia rolled her eyes. "I've heard the word before."

"The moral decay of society most certainly guarantees that not only have you heard the word, but used it as well. I find the word most appropriate when driving in town."

He walked to her and took her by the hand. The warmth she radiated made him want to curl up beside her and sleep. "We do not choose our fates, Alicia, you must realize this. I did not choose to become a vampire. You did not choose to be my guest, which is most unfortunate, because I would have liked to have known you under different circumstances."

"Why past tense?"

"What do you mean?"

"You talk as if I'm already gone."

He released her hand and returned to his chair. "That is one of my many bad habits, along with leaving up the toilet seat." He chuckled. "I should not have told you that last one. Now you will think me uncivilized."

"You can never escape your human side."

"This is true; however, if I had remained human, I would have been gone from this world many years ago."

"You wished you had died."

His right hand balled into a fist. "That would have been better for everyone, I do believe. But I cannot blame my son for wanting to save my life. He is a good boy."

"So he's a vampire?"

"Indeed. He lives somewhere in Australia. I have not seen him since before the Great War. He fought for the Empire. Damn fool. Killed many a Turk. Slipped across no man's land at night for their blood. According to Lenhard's correspondence, he wanted to die in the war. But the Turks failed to kill him and so he lives on, taking lives like his father."

"Are you ashamed of him?"

He tugged on an earlobe. "No, no, like me he did not choose to become a vampire. It is that way with most of us. We are but satellites that orbit in a universe we did not create."

"Like humans with God."

"Yes, well, at least God loves you. The Creator has hated me for a very long time."

The telephone rang upstairs. He rose from the chair with a grunt. "I despise the telephone. The device never brings good news and interrupts my solitude. Please excuse me for a moment."

He trudged up the stairs, each step seeming to take a lifetime. The phone continued to ring as he emerged in the living room. "Hold on, I am coming." He snatched the unregistered cell phone from the kitchen counter and checked the caller ID. It was Stanis, the private investigator. Finally. He pushed the talk button. "What do you have for me?"

Several seconds of silence followed before a scratchy voice said, "We need to meet."

"Meet, as in face to face? Is that really necessary, Mr. Stanis?"

"I've got what you need on the cop."

Mr. Howard leaned against the counter, a big smile on his face. "Something I can use against him?"

"Oh yeah. If I were this guy, I wouldn't want anyone seeing this."

"Very well. I recommend someplace discreet. Are you familiar with the Bingham Hill Cemetery?"

"Uh, yeah, but that seems a little too discreet. How about someplace in town?"

"I do not hand over seventy-five thousand dollars in town. Either we meet at the cemetery or not at all."

"Fine. What time do you want to do this?"

"I can be there in thirty minutes."

Stanis hesitated. "Shit, yeah, I suppose I can make it. You'd better show up."

He didn't like to be threatened, but held back a response. "See you then." Mr. Howard hung up the phone. The call improved his mood. He bustled down the stairs into the basement. Alicia watched him with a puzzled expression.

"You win the lottery or something?"

"In a way, yes," he said, collecting her plate and glass. "I must leave for a bit. You will be fine until I return."

"I'm not going anywhere," she said.

Oh but you are.

He gave her a comforting smile to make her think he found her joke amusing. "Should I leave the music playing?"

"Yeah… sure, it beats silence."

He started up the stairs.

"Professor," she called as he neared the top.

He stopped and glanced over his shoulder. "What is it?"

"Will you please leave the light on?"

His head bowed under the weight of guilt. "Yes, of course."

Chapter 33

Bingham Hill was a pioneer cemetery located ten miles north of town. Surrounded by farms and fields of grass and cottonwood trees, the isolated burial ground was the perfect location to meet someone, especially if you needed to kill them, which might be the case depending on what evidence Stanis brought, and his attitude.

He drove the winding road to the graveyard, warm summer air blowing through his hair, his thoughts on Alicia. Why couldn't she be a foul mouth rube with yellow teeth and warts?

No.

She was beautiful, intelligent, and vulnerable, like Stephanie Coldstone and the others. Something flashed out of the darkness. He slammed on the brakes, tires squealing as the car fishtailed to a stop. A deer stood in the beam of his headlights, black eyes fixed on the danger before it. The creature remained motionless, waiting for him to make a decision. After several seconds, it passed into the surrounding shadows. He released the brake and drove away.

Bingham Hill had no parking lot. He stopped on the shoulder of the road outside the cemetery and turned off the engine. Clouds obscured the stars and the surrounding blackness reminded him of the Paris catacombs. Century-old trees became dark sentinels. Wind rustled their leaves.

He stepped out of the car and strolled to the cemetery gate, which opened with the squeal of rusted hinges. A long, narrow dirt trail led to the graveyard. Alongside it, water bubbled past in an irrigation ditch. The buzz of mosquitoes filled the air. Crickets sang. The branches of a willow bowed over the path near its end. He pushed through the delicate limbs, leaves feathering over his face, and emerged at the entrance of the graveyard.

Bingham Hill was built haphazardly on a sloping grade, gravestones spread here and there amongst patches of rocky dirt and cactus. The majority were tiny stones from the 19th century, weather-worn and cracking. Mr. Howard passed the guest book and took a seat on a nearby bench.

After a few minutes, car headlights cut through the darkness. The car stopped next to his and the headlights went out, restoring the gloom. A black figure emerged and turned on a flashlight, its fuzzy white beam swallowed by the night. Mr. Howard followed the light along the path toward the cemetery. Willow branches shook and a large man appeared. "Over here," Mr. Howard called.

"Who said that?" The flashlight swung wildly from side to side as the man searched for the source of the voice.

"Do not worry, Mr. Stanis. It is me, not a ghost." Mr. Howard winced as the flashlight shined in his face.

"You scared the shit out of me," Stanis said, tromping toward him. The P.I. stopped. He leaned forward to consider Mr. Howard with narrowed eyes and blinked several times. "You're whiter than a baby's ass."

"I do not get out much."

Stanis shrugged. "Whatever." His gaze moved over the graveyard. "This is a hell of a place to meet. You know it's haunted? They say you can hear the ghosts of little children and babies crying and cold hands reach out to touch you."

"Then we should get down to business before that happens, yes?"

The P.I. edged closer. A long trench coat stretched tight across his broad shoulders and barrel chest. His head looked like a bowling ball that had seen too many gutters. Whiskers dotted his sagging cheeks. He reached inside the coat and brought out a cell phone. "I've transferred the tape to my phone so you can watch. You won't believe what's on this."

"Mr. Stanis, you would be surprised by what I believe." He motioned toward the bench. "Take a seat."

The burly P.I. lowered onto the bench next to him, an asthmatic wheeze whistling from his chest. He pulled an inhaler from his pocket and took a hit. "That's some walk over here."

"Is it?" Mr. Howard held out his hand.

Stanis appeared confused as he stared at it.

"The phone."

"Oh yeah right." Stanis's fat fingers punched several buttons on the phone. "Here you go," he said. "What some people won't do to get off these days."

Mr. Howard leaned toward the small screen. It came to life suddenly with a video of a naked man moving about a bedroom. Not just any man, but Willard. Yes, it was most definitely Detective Willard with a… dwarf. He covered his mouth to hide a snicker. This was too good. He watched with amused satisfaction, images of Willard hooking the dwarf woman to some kind of harness and lifting her into the air, but as the film progressed, and they began to make love, his amusement turned to pity. He knew all too well what it meant to be an outcast, and how desperate for love some people became. This tape gave him everything he needed to stop Willard's investigation. His career and marriage would be over. He should be happy, but his victory felt bittersweet and hollow. Willard might be perverted, but he was also the greatest opponent he had ever faced. When the video ended, Mr. Howard handed the phone back to the P.I. "You've done well, Mr. Stanis."

The P.I. beamed. "I was sure he spotted my truck when I followed him. Can't believe the dumb bastard left the blinds up, like he wanted me to film him or something."

"You have to admit, he did put on quite a show. I especially liked the part where he slaps her on the hip and sends her spinning."

"Yeah, I guess if you're into that kind of thing. Personally, I get my sex on the Internet."

"Oh?"

"Pictures," Stanis said, "I look at pictures."

Mr. Howard offered a patronizing smile. "I see. Compared to yours, my life is rather ordinary and dull."

"Most people don't sit out in bone yards watching dwarf porn."

"Good point."

Stanis squirmed. He glanced around as if expecting someone to join them. "So, is this what you wanted?"

"Most definitely, but, I need you to do one last thing."

Stanis massaged the back of his neck, the wheeze returning to his chest. "Look, I'm already nervous about this case. Christ, this guy's a fucking cop."

"Yes, in the video he is a fucking cop." Mr. Howard smiled at his own joke. "What I need you to do is not difficult and will not place you in any kind of danger."

"If he finds out about me, I'm a dead man."

If you don't do what I want, you're a dead man.

"All I need is for you to leave a copy of the disc at the detective's house. Prop it against the door in an envelope marked urgent with his wife's name, Doris Willard, written in big letters."

Stanis puckered his lips and blew out raw onion breath. "She'll be pissed as hell. You really have it in for this guy. What'd he do write you a speeding ticket or something?"

"Something like that."

"All right, I can drop off a disc. I'll just have to be careful not to leave prints or DNA."

"Good thinking."

"Would you like me to send you a copy?"

Do you honestly think I'm going to provide my address?

"No, that will not be necessary, but you should keep a copy for thirty days."

"Why thirty days?"

"Thirty days should be enough time for this video to do what I think it will. If I should need a copy, expect to hear from me before the end of the month. Our business here is concluded, yes."

"Aren't you going to pay me?"

"Certainly. Follow me to my car." He stood and headed toward the path. Stanis fell in behind him, his ragged breaths rising over the sound of the insects and the running water.

"Want to borrow my flashlight?"

"Thank you, but no," Mr. Howard said over his shoulder. "I can see just fine."

"How? It's darker than a Tijuana whorehouse."

Stanis took another hit on his inhaler when they arrived at the road, the wet sound like water sucking down a drain. "How can you see in this?"

"Take it from me," Mr. Howard said, opening the trunk on his car, "you do not want to know." He lifted a suitcase and held it out. "Seventy-five thousand in cash."

Stanis licked his lips. "The money's all here right? I mean, I trust you and everything."

"Do not trust anyone." Mr. Howard popped open the locks on the case so the P.I. could see the neatly stacked rows of one hundred dollar bills.

"Fuck me, that's a lot of money."

"Yes it is, and no, I would prefer not to fuck you." He snapped the locks closed and handed the suitcase to Stanis.

"That was just a figure of speech."

Mr. Howard held back a smile. "Yes, I know. I just wanted to see you stumble for a response."

"Good one." The P.I. tossed the case inside a battered sedan. "Guess I can afford new wheels."

"Perhaps you should invest your money."

"What for?" Stanis asked, climbing into the car. "I may be dead tomorrow."

Indeed, if Willard learns who you are, you will most certainly be dead.

Stanis leaned out the car. "Do you need me to call after I've dropped off the disc?"

"That will not be necessary."

The P.I. gave a quick wave and slammed the door. The sedan started with a roar and backed onto the road. Mr. Howard watched until the taillights faded.

***

Mr. Howard drove east, away from the city, to the open plains of northeastern Colorado. He'd made this journey several times, but this occasion felt different, more purposeful. He passed through the same little farming towns without a moment's thought, his attention on the task at hand. It had to end. Soon.

A veil of stars shined down on the entrance to the grasslands. He turned north, dust rising on the road behind his car. A lump rose in his throat when he spotted the cottonwood tree in the distance. It felt strange to be there without Stephanie. He wondered how her spirit was getting along now that she was reunited with her family, and if she hated him for taking her life. Perhaps she hated him for not leading the police to her grave, but the important thing was that she no longer remained in this desolate place.

He parked and retrieved a glass jar and gardening shovel from the trunk. As he approached her grave, the only evidence of a crime was a piece of yellow crime scene tape tied to a stake. The tape danced and snapped in the wind. The cops hadn't bothered to refill the grave. He stood at the edge of the hole and remembered Stephanie lying at the bottom. The image proved unsettling and so he went to work scooping dirt from the grave into the jar. It wouldn't be hard for the cops to match the dirt to this place, especially with traces of her bodily fluids present.

He finished filling the jar and screwed on the lid. A prayer seemed in order, but the words failed him, and so he trudged back to his car, knowing there was still much to be done. Yes, it had to end. The pieces remained in play. Time to maneuver them toward checkmate.

Chapter 34

The morning sky was blood red, a proper hue to greet a vampire's eyes. Mr. Howard stared out the living room window and yawned. Dead tired, he longed to crawl between warm sheets. He belonged in the dark, hidden from the world, but not on this day, not with so much left to do.

He went to his bedroom to prepare. Although he would not be in sunlight for an extended period, he must dress as if he might. No reason to throw caution to the wind at this stage. He lathered sunscreen on his face and neck before slipping into his long coat. His fedora came last. He tried to imagine what his reflection would look like if he had one. Stylish no doubt. The thought made him smile.

Inside the basement, Alicia watched him approach, her eyes red and glassy. Once again guilt tore through him at the things he must do to survive. He came before her with a heavy sigh. "Such sadness, I see in your lovely face. This is not what I wanted."

She sniffled twice and avoided his gaze. "Do you think this is what I wanted?"

"Did you have a vision during the night?"

She nodded.

"Of your future?"

"Can we not talk about it?" she asked, looking at him. "I so much want to hate you, but I can't because I understand you."

Please do not forgive me. I would never ask that of you.

He reached into his coat for the tin of sleeping powder. "I must take you someplace," he said, opening the tin.

"And for this I must sleep?"

"It is for your own good." He placed a pinch of the powder in his palm.

"Why must life hurt?"

He touched her cheek, the way a father might comfort a crying child. "Perhaps when Christ died upon the cross, he passed his pain onto us. But death, my dear Alicia, is not painful. Dying is like floating in a warm sea, the sun bright on your face. I wish my son had allowed me to die."

"Me too," she said.

He couldn't help but smile at her words. "Now close your eyes and rest."

"Promise me something."

"Anything."

Her gaze locked on his face. Her eyes held the sorrow of resignation. "Don't wake me up."

He pulled back, lines forming on his brow. "I will not kill you."

"I know."

For a moment he considered letting her go, but quickly dismissed that idea. Even if he could flee, leaving Willard in a position to pursue him was not an option. "Close your eyes and fall into a dream. A sweet dream from your youth perhaps, yes?"

Her eyes closed.

"Do you see your mother in this dream? She holds your hand as you walk through a field of wildflowers."

"I see her."

"Feel a gentle spring breeze feather across your hair. The smell of a recent storm remains in the air to blend with the scent of the flowers. Do you smell this?"

She nodded.

He raised his hand and leaned close to her face. "A warm sun caresses the back of your neck." He softly blew the powder toward her. "You are loved Alicia. You are most certainly loved."

***

As he drove, Mr. Howard listened to Blue October's gut-wrenching song about suicide, "Black Orchid." He glanced back at Alicia asleep on the floor of the van. Life's not for everyone, and yet, here he was, the one creature least deserving of life, playing the role of God once more. Unlike a typical serial killer, he took no pleasure in controlling others. Each tear of his victims poured over his soul like freezing rain.

His mood lightened when he was out of the noise and traffic of the city. He even managed to smile while imagining Willard's reaction to the sex tape. He reminded Mr. Howard of Inspector Broussard, who doggedly pursued him for three years without success. Broussard's career in law enforcement came to a sudden end when villagers discovered him passed out nude in a barn with a girl far too young. What was it about cops and perverted sex? Perhaps it took a mind that operated beyond the boundaries of normal behavior to understand the way criminals thought. Perhaps the line between acceptable and criminal was razor thin.

The interstate to Wyoming offered unobstructed views of the Rocky Mountain foothills. Fat morning clouds hovered over the peaks with the threat of an afternoon rain shower. He soaked in the daylight views, foreign to his night eyes. How different things appeared when exposed to the truth of the sun. Darkness provided lies.

He turned off onto the dirt road that led to Van Adams's house. Van Adams enjoyed his privacy, which explained why he lived in a custom-built house on three hundred acres north of the city. Whispered rumors suggested he wanted no one to spy on his activities with the young women from the college.

After driving a couple of miles, he arrived at the estate, a sprawling ranch-style house surrounded by aspen and cottonwood trees. The exterior matched the bland personality of its owner. Mr. Howard steered off the driveway and onto the grass. He weaved around the trees until finding a concealed parking spot. Ten o'clock. Van Adams would return from church within the hour.

Mr. Howard carried the sleeping Alicia across the yard and onto the front porch. An intelligent man would protect his home with an alarm or snapping canine. Van Adams had the common sense of a skunk that liked to smell its own butt. It took but a moment to work the lock open. Mr. Howard stepped into the entryway. The trees kept the house in permanent shade. Gray settled over the big open rooms, stiff and formal with oversized furniture. Copies of Renoir, Sisley, and Bazille paintings decorated the walls. Van Adams liked to impress his guests by throwing out words like, "The Café Guerbois crowd and *en plein* air." The truth was, a monkey could throw its shit on a canvas and Van Adams would buy the picture if he thought it'd help him get laid. Without his gold-plated cock to attract the unsuspecting, Van Adams's palm would be as callused as that of a longshoreman.

Mr. Howard carefully laid Alicia on the couch and went back to the van. He returned with rope and the jar of soil collected at the grasslands. As he sprinkled dirt in various parts of the house, he remembered the last

Christmas party with Van Adams. The bastard was hornier than a buck chasing a doe in heat, his attention focused on Maria Hernandez, who worked in the finance department. The married Hernandez managed to resist Van Adams's advances for a while, a look of discomfort on her face whenever he pressed up behind her and massaged her shoulders. Then she and the assistant dean vanished for nearly an hour before emerging from a back room, faces flushed. Two weeks later, she received a layoff notice. There was a price to be paid for playing the Devil's game.

After spreading dirt around the family room and entry, he picked the basement door lock and stepped down into the subterranean chamber. On the walls, dozens of black and white photographs depicted graphic bondage scenes. Naked women tied and stretched into degrading poses, black leather hoods concealing their identities. Clothespins pinched breasts. Needles pierced places not meant to be pierced. There was blood. There was agony. And this is what Van Adams wanted to see. To him, women were nothing more than objects, no more alive than an inflatable sex doll. What he couldn't know is the cruel photographs, and the bizarre scene they created, would be his ultimate downfall. Now, he was glad he had snuck into the basement during the Christmas party and discovered them. A picture was worth a thousand words and these photographs told volumes.

Mr. Howard sprinkled dirt around the basement floor and on the black leather massage table with stirrups. When he finished, Mr. Howard removed Stephanie's locket from his coat pocket. He opened it and stared at her photograph. "Do not worry, Stephanie, the locket will belong to you once more, I swear. I want nothing more from you than what you've already given me." He placed the locket on the table, collected the jar of dirt, and made his way upstairs.

He carried Alicia down the basement stairs, huffing and puffing as he went. She settled against his chest with a soft whimper like a child in the midst of a nightmare. Retrieving two dining room chairs, he brought them downstairs. He sat Alicia on one of the chairs, stretched her arms behind her, and used rope to secure them. He then tied her ankles to the chair. She stirred but remained asleep.

Back upstairs, he sank onto a leather recliner and waited. It wouldn't be long now. He could feel the pending conflict in his blood, in the way the hairs stood on his arms, and the back of his neck. He had finished his analysis and moved accordingly. The queen was in *en prise* and the endgame in sight. His breathing slowed. He focused on the task at hand. No mistakes. He had come too far to screw up at this late hour.

A car turned onto the road leading to the house. His ears, which could pick up sounds at much greater distances than a human, followed its progress. His fingers gripped the soft leather, knuckles darkening with stolen blood.

Come to me, I am waiting.

The car stopped outside. The engine turned off. A door slammed. Keys jangled on a chain as someone approached the front entrance. The keys turned in the lock. The front door opened with a protracted creaking and closed with a thud. A grandfather clock chimed to announce the hour. "Good morning, Luther."

Van Adams jumped back as if hit by an electrical shock. "What the hell!" He clutched his heaving chest. Eyes dilated, he searched the room until locating Mr. Howard.

"How did you get in?" Van Adams stomped closer. He no longer wore his famous smirk, but rather, a threatening scowl that hinted at his hidden nature. "You heard me. How did you get in?"

Mr. Howard sighed. Engaging Van Adams in any sort of intellectual match was like talking to a jackass about the weather. "Tell me, what is more important, how I got in, or why I am here? Think, Luther, use that little peanut brain of yours and come up with something of substance."

Van Adams drew closer, his scowl giving way to his typical smugness. "You've heard the board has agreed to cut your position, is that it?" He strolled into the family room and dropped onto the recliner next to the one Mr. Howard sat in. "You knew this day would come."

"You act as if I should care."

Van Adams dismissed him with a condescending laugh. "What are you going to do now? Sit up in that big house of yours by yourself and write crappy books?"

"Why does that thought amuse you? I am old. I have an excuse. You are still young and yet, you stay in your big house by yourself and do nothing. You are but a fly born from your father's shit. A pest that buzzes around and annoys people."

Van Adams shook his head. "Sticks and stones, Professor, sticks and stones."

"You are right. My words could never hurt one as dense as you."

"The vote was unanimous by the way."

"The vote?"

Van Adams continued to smirk. "To let you go, the Board voted unanimously. They would have gotten rid of you years ago if not for Dean Harris. I'll never understand what she saw in a freak like you." His neck craned like a swans as his attention traveled to the carpet. "Did you drag dirt inside?"

"No, you did."

Van Adams slid off the chair and went to a knee. A hand brushed over the carpet. "This is wool carpet you bastard." He looked up with a snarl. "You'll pay for this."

"You brought the dirt, not I."

"Crazy son of a bitch." Van Adams stood. He pointed toward the door. "Get out of my house before I call the cops."

Mr. Howard slowly pushed out of the chair. "I will call the police."

"What?"

"To report a murder."

Van Adams appeared sucker punched, the blood draining from his face. "That's it. I'm getting my gun and if you come within five feet of me, I'll blow your goddamn head off." He hustled toward the hallway that led to the bedrooms.

Mr. Howard sprung from the ground to the ceiling. He scurried forward, passing Van Adams before he reached the hall. Van Adams stopped. His mouth hung open as he stared into the inverted face of the vampire.

"Jesus Christ." He took a step back. "What are you?"

"You are calmer than I expected." Mr. Howard dropped onto his feet. "That will not save you."

"Save me from what?"

"From the reality of your situation."

He stepped toward Van Adams, who backed away. "Ah, now you are cognizant of the danger. I see fear in your face, a paleness in your cheeks that rivals my own, widening of the eyes, sweat upon your brow, rapid breaths escaping from your lungs. You are frightened as you should be, the same way you have terrified countless women to satisfy your delusions of love. No one could satisfy you, Luther, for they could not provide the same affection you reserve for yourself. You are in love with your reflection, and because of this, you fail to see the beast that stares back at you. You created in your mind a canvas of happiness and color, but in truth, your life is the nightmare of a Bosch painting. You deserve pity, and yet, I am not in the mood to give it."

Van Adams raised a trembling fist. "Get out of my house, you crazy bastard."

A harsh transformation occurred within Mr. Howard, a warming of the blood that coursed through his veins, a closing of the doors which led to compassion, a long, dark passage emerging in the reaches of his mind, the road to his own personal hell. Like a young wolf that suddenly realizes its capacity to kill, he too became a messenger of death.

Van Adams's fist came down and his entire body quivered. "My God, what is happening to your... face? Your veins are... everywhere, and your eyes... blood red. God no, please, I'll do anything, just tell me what you want."

"What I want?"

Van Adams backed toward the front door. "You can have your job back. I'll talk to the board. They'll listen to me."

"You think I care about retaining my job? I can get a job at any university in the country, including your old alma mater."

Van Adams stopped, his jaw set. "Harvard would never hire you."

Van Adams's arrogance was predictable and amusing. Even in the face of death, he refused to believe anyone could rise to his station. "Luther, I do believe if locked in a room with Albert Einstein, you would maintain your air of superiority, even if the subject turned to quantum theory. But the difference between what you believe and what is the truth matters not. We are in the here and now, and our actions will shape the course of history."

Van Adams raced for the door. Mr. Howard leaped onto his back and placed him in a choke hold. They spun around, crashing into an end table. A porcelain lamp shattered. The battle moved toward the kitchen. Van Adams gasped as he struggled to stay conscious. He whipped around, slamming Mr. Howard against a large mirror. Glass splintered. Mr. Howard held on despite the stabbing pain in his lower back, surprised by Van Adams's strength.

"Uh-uh-uh," Van Adams muttered, his face the color of a beet. He dropped to his knees, shoulders heaving in a final effort to shake him, but Mr. Howard held fast. Van Adams's body relaxed and the guttural sounds ended. Releasing his hold, he eased Van Adams onto the floor. Mr. Howard wiped sweat from his brow onto the sleeve of his coat as he looked down at the unconscious Van Adams. The bastard put up more of a fight than he expected. "Now, Luther, let us take the next step toward your enlightenment."

***

Van Adams's eyes opened with a start, as if he'd been awakened by a hypnotists clap. He blinked several times while gazing around the room. He fought against the ropes that held him, and then suddenly stopped, his attention on Alicia tied to a chair across from him. He stared at her for a long time before shouting, "Mr. Howard, goddamn it!"

"You called?" Mr. Howard stepped out of a shadowed corner so Van Adams could see him.

Van Adams fought the restraints once more with a desperate growl. "Untie me at once!"

Mr. Howard glanced around the basement. "Based on your décor, I thought you were into bondage."

Van Adam's went pale and he appeared in need of a bucket. "You're not going to do anything… unnatural are you?"

"Do not worry, Luther," he said, walking to Alicia. He stood beside her and stroked her hair. "If I intended to do anything, it would be with her. I would rather die than take part in what you imagine."

His words seemed to put Van Adams at ease. Van Adams took a deep breath and blew the air out with a puff of his cheeks. "Who is she?"

Mr. Howard looked down at her. "She is beautiful, yes? And smart too. Smarter than you anyway, which is not saying much. I have seen dogs chasing Frisbees whose intelligence rivaled yours."

Van Adams grimaced. "Must you continue the verbal assaults?"

Mr. Howard left Alicia and strolled over to the table that held the wooden box. Opening the box, he raised the glistening needle for Van Adams to see.

Van Adams stared at the needle with wide eyes, as if sensing the means of his demise.

"What's that for?"

"The needle is an instrument of transformation. With this, your chrysalis shall form and from it, you will emerge a new being. The life you have known will no longer exist."

"Get away from me, you fucking creep show!"

"Our paths intersected for a reason. Call it fate or destiny, the word matters not. We both have parts to play in this drama. That is the way of things."

He unbuttoned a sleeve on his shirt and rolled the material past his elbow. "Please forgive me if I do this poorly. I have only done this once, and swore to never try again, but for you, I must make an exception."

Van Adams attempted to stand, but quickly sank back to the floor.

"Even now, you contemplate escaping. Fool. Not even God hears your call for help. You belong to me, a slave to my will."

Panic turned to anguish, tears welling in Van Adams's eyes. "Don't kill me."

Mr. Howard stepped before him. "I have no intention of killing you." He positioned the needle over a vein in his own arm and jabbed it under the skin. The vein burned as he wiggled it from side to side. When he extracted the needle, blood rushed to the surface of the puncture and trickled down the length of his forearm. Mr. Howard returned to the box, wiped the needle clean, and placed it inside. "Are you ready?" he said facing Van Adams.

"Get away, get away from me!"

He walked to Van Adams and leaned over his face. "Open your mouth."

Van Adams clenched his teeth so hard the muscles in his jaw flexed. He shook his head.

"Open your mouth," he said again, the words harsh and unforgiving.

Van Adams mumbled something.

"All right, have it your way." Mr. Howard pinched Van Adams's nose and held on as he jerked his head from side to side. After struggling for a while, his mouth opened for air. Mr. Howard thrust his arm against Van Adam's lips, his blood flowing past Van Adam's teeth and onto his tongue. "Swallow!"

Van Adam's spit blood into his face. "Fuck you!"

Mr. Howard pushed his arm over Van Adams' mouth. "Fight with all your strength, but in the end, you will swallow."

More blood dripped onto Van Adams's tongue, only this time, Mr. Howard seized Van Adams's jaw. He shoved his lower jaw upward to prevent him from opening his mouth. Van Adams gulped down the blood and Mr. Howard stepped back.

Van Adams met him with a sharp gaze. "You son of a bitch, what did you do to—?" His face contorted into a mask of fine wrinkles and beneath his skin, veins swelled and deepened in color. His entire body shook like a can of paint in a mixing machine. He became a blur, the violent shaking tipping the chair over. "Ah, ah, ah," he cried, as if suffering the start of impalement. Mr. Howard remembered the pain of his own transformation, a fire that sparked in the blood and spread slowly across every nerve. Van Adams flipped the chair from its side onto the back. His feet stamped upon the floor as if dancing over a mound of biting ants. "Stop it! Stop it! The pain, oh God, please stop it!"

The chair went back over and as he kicked and struggled, the chair started to rotate, faster and faster. Van Adams continued to scream, the wails bouncing off the basement walls. This continued for several minutes until the chair came to a stop and the cries faded away, replaced by the sound of Van Adams sobbing. Mr. Howard checked his watch. Half past noon: he was right on schedule.

"I'm dying."

"You are most certainly dying, yes," Mr. Howard answered, "but you are not dead yet. Your blood is turning to dust. Soon there will be nothing in your veins to sustain your life force."

"Jesus Christ, help me."

"You need new blood."

"Blood, yes, give me more blood."

Every newly turned vampire experienced *The Hunger*, the period when their old blood died and had to be replaced. For some, such as him, the stage lasted for many hours, while others, like Van Adams, required blood right away. Still, it was best to keep Van Adams waiting a while longer so his deficiency turned into a blood lust. When that happened, the Devil himself could not keep Van Adams from his prey.

Mr. Howard checked the ropes holding Alicia and patted her cheek to make certain she slept. He owed her that much. Van Adams twisted and fought against his restraints. He snapped at the air, a threatening growl rising from his chest. "Untie me, damn it!"

Mr. Howard retreated to a far corner and waited. Too soon, it was too soon to turn him loose. The overhead light reflected upon Van Adams, who grew paler by the minute. His eyes became red embers that glowed with rage.

"I must feed! I'm dying! Give me blood!" He managed to stand while still tied to the chair. Hunched over, he crept toward Alicia, fangs bared, blood-tinged drool dripping from the corners of his mouth. "Give her to me."

Mr. Howard rushed over. He grabbed Van Adams by the throat and shoved him backward. Van Adams crashed to the ground. He glared at Mr. Howard and snarled. "I'm dying, I tell you. It burns. I'm burning inside."

It wouldn't be long.

Van Adams flicked his tongue in and out of his mouth. He started to babble. "Fucking Howard, fucking trustees, fucking Mom, fucking Dad, fuckers the lot of them. Fuck, fuck, fuck. Jesus forgive me, no, I forgive you, no, I don't. Nah, nah, nah. This is bullshit, bullshit, bullshit. Help me. No, no, no. Mister mojo rising, rising, rising. All that glitters is gold. If the stores are all closed, fuck. La, la, la, I'm a god, I'm a god. Shit."

Van Adams looked straight at him. "You did this, Mr. Howard, you cock-sucking, son of bitch, piece of shit, mother fucker. You did this. Thank you, thank you, thank you. And for our first contestant, we have

Van Adams, fucked in the head, wished he was dead, la, la, la. Jack and Jill ran up the hill. I knocked Jack down, broke his goddamn crown, then fucked Jill ever after. I need blood, mother fucker! I'm God's burning bush, yeah, I'm on fire. Fuck. I'm really on fire. Help me, you fucker!"

Mr. Howard sighed. If Van Adams ever had a shot at going to Heaven, he just blew it, and it saddened him to think one day Van Adams might be his roommate in Hell.

He walked to him and leaned over. "I would rather kill you, however, that would not advance my plan, and so I will set you free. Enjoy what time you have left."

He slammed a fist against Van Adams's temple. Van Adams eyes rolled back and air whistled from his chest as if escaping a valve. He tumbled to the side, face smacking against the floor, and lay still.

"That should hold you for a few minutes," Mr. Howard said leaning over to untie the ropes that bound Van Adams' arms and legs. After rummaging through Van Adams' pockets for his keys, Mr. Howard went to Alicia, who continued to sleep. He knelt before her and bowed his head.

"Forgive me for what I must do." He stood, kissed her on the forehead, and turned away. At the stairs, he looked back into the room, a sickening feeling in his gut. He locked the door and hurried to his car.

***

As he drove home, Mr. Howard tried not to imagine what was happening inside Van Adams' basement. Van Adams, now a blood-starved vampire, would soon awaken, if he hadn't already, and when that occurred, there would be no controlling his fury. Poor Alicia. If only she had kept her visions to herself.

The traffic was light for a Sunday. He stayed on back roads, the sun glaring on the windshield, heat rising through the leather seat. Killgood needed to be home. But would he respond? Of course he would, he was a cop. He turned onto Overland Trail. The body of a deer lay bloodied in the road. Head out the window, he slowed as he passed. Was this the same deer he saw on his way to the cemetery? The sick feeling returned to his stomach.

It took fifteen minutes to make the drive from Van Adams's house to his own. Deep shadows played upon the slopes of the foothills. A northern breeze brought a hint of autumn. He parked in the garage and hurried into his bedroom, where darkness wrapped around him like a security blanket. He peeled out of his extra clothes and sat in front of the phone. After a deep breath, he dialed Killgood's home number.

"Hello?"

It was Susan. Damn, maybe he was out playing golf or something. "Susan, this is—"

"Mr. Howard, what a surprise. Are you looking for Chandler?"

"Yes, as a matter of fact. Is he in?"

"Hold on, I'll go get him."

"Thank you."

A minute passed. He could hear voices in the background and recognized them as Susan and Chandler. Chandler said, "Why is he calling me here?"

Soon after, the phone was picked up. "Hello, this is Killgood."

He'd answered using his cop voice and last name, which meant his mind was on the job, even though it was his day off. This was good. "Chandler, Mr. Howard here."

"What can I do for you?"

"I hope I am not interrupting anything important."

"I was watching the Broncos game."

Mr. Howard paused to collect his thoughts and to add drama to the moment. "Chandler, I must tell you something terrible."

A long silence followed before Killgood said, "You've had a vision?"

"Yes, and I do not believe this vision is of something that has already occurred."

"I see. Now you're seeing the future?"

"No, well... more like the present, I fear. I think what I saw is happening now."

Another long silence. "Right now, as we speak?"

"That is correct."

Killgood groaned softly. "All right, tell me what you saw."

"A young girl is being killed."

"At this very moment?"

"I believe so, yes."

Killgood took in a deep breath, the sound like a wet whistle as it passed his teeth. "That's not much to go on."

"I saw the killer. I saw him clearly. He is the man who killed Stephanie Coldstone."

"Are you serious?"

"I am serious about this, yes. He is killing a girl right now, inside his house."

"How do you know he was inside his house?"

"I have been there."

"Christ. You're totally serious."

"Yes."

"Who did you see?"

Mr. Howard smiled as he twirled the phone cord around a finger. "Luther Van Adams, assistant dean at the college."

"Shit, I don't know, Mr. Howard. That seems like a stretch to me. Are you sure about this?"

"The man has a reputation with young women, if you know what I mean."

"And he's killing this girl now?"

"She is a young woman. He called her Alicia."

"Alicia… fuck me."

"What is it?"

"The psychic, the one who led us to Stephanie's body, her name is Alicia Whitmore." There was a pause. "Where does Van Adams live?"

He gave Killgood the address. "I realize this is all sudden, but I do not control my visions."

"I understand," Killgood said.

"So you will have someone check it out?"

"I'll go myself."

Christ no, he hadn't meant for Killgood to go to Van Adams's house, and certainly not by himself. It was too dangerous for one man to face a newly turned vampire. A vision of hundreds of cops in dress uniform, black tape over their badges, saluting a flag-draped coffin came to him. Susan and the kids sat near the coffin, tears rolling down their cheeks.

"Chandler, you should not go alone."

Killgood's voice lowered to a whisper. "Listen, I'm still in the dog house over this shit with Ryan. The last thing I need is to call out the troops on a bogus murder investigation. I might as well turn in my badge now."

He could not persuade him to send in a marked unit first, and there was no way he could go to Van Adams's house to assist him. If Van Adams saw him, there was no telling what he might say. "Take your gun."

"Always."

"Your shotgun."

Several seconds passed. "You're serious about this?"

"Most definitely."

"Don't worry, I'll be fine."

"You will call to let me know."

"I'd better get going. With any luck, I'll be able to catch most of the second half of the game."

Mr. Howard hung up the phone. He would have said a prayer if he thought it would do any good. The hands on the clock ticked off the seconds. There wouldn't be long to wait.

Chapter 35

Killgood eyed the shotgun on the seat beside him. A part of him felt foolish for having brought it, while the other part was damn glad to have the shotgun for company. Nothing said hello like a round of twelve-gauge buckshot. If this assistant dean, this Van Adams, tried to give him any shit, he'd shoot first and take his chances with the grand jury. Having a throw down in his ankle holster was added insurance in case something went wrong.

But, what could go wrong? He'd done a quick check on Van Adams before leaving the house. How many Harvard educated, multi-millionaire serial killers were out there? To his knowledge, a big fat zero, all of which made Mr. Howard's vision sound absurd.

As he drove, Willard's voice filled his head. *You're going down the wrong road. Mr. Howard's the killer, I'm telling you.* Willard's insistence on Mr. Howard's guilt nagged at him. He didn't want to believe Mr. Howard was capable of murder and had no reason to, based on the flimsy evidence Willard offered, yet the idea proved difficult to dismiss. He had hoped Alicia Whitmore's involvement might help solve the case, but other than leading them to Stephanie's body, her visions were as cryptic as Mr. Howard's. Now, she might be in danger. Crap. This wasn't even his case anymore, yet here he was, driving off to find who knows what, missing the goddamn football game and all because Mr. Howard had a vision.

You'd better hope I find someone dead out there, Mr. Howard, or I'll never listen to another word from you.

He read his scribbled notes with the directions to Van Adams's house. For once, he wished he'd listened to his wife and bought a car with GPS. After taking two wrong turns and ending up in a field surrounded by cows, he finally arrived at a long dirt road that headed toward the foothills. The name Van Adams was stenciled on the mailbox. He took a deep breath and let it out. "All right, time to get this over with."

The afternoon sun swung westward, rays of light beaming down through the leaves of aspen and oak trees on either side of the road. In a couple of months, the trees would stand barren, piles of red and yellow leaves littering the ground. He remembered Reann helping him rake leaves when she was a little girl. He raked them into big piles and before he could toss them into a trash bag, she came running, and dove into the piles with a squeal. Odd that he should think of that now.

A soft whistle escaped his throat as the large house came into view. What was he going to say to Van Adams if there was nothing wrong? Sorry to interrupt your day, Mr. Uppity Millionaire, but a psychic said you were busy murdering a girl. His name? It's Mr. Howard. Do you know him? You do? Great. Now about that murder. What's that you say? You're going to sue my ass for trespassing and invasion of your privacy? Why, thank you, sir. It's not as if I need my job or anything.

He parked the car and climbed out. "I feel like a total ass," he said, walking up the porch steps. At the top, he froze, his gaze on the door standing ajar.

Shit.

He ran back to his car and grabbed his police radio and the shotgun.

Why is the door open? Rich bastards don't leave their doors hanging open.

He gave the door a gentle shove and peeked inside the house. A Tiffany lamp lay shattered on the entry tile. He took two steps and spotted a splintered mirror on the wall in the dining room. "Jesus Christ." The shotgun clicked as he racked in a shell.

This is bad. This is really fucking bad.

Blood hammered through his veins. Sweat popped out along his brow. He turned on the police radio and brought it to his mouth. "Baker 313."

"Go ahead, Baker 313."

The dispatcher responded. "Baker 313, I'm at 2932 Stoltey Lane on a signal 51. Send backup."

"Ten-four Baker 313. Do you need those units code 3?"

Code 3 meant responding with lights and siren. He saw no reason for that yet. The patrol units would drive like wild men if they thought he was in danger. "Negative dispatch, not at this time."

"Ten-four. Charlie 112 and Charlie 115 copy call. Charlie 112 has the sheet. Signal 51 at 2932 Stoltey Lane. You'll be assisting Detective Killgood."

He crammed the radio into his back pocket and crept into the family room. His eyes narrowed at the sight of dirt spread across the tan carpet. Inside the dining room, he stared at the shattered mirror.

What the hell is going on?

He looked at his watch. The patrol units wouldn't arrive for another ten minutes. Should he check the rest of the house? No, better wait until backup arrives. A high-pitched scream carried from behind a closed door. Part animal, part human, unlike anything he'd heard before.

"Son of a bitch."

Another cry, followed by a deep growling.

"Shit." He ripped the radio from his pocket and brought it to his mouth. "Baker 313, close the channel and send those units code 3."

"Ten-four Baker 313. Attention all units, the channel is closed for emergency traffic only. Charlie 112, Charlie 115, you are authorized to go code 3."

A scream rolled up from behind the door. Killgood checked his watch again. He edged toward the door, shotgun raised. With one hand, he turned the knob.

Locked.

They'll never make it in time.

Sweat trickled down his temples. His heart pounded so hard his chest ached. What to do? What to do? A woman may be getting killed.

Damn it.

He reared back and kicked the door as hard as he could. The wooden frame cracked, but the door held. Another kick and the door snapped open. Stairs led down into a basement. A light burned inside the room, but he couldn't see much beyond the last step.

Where's my backup?

He considered waiting until the patrol units arrived. The growling returned, wet and threatening.

"Fuck."

Swallowing his fear, he took a step, his legs wobbling. Two steps down and more of the basement came into view. Another step and he paused. Long streaks of red paint rained down one wall.

That's not paint. It's blood.

Another step. He stared wide-eyed into the dimly lit room. Something bloody and torn lay on the floor. One arm, legs, but no head.

"Holy shit." He glanced over his shoulder, waiting, hoping for help to arrive. Nothing. No distant wail of sirens to assure him everything would be all right. He was on his own.

Killgood slinked farther into the basement, back pressed against a wall, shotgun elevated in trembling hands. He reached the bottom step and hesitated, resisting the urge to run like a frightened boy from a bully. Images of Susan and the kids flashed through his mind. Why did he take Mr. Howard's phone call? He could be safe at home, watching the football game, and eating nachos.

When he took the last step, it felt as if he had stepped into his own grave. He inched closer to the body. A severed head lay nearby. Blood streaked short black hair and spread over the face. Acid scaled the walls of his throat. Mr. Howard was right. The body belonged to Alicia Whitmore.

A threatening growl made him spin around. Something approached, part animal, part human, white skin, the color of wind-driven snow, fierce eyes that glowed red. Blood dripped from an open mouth.

It's a fucking zombie.

The man leaped toward him, covering the distance so fast, he barely had time to react. His shoulder recoiled, the shotgun booming as if someone set off a mortar shell next to his head. The monster fell back and howled, a hand pressed against its left shoulder. The hand came down, exposing a missing chunk of flesh and bone at the shoulder blade. The creature snarled. "You've come to kill me, and though you may try, in the end, it is you who will die."

He aimed from the hip and fired. Shotgun pellets ripped into the right thigh of the killer, blood spraying from the wound. The blow knocked the beast onto his stomach.

The zombie or man, or whatever he was, lay motionless. Killgood took a step forward and froze, his throat constricting with sudden fear as the beast pushed off the ground and stood.

"You are powerless against me."

"Let's see how you do with a round to the chest." Killgood raised the gun to rack in a new round. The monster exploded forward and slammed into his shoulder. Killgood hit the wall, a stabbing pain racing along his spine. Blood-stained fangs flashed against the gray backdrop. Killgood thrust the shotgun upward, the stock crashing against the beast's jaw. Arms crushed around his ribs.

Killgood screamed as a fire raced along his spine. The shotgun flew from his hands. He was elevated off the ground, kicking and clawing at the air and then hurled across the room. His face slammed against the floor and he rolled several times. He tried to sit up, but collapsed onto his back. The metallic taste of blood flooded his mouth.

From the shadows, the pallid face of what resembled a man appeared. "I said you would die, but you wouldn't listen. I might have shown mercy and killed you quickly, but now I will take my time. First, I'll tear off your flesh, then your arms and legs. I'll only rip out one of your eyes. I want you to see what comes after that."

Killgood slowly lifted his head to stare into the glowing red eyes of the beast. "Fuck you."

The killer reared back, a deep growl bursting from his chest. Killgood closed his eyes.

"Freeze, mother fucker," a voice shouted followed by four loud pops.

Another growl tore through the room followed by several more pops.

A hand gripped his shoulder. "Detective Killgood, are you all right?"

He opened his eyes. Officer Couch leaned over him, a worried look in his eyes. Killgood smiled. "Never felt better."

Chapter 36

Willard grimaced as he drove along the interstate. It had been one of the worst days of his life with the promise of getting worse. The shit started when Doris telephoned and woke him from a dream of sex with the Siamese twins.

"Why are you at home?" she asked, voice whiny.

"Where else would I be?"

"Damn you."

"What'd I say?"

"Didn't it ever occur to you to come visit your sick wife in the hospital?"

"Must have slipped my mind."

Her silence spoke volumes.

"Jesus Christ, Doris, I can't drop everything just because you had a little surgery."

"A little surgery?" Her voice elevated to an ear-splitting level. "I had open-heart surgery, you selfish bastard. You don't even care if I die, do you?"

He sighed while debating how to answer. "I don't want you to die. If you died, who would do the laundry?"

"Get your ass up here."

"I'll try, Doris."

"I hate you."

"How can you hate me when I'm so lovable?"

The conversation ended with her slamming down the receiver.

Against his better judgment, he dragged himself into the shower to get ready. Maybe I should bring her flowers, he thought, or a box of Ding Dongs. He laughed. Despite all of her faults, Doris was always good for a chuckle. After cleaning up and getting dressed, he sat down at his desk and turned on the TV. While the football game played, he opened up the swinger's website. A smile crept over his mouth when he saw someone had left him an email.

Hey Swinging Dick,

You really are a jerk. You treat people like crap and you're not the stud you think you are. Honestly, I've had better sex with men who were impotent. But as much as I hate to say it, I kind of had fun with you. It was different. I dreamed last night of flying around naked. Anyway, despite your shitty attitude, I would consider hooking up with you again. Think about it.

Yours truly,
Ride Me Like a Shetland Pony.

He started to type in a reply when the phone rang. "Damn it, Doris, give me a break." He snatched the receiver off its cradle and in a gruff voice said, "Yeah."

"Willard, it's Killgood."

"Why are you calling me on my day off?"

"You need to get to Fort Collins right away."

He stared at the email on his monitor and shook his head. "Look, I have—"

"Something's happened with the Coldstone case."

If he didn't show up at the hospital soon, Doris would be pissed. She might be mad enough to have another heart attack. "It's not my case, remember?"

"We arrested a suspect."

An image of Mr. Howard in handcuffs came to him. "Who is it?"

"You need to get up here."

He closed the swinger's website on his computer with a sigh. "Give me the goddamn address."

When he backed out of the drive, he spotted a large man placing an envelope against the front door. The man turned around and they made eye contact. He went ashen before hustling down the sidewalk. Willard considered rousting him, but decided to blow it off. Whatever the man delivered could wait until he returned from meeting Killgood.

As he drove north, weaving around slower cars, Willard stewed on the day's events. *I probably should have called Doris to let her know what was going on. Nah, she'd never believe me. Oh well, it's not like she's going anywhere. Maybe I'll pick up a little bouquet of flowers. Something simple and cheap. With any luck, she'll be asleep when I arrive, and I can leave them in her room with a card. But what to write on it? I know, I'll put, get well soon, lard ass.* He chuckled out loud as he cut off an elderly couple in a Subaru.

Black and green storm clouds blew in from the west, swirling across the mountains and onto the plain with surprising speed. Fat drops of rain began to splatter against the windshield followed by an assault of pea-sized hail. Brake lights glowed red against the sudden gloom. Traffic slowed almost to a stop. His cell phone started to ring. He checked the number. "Damn bitch, won't give me a minute of peace." He debated answering before pushing the talk button. "Hello."

"Where in the hell are you?"

"Killgood called. He needs me in Fort Collins. Something about the Coldstone case."

"Liar."

"I'm not lying, Doris."

"Bullshit. Lying is the only thing you do well anymore."

Score one for the fat bitch.

"I'll try to swing by the hospital later. Are the kids coming home tonight?"

"They're probably already home."

"Good, good," he said, watching the dark clouds tear apart. Patches of blue sky emerged as the storm blew past. "I miss having the kids to yell at."

"You don't miss me."

"I'm not sure how to answer that, Doris."

"You just did," she said and hung up.

He tossed down the phone. His marriage was a joke, but he'd never divorce Doris until Margo turned eighteen. Custody battles were a pain in the ass, not that he would fight her for the kids. What concerned him was the possibility of paying child support every month, which he knew would go toward buying Doris food. She could stuff her pig face on her own dime.

It was after five when he arrived at the address Killgood provided. A dozen patrol cars were parked out front along with several unmarked cars, a fire truck, and an ambulance. "What the hell?" he said, pulling to the side of the road to park behind one of the unmarked cars. He climbed out of the car, slipped on a jacket, smoothed his necktie, and strolled toward the entrance.

Four uniformed cops lingered near the front door. A big, square-headed cop with Popeye arms acknowledged him by jutting out his chin. "Can I help you?"

He reached inside his jacket and produced his badge. "Willard, State Police. Where can I find Killgood?"

Square Head gestured toward the door. "Check the basement."

Willard passed the cops and stepped inside the house. The stench of blood hung in the air. Someone had died, that was pretty damn obvious. Men in suits stood in small groups talking. Detectives. Another man wearing a navy windbreaker knelt beside a broken lamp and dusted it for prints.

The dining room mirror is shattered and there's dirt all over the rug. There was a struggle. Maybe a break-in.

An older detective watched him approach. He broke from the group of men he was talking with and walked over. "You Willard?"

"That's right."

"You'll find Killgood in the basement." He pointed at an open door.

Willard nodded. "What happened here?"

The cop removed his glasses and massaged the bridge of his nose. "Killgood caught the man who murdered Stephanie Coldstone."

"That so?" Willard said and frowned.

"The bastard's paler than snow and growls like a wolf. Don't know if he's a man or animal."

This news turned his frown into a smile.

Maybe they did catch Mr. Howard.

"Thanks, I'll find Killgood."

Willard hesitated outside the basement door, his gaze on the broken door frame. He examined the lock for a moment before starting down the basement stairs. Killgood stood with three suits. They talked in low voices. Killgood spotted him and waved him over. "Glad you're here."

"What the hell is going on?"

Willard moved alongside him. He squinted at the body of a woman on the floor. She was a piece of ground beef, torn and shredded almost beyond recognition. He looked at Killgood. "Who is she?"

Killgood motioned toward a severed head. Willard took a step toward the head and stopped. A sharp tremor tore through his gut as he recognized the blood-soaked face. He turned to Killgood. "Alicia Whitmore?"

Killgood nodded. "We don't know how the son of a bitch found out about her involvement in the case."

"The son of a bitch? You mean Mr. Howard, right?"

A puzzled expression settled over Killgood's face. "Mr. Howard helped catch the bastard."

The pain in his stomach became white hot as if a blade twisted through his intestines. "Bullshit."

"He called me this afternoon and said he had a vision of this guy Van Adams killing Alicia. Van Adams is the assistant dean at the University. Mr. Howard's been to his house before, so he was able to give me directions. I drove out here to investigate and discovered Van Adams in the basement. The fucker went insane. I managed to put a couple of rounds in him, but he kept coming. If the patrol units hadn't arrived, I'd be dead too."

"You're telling me Mr. Howard had a vision that led you to Van Adams' house, and when you arrived, you found Van Adams in the basement with Alicia's body?"

"That's what I'm saying." Killgood reached into a pocket. He pulled out a plastic evidence bag and tossed it to Willard. "That locket belonged to Stephanie Coldstone. We found the locket here."

Willard tossed the bag back to Killgood. "I'm not buying it."

"Not buying what?"

Willard pitched the necklace back. "Any of it. There was a struggle upstairs. Who fought? Van Adams and Alicia Whitmore?"

"It's possible."

"Yeah right. Tell me, when you arrived, you found Van Adams in the basement with Alicia, right?"

"That's right. He was covered in blood."

Willard walked over to a wall and stared at one of the bondage photographs. "Nice guy."

"Apparently, he has a reputation with young coeds."

Willard glanced over his shoulder. "Don't most professors?" He approached Killgood. "The basement door was locked when you arrived correct?"

Killgood's forehead creased into a series of fine wrinkles. "Yeah, I had to kick it in"

"The door can only be unlocked with a key. Did you find a key on Van Adams?"

Killgood shook his head.

"Then someone locked him inside the basement with Alicia's body."

"Wait a minute. You weren't here when I confronted this asshole. He's a lunatic. I'm telling you, the patrolmen and I had to shoot the fucker several times to stop him. And the bastard still didn't die. They've taken him to the hospital for surgery."

"Maybe he's on PCP."

"What's your point? He was found with a murder victim, covered in her blood, and there's evidence he may have killed Stephanie Coldstone."

Willard gestured at the pictures behind him. "This crime scene has been staged."

"You're out of your mind." Killgood presented his back and shook his head. "You're determined to prove Mr. Howard had something to do with this and it's blinded you to the truth. Mr. Howard is a real psychic. He led us to Van Adams through a vision." He turned to face him. "Keep digging, Detective, and you'll soon find that you've dug your own grave. Every cop in this room thinks Van Adams is guilty."

"The dirt upstairs?"

"Crime scene boys think the dirt may be from Stephanie's grave."

"Guess Van Adams doesn't believe in vacuuming. Did you find the necklace in plain view?"

"On top the table over there."

A flash of white light filled the air as a crime scene officer took a photograph. Black spots floated in front of Willard's eyes for several seconds. He looked down at Alicia's body.

What a waste.

"What can you tell me about Van Adams? He obviously has money."

"His family's worth several billion."

"Anything else?"

"He graduated from Harvard and has worked here at the college over a decade."

Willard tapped his chin. "I don't recall many serial killers coming out of the Ivy League."

"There's always a first."

"Do Van Adams and Mr. Howard have a history?"

Killgood appeared confused. "A history?"

"Is there bad blood between them?"

"I don't know and I don't care. Van Adams killed Alicia, not Mr. Howard." Killgood came face-to-face with him. "Even now, with a killer caught in the act, and all kinds of evidence, you refuse to admit you could be wrong. I feel sorry for you, Detective, I really do."

"Don't feel sorry for me," Willard said. "I'm not the one who's going to look like a fool when Mr. Howard gets arrested for these crimes."

Killgood pointed toward the stairs. "You're out of your jurisdiction and no longer working this case. Get your ass out of my crime scene."

"I work for the state, remember? So my jurisdiction is pretty much in your face, asshole. Enjoy your moment of glory. I'll be in touch."

"No, you won't. Now get the hell out of here."

Willard glanced at Alicia's mutilated body, grimaced, and headed for the stairs.

Back inside his car, he sat staring at the house. The sun edged toward the distant mountains and long shadows stretched across the yard. *They're all fools. Mr. Howard set this entire thing up. After Killgood told him Alicia helped us find Stephanie, Mr. Howard knew he'd have to get rid of her or risk exposure. She'd already said the killer was an older man with long silver hair, just like Mr. Howard. I'll bet he has an ax to grind with Van Adams. It wouldn't surprise me if Van Adams tried to get him fired.*

He smacked a palm against the dash. "That one cop said Van Adams looked like a monster with pale skin and he..." Willard touched his temples and grimaced as a thought rolled through his head. "That fucking son of a bitch. It's true... it's really true."

Chapter 37

Mr. Howard retrieved a bottle of Dom from the basement. He poured a glass and mixed in the last vile of Stephanie's blood. Word of Van Adams arrest put him in a celebratory mood. Receiving the news from Killgood, made it all the better. He stirred the blood in the champagne and retired to the living room. Sinking into a leather recliner, he let out a deep sigh. For the first time in weeks, he could relax. Based on what Killgood told him, the cops considered the case against Van Adams airtight. The thought of Van Adams writhing in pain at the hospital made him smile.

Not the kind of life you expected, eh, Luther?

Of course, the court would rule Van Adams insane and order him committed to a mental institution. In a few months, when he needed to replenish Alicia's blood, and was unable to do so because of his restraints, Van Adams would die a slow, painful death, his body withering like an autumn leaf until, at last, crumbling to dust. That is if the hospital staff hadn't already killed him by exposing him to sunlight.

Thinking about Alicia took his smile away. He wasn't surprised when Killgood described the condition of her body and only hoped she didn't wake during the attack. Too many people had suffered on his account. The telephone rang.

"Hello."

"I heard what happened. Are you all right?"

"Jennifer, how nice to hear your voice. Yes, I am fine."

"Thank God. Can you believe the news about Van Adams? And to think I used to sit alone with him in my office. Jesus."

"We all can be fooled, I think."

"But not you," she said, her voice becoming softer like a lover whispering promises across a bed. "Is it true you had a vision that led the police to him?"

"Where are you getting your information?"

"Chief Kaufman called."

"Ah, yes, Chief Kaufman, head of the campus police. The world is a safer place with him on duty."

"Do I detect sarcasm?"

He took a sip of his champagne. "To answer your question, it is true. I had a vision of Van Adams with a young woman."

"I heard about the girl. What a tragedy."

"Indeed."

"Well, the good news is," she said, becoming suddenly cheerful, "I heard that the Board won't cut your position now. With Van Adams gone, you can stay at the University for as long as you like."

He'd anticipated this outcome, but for some reason, found the news unfulfilling. If his sole purpose in framing Van Adams was to save his job, and Alicia had died so he could keep teaching, he would have felt even more selfish than he already did. "I appreciate everything you have done for me."

There was a pause. "I can do more, you know. Much more."

He remembered her soft body moving against his and the warmth that radiated from between her legs. "We should discuss that on another night. I am tired, bone tired, and need sleep."

"I thought you slept during the day?"

"Normally that is true, but my vision kept me awake on this day."

"Yes, I can see how it might. Get some rest and we'll talk more tomorrow."

"Thank you, Jennifer. Good night."

When she hung up, he pressed against the cool leather of his chair. The thought of being with her would haunt him throughout the night. He got up to fetch his copy of Nietzsche's *Beyond Good and Evil*. The buzzer went off by the front door to announce someone at the gate.

Who could be visiting at this hour?

He walked to the door and pressed the button. "Yes?"

"It's Willard. We need to talk."

Had his wife received the disc and watched his performance with the dwarf? "It is late, Detective. Can't this wait until tomorrow?"

"It's about Van Adams and Alicia Whitmore."

"Van Adams and who?"

"Don't pretend you don't know her, Professor."

He hesitated. "Alicia... oh yes, she is the psychic woman. What about her?"

"You know she's dead," Willard said. "You called Killgood and told him Van Adams was murdering her."

"No, I called Killgood and told him Van Adams was killing a young woman he called Alicia. Seeing as I never met this psychic, there is no way for me to have known her identity."

"Oh really?" Willard said. "Killgood already told me he mentioned Alicia to you after she helped us locate Stephanie Coldstone's body. After you kept Stephanie a prisoner in your house to extract information you used to make us believe you're a psychic."

Well played, Detective, but your move comes too late to change the outcome of our contest. "Detective, I am very tired and would—"

"Did Van Adams kill her in a blood lust? Did The Hunger drive him insane?"

Mr. Howard's jaw set. Obviously, Willard was unaware of the sex video or he wouldn't show up with questions about Van Adams, but the references to vampirism concerned him. Had he made the connection? Did Willard realize he was, in fact, a vampire?

"I read your book, Professor, the one about vampires. The clues are there for someone willing to decipher them."

Christ, it's as if he can read my thoughts. Can he also anticipate my future actions? My fool-proof plan is suddenly not so fool-proof, it seems.

"I will unlock the gate." He pressed the button to open the gate and waited. A car rumbled up the road and stopped outside. He opened the front door before Willard rang the bell. "Good evening, Detective." Mr. Howard stepped aside and motioned for him to enter.

He closed the door and took a position in front of Willard. "Would you care to sit down? I can fix you a drink."

"You don't seriously think I'd trust you to make me a drink?"

"No, I suppose not." He went to shove his hands inside his pockets and Willard jumped back. "A bit on edge, are we? They have medicine for that."

"You killed Stephanie Coldstone."

"And you expect to prove this?"

"No."

"Why did you refer to my book when talking about Van Adams?"

Willard gazed around the house. "That's why he killed her, isn't it? You learned Alicia was helping us and had to stop her before she exposed you. So, you kidnapped Alicia and took her to Van Adams's house. Why not kill two birds with one stone? She'd be dead, Van Adams would get arrested, and the real killer walks. The perfect plan."

"Not so perfect if someone like you could figure it out."

Willard met him with a cold stare. "You knew no one would believe me when I told them you're a vampire."

"Is that what you think?"

"Cut the bullshit, Professor."

"Very well. What is your intention? You must have a reason for coming to my home?"

Willard reached inside his jacket. He drew a pistol. "Someone has to stop you."

"I have lived four centuries. I have witnessed the horror of war and the rise of technology. During the course of my life, the world has turned from a love of God to a love of gold. I have known kings and beggars, saints and sinners, but I have never known anyone quite like you. Your dogged pursuit is to be applauded. Your use of logic admired. But if you believe I will let you kill me, you are the biggest of fools."

The gun shook in Willard's hand. "Yeah, I figured that's what you'd say."

"And still you have come."

"Like I said, someone has to stop you."

He focused on the barrel of the gun. "Are you certain a gun will kill me?"

Willard smirked. "According to your book it will."

"Ah, yes, my book. I forgot you knew how to read. Very well, shoot me."

"What?"

"You heard me. Shoot."

Willard's left eye closed. A vein that snaked down the side of his neck started to twitch. "This is for your victims."

The gun went off with a boom. Mr. Howard staggered, his chest on fire, but remained upright. He examined a smoldering hole in his shirt. "Direct hit in the heart. Impressive shooting."

Willard stared at the gun in disbelief. "What the fuck?"

"Did you really think I would write instructions for how to kill me?"

Willard aimed again and fired.

A flash of fire. Flesh tore apart where the bullet ripped into his cheek. Bone exploded as the shell exited behind his ear. A heavy pressure, as if his head were being crushed in a vice, spread across his skull. Blood filled his mouth with a metallic taste. He touched a hand to the wound. "That may leave a scar."

Willard turned to run. Mr. Howard flew past to block his escape. The detective raised the gun and Mr. Howard ripped it from his hand. "Son of a bitch."

Mr. Howard laughed. "Yes, you are most likely the son of a bitch." He pulled back the slide to unload the gun and pushed the switch to drop the ammunition clip. "Take it," he said, handing the empty pistol back to Willard.

Willard stared at the gun for a moment before snatching it back.

"Do not worry, Detective. I have no intention of killing you. The last thing I need is a dead cop in my house. Besides, you cannot hurt me, and you know it. Tell the world what I am and see what happens. You will soon find yourself locked away with Van Adams."

Willard slipped the gun back into its holster. "You figure this is the end, but you're wrong. I'll never stop coming after you."

Mr. Howard walked to the door and held it open. "I tremble at the thought. Now leave before I change my mind and decide to tear you apart."

Willard stomped past with a scowl. He slammed the door on his car and tore out of the driveway, gravel spitting. Mr. Howard waited until he drove through the gate and closed the door. His chest and face ached where he had been shot. He stared at his palm, red with Stephanie's blood, and was glad he couldn't see his reflection.

Chapter 38

Willard's heart raced as he drove home. He couldn't believe how stupid he'd been to trust Mr. Howard's book. Of course he wouldn't tell anyone how to kill him. But there had to be a way to kill a vampire and he was determined to find out how.

Then it hit him. Mr. Howard was a vampire. A *real* fucking vampire who could've killed him. Jesus H. Christ. He shivered despite the August heat while remembering what Van Adams had done to Alicia Whitmore.

He arrived home to a dark house. For once, he wished someone was awake to talk to, even if it was Doris. He needed to try and explain what he'd just experienced. He grabbed a bottle of Jack Daniels from the pantry and retreated to his office, where he spent an hour drinking and researching how to kill vampires.

The more he read, the more he became convinced that there must be something to the old methods. If he could break into Mr. Howard's home while he slept and drive a stake through his heart, then maybe, just maybe, he could end the nightmare. The bastard had to die, that much was certain.

When he tired of researching vampires, he opened the swinger's website. After reading the message from Ride me like a Shetland Pony again, he fired off a quick response asking if she would like to get together. He next checked the profile page of the Siamese twins and sent them a message asking if they would also like to hook up. A smile flickered over his lips as he imagined himself engaged in a ménage a trios with the dwarf and the Siamese twins. But would it be a ménage a trios or did the Siamese twins count as two people? Maybe the dwarf only counted as half a person. This thought stayed with him as he turned off the computer.

He staggered into the hallway, stopped outside the kids' rooms, and peeked inside. The sight of them asleep in their beds filled him with a sense of satisfaction. Maybe tomorrow he would take them to the hospital to see their mother. Hell, after surviving Mr. Howard, he could survive a few minutes in a room with Doris.

He stumbled into his bedroom. The whisky made his head spin. He nearly fell over as he stripped down to his boxers. He collapsed onto the bed and quickly drifted into a deep sleep.

***

He awoke and tried to move. Something cold and hard restrained his wrists. Willard opened his eyes and looked up. His wrists were handcuffed to the headboard, and ankles bound. He immediately thought of Mr. Howard. Had the vampire come to finish him off? He raised his head and shouted, "Dave, Margo!"

Nothing.

He tried again. Still no answer.

The bedroom door creaked open. Dave and Margo crept into the room with grim expressions. "What in the hell is going on?" he shouted. Dave turned on the television on the dresser. "Take these goddamn handcuffs off me."

Dave slipped a disc into the DVD player. After several seconds, the screen came to life. Willard's jaw dropped at the image of him fucking the dwarf. He turned to his kids. "Where did you get this?"

They remained silent.

"Where did you get this video!"

"How could you do this to Mom?" Dave asked. "While she's been lying in the hospital, you were out screwing some midget?"

He struggled against the handcuffs. Steel rattled against wood. "You don't understand what's happening here. Your mother hasn't always been good to me. I've tried to help her, I really have, but—"

"Shut up!" Margo screamed her eyes wild and glassy with tears. "We've seen the way you help people and we're sick of it."

He tried to yank his hands out of the cuffs, but they dug into his flesh like dull razor blades. "Listen to me. This isn't what you think it is. I've been framed. Now, turn me loose and we'll talk."

Dave walked to the dresser and picked up something. He returned with an opened box of Ding Dongs. "We're done talking to you, asshole." Dave climbed onto his chest.

"Get off me, damn it!"

Margo approached the bed with one of his leather belts. She snapped the folded belt across his thighs and he flinched. "Stop hitting me, you little shit!"

"I love you, Dad," she said, whacking him again. "This is because I love you." Again and again, she whipped the belt over his legs.

His thighs burned.

Dave pinched his nose. "Open your mouth!"

"What?"

Dave crammed a Ding Dong past his teeth and reached for another. Willard sputtered and gagged as the sweet cake filled his throat. Dave shoved another Ding Dong into his mouth. "Sumo wrestling, huh? Well I'm going all sumo on your ass!"

Willard twisted and fought against his son and the handcuffs, while trying to spit out the Ding Dongs. Dave mashed another one down his throat and turned to Margo. "Get me the tape."

She grabbed a roll of duct tape from the dresser and tossed it to him. Dave ripped off a long piece and pressed the tape over Willard's mouth. "Now the bag." She handed him a plastic bag and Dave worked the bag over his father's head, duct taping it around his neck. Willard tried to scream, but nothing came out. For a moment he was a boy again, locked inside a toy chest.

They're killing me. The little shits are killing me.

Dave climbed off his chest. He joined Margo beside the bed. They stood side by side holding hands. White light flashed before Willard's eyes. Blood hammered through his skull. On the television, the dwarf flew overhead like a circus performer. He would reach for her. He would bring her against his chest and everything would be all right. Ménage a trios. Siamese twins. Fuck.

Chapter 39

Evening rain came down over the campus. Raindrops pattered against the roof. Water pooled on sidewalks captured the reflection of lamplight. Mr. Howard turned from the window and walked to the podium. His students waited patiently for him to begin. He thumbed through his textbook.

"Ah yes, we were about to discuss Caribbean Voodoo and the spirits of love, a subject most of you should find interesting. For those who remain bored, I will change their name to the spirits of sex. This will please you, yes?"

A soft chuckle rose throughout the classroom. "You find the subject of sex amusing?"

"Only when taught by someone as old as you," Spriggs shouted.

Mr. Howard reached for his reading glasses and put them on. "I may be old, Mr. Spriggs, but unlike you, when I make love, it is to a woman and not my hand."

He ran his fingers over a page in the textbook and started to read. "Among the family of spirits, the Erzulie were the most common, and among the Erzulie, the most important spirit is Erzulie Freda. She wears three wedding rings, which symbolize her marriage to the serpent spirit Damballa, the sea spirit Agwe, and the warrior spirit Ogoun."

The door opened and Killgood slipped into the room. He took his familiar position against the far wall and waited.

My business with the police is finished and yet still he comes. Perhaps he's here about Willard. Why didn't he wait until my class had ended? Did he come to thank me for making him a hero? Probably not.

Mr. Howard acknowledged him by dipping his head and continued with his lesson. He lectured on Voodoo ceremonies and explained how the spirits took possession of the participants and spoke through them. He went on to discuss the association of Voodoo with black magic, or Hoodoo, and Satanism. The class appeared enraptured when he explained how certain Voodoo sorcerers were said to create zombies. When the bell rang, students rushed toward the door.

"Interesting lecture," Killgood said, approaching the podium. "Voodoo, zombies, sounds like something straight out of a movie."

Mr. Howard took off his reading glasses and slipped them into his shirt pocket. "That is why my class is popular. It exposes impressionable minds to infinite possibilities."

Killgood stopped several feet away, his expression solemn, eyes moving back and forth as if seeing Mr. Howard for the first time. "Infinite possibilities such as the reality of vampires?"

Mr. Howard retreated to his desk where he gathered loose papers into a pile. "Something like that, yes." He looked up and forced himself to smile. "So, Chandler, what do I owe the pleasure of your visit? Are you here on official police business?"

"Did you hear what happened to Willard?"

Mr. Howard struggled to hide his enthusiasm. If he still had the body of a human he knew his cheeks would flush. Of course he knew what had happened to Willard. He read the article on the Internet a half-dozen times. "Strange what children are capable of these days. Imagine, killing your own parent. A tragedy. Have the investigators pieced together a motive?"

Killgood jammed his hands inside his pockets. "From what I've heard, Willard would never have been nominated for father of the year."

"Oh?"

"Apparently he treated his wife and kids like shit."

Mr. Howard stashed the papers inside his attaché. "And for this he was killed?"

Killgood's left eyebrow arched. "Don't you know?"

"Should I?"

"Someone filmed him having sex with a dwarf and dropped the disc off at his house. Willard's kids found the disc. Apparently watching their father with the dwarf drove them over the edge. Now they're in jail for God knows how long."

"Dwarfs are best left to fairytales."

Killgood didn't crack a smile and a nervous flutter rose in Mr. Howard's stomach. "I should not make jokes. A man has died."

"Someone set him up."

Mr. Howard closed his eyes and took a deep breath. His carefully spun tapestry of lies was coming unraveled. "Do you have evidence of this?"

"A private investigator, Jason Stanis, has gone missing. Does the name ring a bell?"

He opened his eyes. "Should it?"

"Come, Professor, I can't believe a man of your intelligence doesn't see it. The sex tape, Willard's death, the PIs disappearance all happening around the same time are more than coincidences."

Mr. Howard went over to the window. He pressed his hands against the glass to frame the shimmering moon. The rain ended and the moon bathed the campus in ghost light. "Why would someone want to blackmail Detective Willard?"

"I was hoping you might know."

"What does your experience tell you?" Mr. Howard asked, turning around. He strolled to his desk and sat.

Killgood folded his arms over his chest. "Perhaps Willard was close to solving a case and someone needed to stop him."

"Or perhaps the dwarf has a jealous boyfriend."

"I doubt that. Have you ever seen a naked dwarf?"

"No," Mr. Howard said, "and just the thought of it makes me nauseated."

Killgood did smile at this briefly before his stony countenance returned. "Willard may have been an asshole, but he was a good cop. He saw things others missed."

Mr. Howard nodded. "He had passion for his job."

"Willard thought you killed Stephanie Coldstone," Killgood said without emotion.

Mr. Howard straightened in his chair. Killgood had come to arrest him. No. On what evidence? Then what was it? To kill him? Killgood.

His friend? Not likely. "I seem to remember you coming to my house with similar concerns."

"Willard put together an interesting case against you."

"But not interesting enough to take to the District Attorney."

The muscles on the sides of Killgood's face flexed as his jaw set. "You do know your way around the law, Professor."

Mr. Howard considered the detective's demeanor. Whatever friendship they enjoyed faded like a winter sun across a gray and desolate plain. "Do you believe I killed Stephanie Coldstone?"

"It doesn't matter what I believe, only what I can prove." Killgood walked to a chair and sat. He slouched in the seat. "I lied to Willard," he said, and blew out a breath with a puff of air. "Willard asked if I had ever read your book about vampires and I said no. The truth is I read it several years ago."

"What did you think of the book? And please, be honest."

"I always wondered," Killgood said. He sighed, his gaze on the table before him.

"If I was a vampire?"

Killgood nodded. "But everyone knows vampires aren't real."

To hear these words brought Mr. Howard a fleeting sense of relief. "And when Willard came to you suggesting I was a vampire you—"

"Stopped investigating."

"Because you believed Willard had lost his mind?"

"Because I was afraid," Killgood said in a low voice.

"Afraid?"

"Of something I didn't understand. I knew vampires weren't real and yet—"

"You considered me a threat to your family?"

"The thought did cross my mind."

Mr. Howard tapped a finger against his lips.

"You were the one, not Susan, who did not want Reann and Gail coming to stay with me."

I should have left for Florida last week. I could be on the beach right now with a stiff drink and soaking up the moonlight.

"That's right."

"I never would have harmed them."

Killgood twisted his wedding band on his ring finger. "You killed Ryan, didn't you? You killed him to protect Reann."

"Do you honestly believe I would make that confession?"

Killgood pushed out of the chair. He paced in front of the table. "You kidnapped Alicia Whitmore to stop her from leading us to you. You took her to Van Adam's house. There, you waited for his return and overpowered him. Inside the basement, you used your blood to transform Van Adams into a vampire. Knowing he would need fresh blood, you turned him loose on Alicia, locked him inside the basement, and rushed home to call me."

Mr. Howard's gaze returned to the window where mosquitoes pounded on the glass in a desperate search for blood.

First Willard figures out my plan and now Killgood. These cops are getting smarter by the minute.

"How did you come up with this theory?"

Killgood stopped pacing. "I blasted Van Adams a couple of times with my shotgun. The responding officers shot him as well. The man was nearly dead when they loaded him in the ambulance. An hour later, the E.R. doctors couldn't locate a single wound on his body. People don't spontaneously heal."

"Are you sure you shot him? Perhaps you became confused due to all the blood in the room?"

Killgood scowled. "Don't play games with me, Professor."

"Van Adams is institutionalized, correct?"

"Yeah, up at Brook Haven. He attacked an orderly when they tried to wheel him outside. Started screaming, said he couldn't be out in the sunlight. Chewed the poor bastard's nose off. Now he wears a straight jacket and lives in a room with padded walls."

"A most fitting end for the man, I must say."

"You and Van Adams had a history," Killgood said. "He tried for years to get you fired from the college."

"And this is the reason I transformed him into a… vampire?" Mr. Howard leaned forward and flattened his hands on his desk. In the false light of the classroom, the purple in his veins deepened. "Are you here to arrest me?"

"If I could find a way to arrest you, I would." Killgood shook his head. "I trusted you. You were a guest at my home."

Mr. Howard rose from his chair and took a step toward Killgood who backed away. His right hand shot up toward his coat as if reaching for his gun. Mr. Howard stopped. "Are you frightened?"

Killgood swallowed hard. "Considering everything that's happened, yes."

"I have no reason to harm you."

Killgood glanced toward the door as if looking to escape. "I heard you're moving to Florida. Something tells me it won't be long until the police in Florida make your acquaintance."

"Why would you say that?"

"Death follows you." Killgood's hand came down. "I think it's time you get out of the psychic business."

"Anything else?"

"Yeah. Don't come back to Colorado. If you do, I'll be waiting with a wooden stake."

"Maybe you should have brought one with you."

"Maybe," Killgood agreed.

Mr. Howard returned to his desk and sat. He surveyed the classroom and tried to remember the faces of his students, but nothing came back to him. How could he forget them so soon? He would miss teaching, but it was time for a new beginning. Life would go on, at least for some. "Please give my best to your family, Detective."

Killgood stared at him for several seconds with the expression of a child who had awakened from a nightmare before hurrying from the room.

Chapter 40

An orange moon rose in full glory above the black water, casting pale beams onto the sandy beach. Mr. Howard walked barefoot, the tide surging onto land and creaming around his ankles. Behind him, the lights of beachfront houses and condos burned brightly against the night. Had Leslie already gone to bed? If she didn't need to wake up early in the morning to babysit her granddaughter, he would drop by unannounced and sweep her into his arms. He was feeling lascivious and needed her to help release the tension building inside him. Four weeks in Jacksonville and they had only made love three times. That would not do.

The air, heavy with humidity, wrapped around him like a warm blanket. He resisted the urge to go for a late-night swim. As he strolled along the beach, feet sinking into wet sand with each step, Killgood's warning repeated in his head. Would Killgood follow the Jacksonville news to see if the city experienced a sudden surge in homicides? Would he contact the Jacksonville police and give them his name?

No, if he wanted to see him captured, he would have helped Willard with his investigation. Poor, foolish Willard, with a mouthful of Ding Dongs, and the memory of a naked dwarf to sustain him in the afterlife. At least Killgood was smart enough to fear the consequences that came from persecuting a vampire.

He paused to watch the incoming waves. He had walked the earth nearly four hundred years and what was his legacy? A trail of tears marked his passage. There had to be more to this life. There must be a purpose.

He continued up the beach. A breeze coming off the water warmed the back of his neck. The sound of someone crying carried above the crashing waves. He went to investigate. A young woman in a white evening dress sat on the sand. She leaned onto her knees as she sobbed. "Are you all right?"

She looked up at him with glossy wet eyes. "Do I seem all right?"

Early twenties, five foot six, one hundred and twenty pounds, muscular calves, she could be a new lover or something more, a giver of life.

"No, of course you are not all right. How stupid of me to ask." He shoved his hands inside his pockets and stared past her at the city lights. "This is a beautiful night for crying, yes?"

She stopped sniffling. "What?"

He gave her a smile. "I mean, if you are going to be crying, you could not find a better place, or more perfect evening. The moon, the ocean, a warm wind on your face, yes, you have picked a good night to cry."

"Thanks... I guess." She looked at him as if he was crazy.

"My name is Mr. Howard," he said, extending his hand. She just stared without offering her own. He pulled his hand back and smoothed the front of his shirt. "I am a retired professor. What do you do for a living?"

"I'm a professional crier, can't you tell?"

"I see. Based on your performance tonight, I believe you must be quite good at your job. You must be a millionaire."

A smile flashed over her mouth. "You're a nut."

"Some might say that." He breathed in the salty tang of the sea. "You are having boyfriend trouble, yes?"

"Don's a jerk."

"I have known many Dons and all of them qualified as jerks."

She smiled again. "Thanks." She took a deep breath and wiped the tears from her cheeks. "I guess he's not worth crying over."

"Is any man worth crying over?"

"None that I've met."

"May I ask your name?"

She looked up at him. "Season."

"Season is a most unusual name. Are you part of the Phoenix family?"

She blinked several times.

"You know, River, Leaf... it means nothing to you?"

"Sorry."

"I suppose they were a little before your time." He wiggled his toes deeper into the sand. "Tell me, Season, do you plan on spending the night here, alone with the moon and your tears?"

She chewed her lip as she thought. "I can't go back to the apartment. Not tonight."

"I see. Then you should join me at my condo for a drink. I live right down the beach." He pointed to distant lights.

"I appreciate the offer, but I think I'll pass."

"You are afraid, which is understandable. A beautiful young woman cannot be too careful in this cruel world of ours."

"Thanks for understanding."

"But the real question is, are you safer alone on this beach or back at my condo?"

She sighed. "I don't know. I'm so confused right now."

He held out a hand. "Look at me, I am an old man. How dangerous can I be?"

She stared at his hand several seconds before accepting it. "What the hell, anything beats sitting out here alone."

He helped her stand, a smile on his face as her warmth transferred to him. They started down the beach toward his place. "Tell me, Season, do you like Rachmaninoff? I find his music inspiring."

"I'm not familiar with his music."

"Is that right? Then you must tell me what kind of music you enjoy. I want to know everything about you."

The End

This book would not have been possible without the help and support from many people. I would like to thank my critique group, the Rain-Tree Writers, Patricia Stoltey, Brian Kaufman, April Moore, Beverly Marquart, and Laura Powers for their keen insights and observations. Dr. Patrick Allen, Larimer County Medical Examiner, who assisted me with questions regarding body decomposition and autopsies. Dr. Boris C. Kondratieff, Professor of Entomology, Colorado State University, who helped with Forensic Entomology questions. My family, wife, Monika, daughters, Sarah, Michelle, Amanda, and Rebecca, and my parents, Paul and Jan Harmon, provided the love and encouragement I needed to get this done. I would also like to thank Christopher Payne of JournalStone for taking a chance on me, and Russ Thompson of JournalStone for his support and guidance.

Kenneth W. Harmon is a retired police officer who lives in Fort Collins, Colorado with his wife and daughters. His previous publishing credits include a nonfiction book and numerous short stories. He has been a finalist for the Pikes Peak Writers Paul Gillette Memorial Award and the Pacific Northwest Writers Association Zola Award. You can learn more about Kenneth at www.kennethwharmonauthor.com

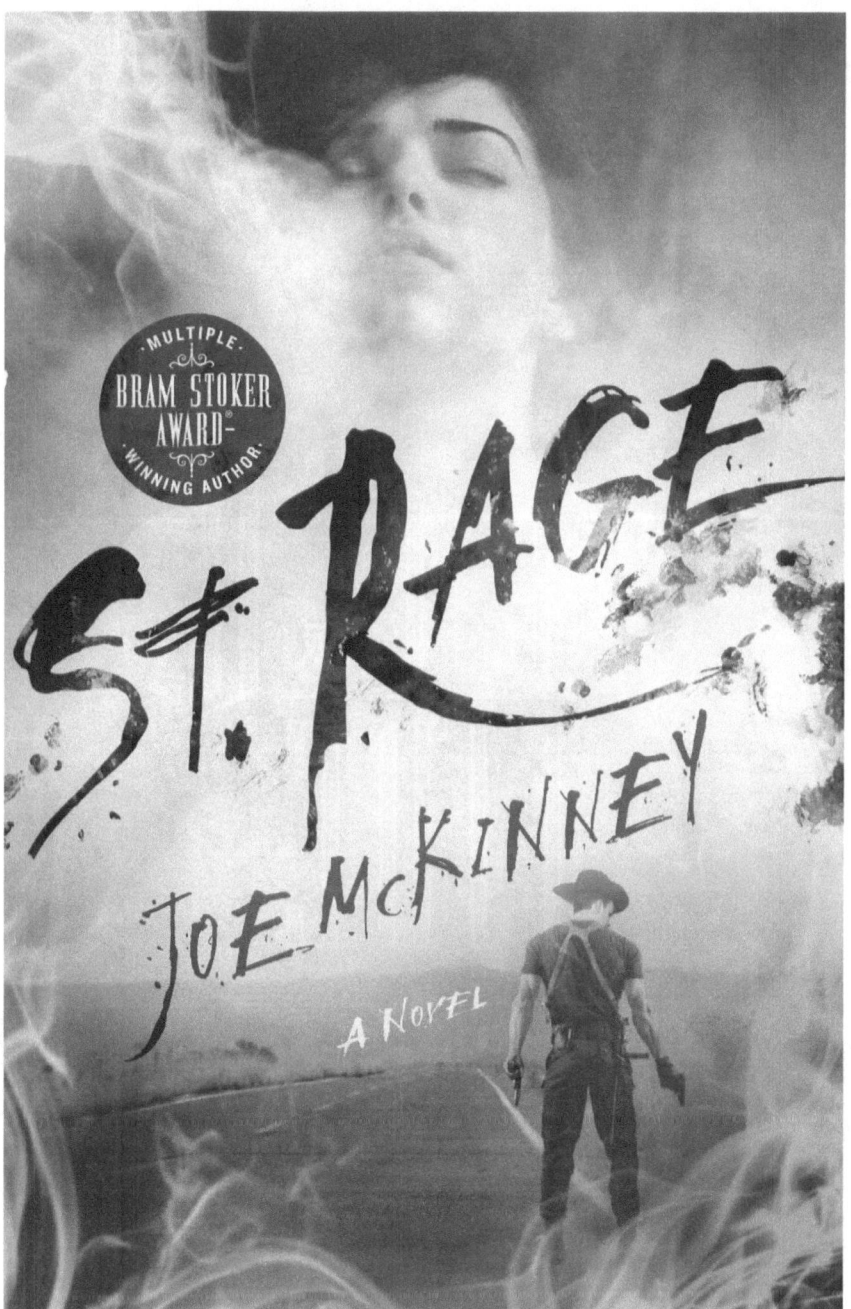

St. RAGE

JOE McKINNEY

A NOVEL

BLACK TIDE

PATRICK FREIVALD

• A MATT ROWLEY NOVEL •

www.ingramcontent.com/pod-product-compliance
Lightning Source LLC
Chambersburg PA
CBHW020823260626
47169CB00003B/800